Kissing Shakespeare

Kissing Shakespeare

PAMELA MINGLE

DELACORTE PRESS

Text copyright © 2012 by Pamela Mingle
Jacket photograph copyright © 2012 by mercier

All rights reserved. Published in the United States by Delacorte Press,
an imprint of Random House Children's Books, a division of Random House, Inc., New York.

Delacorte Press is a registered trademark and the colophon is a trademark of Random House, Inc.

Visit us on the Web! randomhouse.com/teens

Educators and librarians, for a variety of teaching tools, visit us at
RHTeachersLibrarians.com

Library of Congress Cataloging-in-Publication Data
Mingle, Pamela.
Kissing Shakespeare / Pamela Mingle. — 1st ed.
p. cm.
ISBN 978-0-385-74196-5 (hardback) — ISBN 978-0-375-98881-3 (ebook) — ISBN 978-0-375-99034-2 (glb)
[1. Space and time—Fiction. 2. Shakespeare, William, 1564–1616—Fiction. 3. Theater—Fiction. 4. Actors
and actresses—Fiction. 5. Love—Fiction. 6. Great Britain—History—Elizabeth 1558–1603—Fiction.]
I. Title.
PZ7.M6568Kis 2012
[Fic]—dc23
2012007891

The text of this book is set in 12-point Adobe Jenson Pro.
Book design by Stephanie Moss

Printed in the United States of America
10 9 8 7 6 5 4 3 2 1
First Edition

For Jim

Time is out of joint.
—Shakespeare, *Hamlet*

My tongue will tell the anger of my heart,
Or else my heart, concealing it, will break . . .
—Shakespeare, *The Taming of the Shrew*

Chapter One

Boston, Present Day

I WAS ALL ALONE BACKSTAGE. Flinging props and costumes around, slamming cupboard doors, kicking a row of empty water bottles. I'd planned to clean up, but instead I was wrecking everything.

We opened *The Taming of the Shrew* tonight. A few months back, when I found out I'd gotten the role of Katherine, I knew I was headed for trouble. I hadn't even auditioned for it. I wanted to play Bianca, the sweet daughter, the one all the suitors are after. But Mr. Finley, our drama teacher, wouldn't even consider it. "Miranda, you *will* play Katherine," he'd said. "The role was one of your mother's triumphs, and you must carry on the tradition." Inside, I'd fumed. My mother again. It was always about her.

So here it was, opening night, and I'd totally screwed up. Rather than playing Katherine with the subtleties the role deserved, I'd played her as the traditional shrew turned submissive. The woman completely tamed by her husband. Afraid to make the role my own, I practically sleepwalked through the performance. When the curtain fell, I raced offstage, defying anybody to look at me. No way could I deal with polite smiles, insincere congratulations, and, worst of all, pitying eyes that quickly darted away.

My cell phone vibrated in my jeans pocket. It was Macy, my friend and fellow actor, so I answered.

"Miranda? Are you all right?"

"Yeah," I fibbed. I hated it when people asked me that, even friends who actually cared. *No, I'm not all right. I feel like a failure and an idiot. And I let everyone down.*

"Where are you?"

I heard loud music and laughing in the background, so I knew where *she* was. The opening night party. "I'm still changing and putting stuff away. What a mess." I didn't mention that my foul temper had caused the mess in the first place.

"You're not thinking of skipping the party, are you?"

I drew a deep breath and squeezed my eyes shut. "Macy, please don't freak out, but I'm not coming."

"What do you mean you're not coming? You have to come! It's opening night." She broke off to talk to someone, then said, "John wants to talk to you."

"No! Tell him I'm sick or something." John had played Petruchio, and we'd been dating, sort of. He was a nice guy, but he wanted more than I was willing to give. I heard Macy making excuses for me.

I waited a few seconds, until she was back. "What's the matter with you?" she asked. "I'm sure he knew I was lying."

"I ruined the whole performance, Mace! I sucked. I can't face anybody right now." *Or maybe ever.*

"You weren't that bad."

"Thanks. I feel *much* better. Look, after Sunday's closing, I'm driving up to Maine, to our place at Acadia. I need to be alone for a while. I think I want to quit acting, Mace."

"Oh my God, Miranda, give it a little time. Everybody has their off nights. Remember how good you were in *Much Ado About Nothing*?"

I spoke over the lump in my throat, my voice sounding raspy. "I had about ten lines in *Much Ado*! And this was more than just an 'off night.' I stunk from the first rehearsal."

"This is because of your mom, right? You think you can never measure up to her. That's so not true."

"Mace, can we talk about this later? It's late, and I want to get out of here."

"Please come to the party. You'll feel better."

"I'll talk to you tomorrow," I said, ending the call. If I listened long enough, she might wear me down.

Driving up to Acadia National Park had popped into my head while Macy and I were talking. There was no reason I couldn't go. My grandparents, who kept an eye on me when my parents were on tour, wouldn't care. Spring break started next week, and the play, mercifully, would be over. I loved it up there. With its dense forests and deep lakes, Acadia was a great place to hide out. I could use the time to reflect on life after acting and on how I could get out of going to Yale Drama. And on what I dreaded most: telling my parents I didn't want to be an actor. The tears I'd been holding back overflowed, trailing down my cheeks.

"Miranda?"

I spun around, my heart racing. But it was only Stephen Langford, another actor. Someone else who hadn't gone to the party.

I brushed my cheeks with the back of my hand. "You scared me. I thought everyone had left." He was still in costume, I noticed. That wasn't his *Taming of the Shrew* outfit, though. It looked Tudor, like something a man at Queen Elizabeth's court would wear. The first Queen Elizabeth.

"I need to talk to you," he said. "Urgently."

I started throwing the plastic water bottles littering the floor into a recycling bin. What could be so urgent? I barely knew him. He'd shown up at the Dennis School early last semester, just in time for auditions. Finley practically drooled when he heard that posh British accent, so it was no surprise when Stephen won the role of Lucentio. Outside of rehearsals, he never hung out with us, so none of us knew him very well.

"Why are you wearing that costume?" I asked.

"It's not a costume. These are my real clothes." He gestured at his outfit, and I sensed a challenge in his expression. Did he want me to question that ridiculous statement?

Stephen had grown a mustache and short beard for the play, and I now realized he looked years older than a typical high school senior. He was a good-looking guy, with full lips and a straight nose. One of his front teeth slightly overlapped the other, but that didn't spoil his smile. Macy said she'd caught him staring at me a few times during rehearsals, but I'd never noticed.

I lowered my eyes. "Right." I moved on to the dresses I'd thrown to the floor and started hanging them up on the wardrobe rack. They'd be in the wrong order, but someone could fix that tomorrow. "So what do you want to talk to me about?"

"Will you stop fussing with those damnable costumes!"

I felt my jaw tense. "What's your problem?"

"Sit down. Please." He tilted his head toward a trunk. "I need your help with something."

I could see he wasn't going to give up until I agreed to listen. With an irritated sigh, I tossed the last gown aside and plopped down on the trunk. "What is it?"

Stephen dropped to his knees in front of me, and I instinctively drew back. "How would you like to meet William Shakespeare?"

A laugh burst from my mouth. "You're crazy." I tried to stand up, but he put his hands on my shoulders and pushed me back down. My rear smacked the trunk, hard. "Shit!"

"Sorry," Stephen said. "But I'm not crazy. Shakespeare needs our help. Desperately. All the plays and sonnets could be lost forever if we do not act now." This guy was either the biggest drama nerd in existence or a lunatic. Probably the latter. *Wonderful.*

"Last time I checked, the Bard lived in a different century. Like the sixteenth?" All of a sudden, I got it. "Wait a minute. Is this for one of those cheesy reenactment things?" Reenactors are big in Boston. They're all over the Common, dressed like Redcoats or Patriots, acting out battles or meetings or whatever. Doing a Tudor-era reenactment here seemed kind of strange, though. "Thanks, but I'm not interested."

Just then, my cell phone rang. *Probably Macy again.* But when I pulled it out of my pocket, I saw it was my parents, with their usual great timing.

"I have to take this. It's my mom and dad." Why would they be calling at this hour? I wondered. Principal actors in the New England Shakespeare Company, they were in Rome, starring in *Antony and Cleopatra*. Egomaniacs playing egomaniacs. *Perfect.*

Stephen muttered something under his breath but wandered

toward the hallway. I checked him out as he strode away from me. His reenactment costume, or whatever it was, did look authentic. He was wearing a velvet doublet, embroidered with silver and gold threads, over a white linen shirt. His hose were silk, and his boots rich leather, polished to a high sheen. None of our school costumes were that realistic or expensive looking.

I shrugged and took the call. "Mom?"

"Darling!" My mother's exaggerated greeting resounded over the ocean, bridging the space separating us. "We just got in. Daddy and I want to hear all about your opening." I detected an intake of breath and figured she was yawning. It must be around four o'clock in the morning there. Already Saturday.

"Fine. It went fine." I wasn't about to tell her how awful I'd been. Especially since she was the one who'd convinced me to stick to the traditional interpretation of Katherine. I glanced over at Stephen and noticed him pacing, shooting me edgy looks. He was beginning to scare me.

"Miranda? Are you there?" Mom asked.

"I'm here. How was *your* opening? Did Rome's rich and famous turn out for the performance?" Not that I cared, but I knew my mother expected me to ask.

"Of course! The mayor, the city councilors, actors, opera stars. Your father even thought he saw the prime minister."

"That's so exciting," I said, trying to sound thrilled. "How many curtain calls?" But my mind was somewhere else. *How would you like to meet William Shakespeare?* I felt sweat gathering under my arms and breasts. Maybe I was dealing with a real whack job here. After all, what did anyone really know about Stephen Langford?

"Oh, maybe a dozen," my mother said, pretending to have lost count when I knew darn well she always kept track. "Hold on a second. I'm putting your father on."

"Hi, sweetheart. How did it go?"

Hearing my dad's voice perked me up a little. I repeated my "fine" mantra.

"Did your grandparents make it?"

"Grandpa did. Grandmother had some social event she had to attend." I heard my father snort from his end. My maternal grandmother, a true Boston snob, was still busy, at age seventy-two, impressing the city's elite.

"I just wanted to make sure someone was there for your opening. I wish you could have seen your mother tonight. She dazzled, she hypnotized . . . well, she was magical. The audience couldn't get enough of her."

Because they're not related to her. I turned toward the hall and caught Stephen watching me. "Listen, Dad, there's a boy hanging around—" Even as I said it, I realized how incongruous the word *boy* sounded when applied to Stephen.

I heard my mother shrieking. "Oh, Geoffrey, look! Roses from the prime minister!"

"Wonderful, darling. You were saying, Miranda?"

I turned my back to the doorway, hoping Stephen couldn't hear me, and lowered my voice. "One of the guys in the play is hanging around me. He's acting strange, talking about . . ." How could I possibly explain it?

Dad said, "Talking about what, Miranda? I'm having trouble hearing you."

"Nothing. Never mind." What could he do, anyway, from Rome? I'd have to deal with Shakespeare Boy by myself.

"Hey, Dad, I've got to go. The party, you know?"

"Of course. We'll be here for two more performances, and then we're off to Florence. After that we fly to Milan." But I wasn't listening anymore, because I heard footsteps. When I turned, Stephen was striding toward me, his eyes glittering crazily.

"'Bye, Dad. Tell Mom I said goodbye." Feeling a surprising pang of loneliness for them, I disconnected just as Stephen grabbed my arm. I flinched. "Don't touch me!"

He jerked his hand away. "I'm sorry, Miranda, but we don't have time for this."

I walked over to the cupboards, now desperate to get away from him. I reached in, snatched my backpack, and threw it over my shoulder. Where was the custodian? He was usually the last one to leave after performances, busy with cleaning and closing up. I couldn't possibly be here alone, could I? When I turned around, Stephen was standing directly in front of me, blocking my path.

"You're in my way."

"Enough of this!" he said. "I have need of you, wench."

Before I knew what was happening, he bent down, grabbed me around the legs, and hoisted me over his shoulder. "Put me down! Right now!" I pummeled his back with my fists, but I might as well have been punching a brick wall.

Next thing I knew, we were climbing up some stairs, and when Stephen finally set me down, we were on the roof of the school. My legs immediately collapsed under me, and I held still for a few minutes, catching my breath and getting my bearings.

A strong gust of wind nearly blew me over when I finally stood up. It didn't take long to spot Stephen, perilously close to the roof's edge, fiddling with something. My legs were wobbly, but I grabbed on to one of the vents sticking up from the roof and, going from one to the next, I gradually made my way closer to him. Even though I was scared, I was also more than a little curious.

"What are you doing?" I screamed.

"Get back!"

"Not until you tell me what's going on! Why are we up here, and what's that thing you're holding?"

He eyed me, apparently weighing whether to reveal anything. "It's an astrolabe," he finally said.

It was small and round, and made of a shiny metal—brass, maybe. Even in the dark, it reflected light from the stars and the street below, and whenever Stephen's hand moved, it gleamed like the flash of a firefly.

"I'm finding the position of Mars. I measured the altitude of this building weeks ago."

"Well, that explains a lot!" My sarcasm was lost in the wind.

"I must find the portal."

When I didn't respond, he said, "For us to travel back."

He spun around and continued peering through an opening in the astrolabe while adjusting a narrow arm that stuck out from one side. After a minute, he seemed satisfied.

"Let's commence. 'Tis the right time, and the planet is positioned as it should be. Now I need only say the words." He stepped back from the edge, and I sneaked slowly toward my backpack. I planned to run like crazy for the door and then dash down the stairs. Midstep, I sensed Stephen's presence behind me. Before I could escape, he clenched me tightly. And then I heard his voice:

"*From this age we take our leave; to Shakespeare's time we do proceed!*"

In a blast of cool air, I felt myself being lifted off the ground, like that amusement park ride, except Stephen's arms were holding me. We were flying above the earth, around it, a blue-and-white sphere with swatches of green. And there were huge splashes of light. I was cold. Freezing. It was like someone had wrapped me in an ice blanket. Time sped past, and I was tumbling through its layers. I realized the light was from the Milky Way, spilled out before me like fairy dust, and it was dazzling. I started to laugh, and then I felt myself slip into oblivion.

Chapter Two

Lancashire, England, 1581

SOMETHING WAS POKING INTO MY BACK. *I must have fallen asleep on my cell phone or keys.* I rolled onto my side, toward the early light filtering through the open windows. It sounded like every bird in the neighborhood had roosted in my room. Shivering, I reached down to pull my blanket up, but . . . there was no blanket. No wonder I was freezing.

When I opened my eyes, Stephen Langford was leaning over me, staring into my face. I screamed, and he covered my mouth with his hand. "Hush! We must not be discovered."

I nodded and he removed his hand. Gradually I woke up enough to realize we were outside, in a forest so thick that light barely penetrated. He must have driven me here, probably in my own car. Memories of last night began surfacing, and I recalled a creepy discussion involving Shakespeare, as though he was alive and we had to rescue him from something. And another thing. "Did you call me a wench?"

The corner of his mouth quirked. "I did. Pray forgive me. Allow me to help you sit up."

I had to get away from this guy. Jumping to my feet, I decided to make a run for it. And immediately fell. Luckily, the ground was covered with leaves, so I didn't really hurt myself. When I tried to get up, my head spun and my arms and legs wouldn't move properly. Like they weren't receiving signals from my brain.

"I warned you." I could have sworn he snickered, right before he stooped down and, in one fluid movement, lifted me up as if I weighed nothing. Last night he'd picked me up too, but I couldn't remember what happened afterward. Stephen glanced around and finally set me down with my back against a towering oak. "Drink some water," he said, nodding toward my backpack.

"How considerate of you to have brought it," I said, smirking. I snatched my water bottle and drank. He'd abducted me and dragged me off to this godforsaken forest. But why?

We rested in silence for a few minutes, Stephen watching me the whole time. "You changed your clothes," I said. He'd replaced the fancy doublet with a leather one, and his boots appeared worn, more like work or riding boots.

"Aye."

When he didn't say anything else, I rose cautiously and crept forward, testing my neurons. They seemed to be firing normally. I moved more confidently now, right to the edge of the trees. What I glimpsed through the drooping branches blew my mind. I was looking at a massive stone building, with gates and archways and flags fluttering in the breeze. To complete the picture, an intimidating-looking stone tower kept watch near the front of the house. Or castle. Or whatever it was.

I raced back to Stephen. "Tell me where we are. Right now, or I'll start screaming."

"We're in Lancashire, England."

"Sure we are," I said. "I wish you'd quit saying such outrageous things."

"The year is 1581. The time of the danger to Shakespeare."

"Stephen, you're delusional. Did you bring me here, wherever we are, for one of those reenactment events? Why didn't you just ask me? And, by the way, where's my car?"

He laughed. "I do not have your car, Miranda. Let me explain."

"You kidnapped me! I'm calling 911." I fished in my pocket and pulled out my phone.

Stephen reached out and stopped me. "It will not work in this century."

I batted his hand away. "Whatever." Phone in one hand, backpack in the other, I hurried away from Stephen and his castle. Even though I could see there was no signal, I pressed 911 over and over. It must be this forest. No reception here.

"Come back, Miranda!" Stephen called. "Do not be a fool!"

I ignored him and kept walking. I'd have to get to the nearest town, where I could call Macy to come and pick me up. I heard footsteps shuffling over the leaf-covered ground and knew Stephen was following me, so I stayed on the lookout for a sturdy branch. If I surprised him . . . I didn't want to hurt him, only stun him long enough to get away. It wasn't like he was a serial killer or anything. Only weird. Then I spotted just the thing—a fallen limb with a rounded end. Dropping to the ground, I pretended to give up. Meanwhile, I grasped my weapon with both hands and waited.

Behind me, Stephen said, "It is much too dangerous for you to strike out on your own. Look at the way you're dressed. You could be arrested for a witch. Mayhap you would end up in the stocks, or worse."

I leaped to my feet, spun around, and swung, catching Stephen on the side of his head. Eyes filled with shock and alarm, he staggered for a second and then dropped to the ground.

Tossing the branch aside, I ran, cutting diagonally through the trees. *Dear God, what if I killed him?* Once, when I turned to check behind me, my foot snagged on a root and I went down. Stephen was nowhere in sight. I flew up and kept going. Before long a road came into view, but it was only a driveway leading to the manor house.

I raced on, at last reaching the real road. After taking a moment to catch my breath and get my bearings, I looked back toward the house and woods and saw no movement, no one running after me or shouting my name. This place, wherever it was, seemed completely isolated, about as far from civilization as you could get. And the road was nothing but a dirt track, barely wide enough for a small SUV. I grabbed my cell phone and once again tried dialing 911. Still no signal.

And then I heard voices. A couple of men, both short and stocky, were walking toward me. Tweedledum and Tweedledee. Dressed in brown wool doublets and dirty hose, they were leading a two-wheeled oxcart. *Oh, great. Reenactors. Where on earth did they find an ox?*

Since I didn't see anybody else around, they'd have to do. "Help!" I called, waving my arms. I could smell the pungent stink of the ox. It was massive, broad and as tall as the men. They stopped beside me, and up close, I saw that one was much older than the other. So maybe father and son instead of twins.

They studied me with puzzled looks. The older one said, "Good morrow, mistress."

"Uh, good morning to you too. Can you give me a ride to town?"

After glancing at each other, the same man asked, "From whence have you come, mistress? Your manner of speaking is odd."

"I'm from Boston." I couldn't quite place their accents either. Maybe Irish? "I have no idea where I am, and I can't get a signal on my cell phone. Can you guys help me?"

They stepped aside, like they had to consult with each other before making such a momentous decision. While they talked, I glanced up the road toward the house. No Stephen in sight. After a minute, the older man again turned to me, looking a little wary.

"Mistress, 'tis strange garments you wear. Is this the style of dress in your village?"

"Okay, you can drop the reenactor stuff," I said, not even trying to conceal my irritation. "Some guy who mistakenly thought I wanted to participate dragged me out here. I'm trying to get home. I have to be in a play tonight."

"You are a player?" the younger one asked, looking horrified. "But females are not permitted to act on the stage." Again, the two of them locked eyes before looking back at me.

The one who seemed to be the spokesman said, "I cannot account for your behavior, mistress. Mayhap the cunning woman in town can see to what ails you." While he was speaking, I marched up to the cart. Maybe I could ride in it instead of walking. Just as I approached, he shot me what I clearly should have recognized as a warning glance.

"We will escort you, though you will have to walk. The cart carries the body of a friend dead of plague."

Too late. I'd already leaned my elbows on the rim and was peering in. Although the sickening smell nearly knocked me backward, something held me there. Probably morbid curiosity. A shrouded body lay wedged into the bottom of the cart. The cloth had come loose around the head and neck, and I could see it was the body of a man. His wide-open eyes stared out from a bloated face, and his tongue protruded hideously from his mouth. A purplish lump bulged from one side of his neck, and I flinched involuntarily. My own personal *Night of the Living Dead.* I half expected him to rise up and attack me. *This can't be. . . . We don't move dead bodies around in carts pulled by oxen in the twenty-first century. We just don't.* My stomach heaved.

I took a giant step backward and smacked right into Stephen.

"Good men, well met!" he said, ignoring me.

"There's a dead person in that cart!" I turned toward him and barely got the words out before my stomach heaved again and I threw up all over his chest.

Stephen leaped away from me. "God's breath, Miranda!" He pulled out a handkerchief and brushed at the clumps of vomit covering his doublet.

"You know this young woman, sir?" the older guy asked.

"Aye, 'tis my misfortune." He fired a wicked glance my way. "She is our servant, recently arrived from the New World and with many strange ways about her—she is often quarrelsome and peevish. A good flogging will put her in her place."

I felt my blood pressure rise. "That is absolutely—" I broke off when Stephen's look registered. It was a "let me handle this" kind of look. I fumbled in my pocket for a tissue and wiped my mouth.

"If it please you, I shall take her off your hands," Stephen said.

He grasped my arm, and when I tried to wrench free, he dug his fingers in. Hard.

"Ouch!"

"Good day to you, then," the older guy said, looking perplexed. He and his friend resumed the slow journey with their gruesome cargo, walking alongside the mammoth ox and urging him on with a stick.

"Excellent stroke with the cudgel," Stephen said. "But only a superficial wound."

"I should have hit you harder," I hissed. "I wish I'd killed you!"

He half dragged me off the road and down an embankment. At the bottom, a stream rippled past, and we stopped beside it. After giving me a warning glance, Stephen let go of my arm, and I plopped down on the ground. He stooped and dipped a cloth in the water. When he removed his hat, I gasped. I'd really done a job on his head. He dabbed at the wound and then rinsed out the cloth. Walking over to me, he held it out and said, "Wipe your face with this. The cool water will revive you."

I buried my face in the cloth and wished I could wake up from this nightmare. After a minute, I found my water bottle and rinsed out my mouth. I still felt slightly sick and light-headed, topped off with a rising sense of panic.

Stephen unfastened his doublet and dunked it in the stream, letting the flow of the water get rid of the rest of the mess. Then he squatted down on the ground in front of me, again with that fluidity of movement. His knees didn't even crack.

"You're in Lancashire, in the north of England, in the year 1581. Accustom yourself to the idea." His eyes held a fierce gleam, and his voice was hard. I decided not to argue. "If you have any more doubts after that little encounter, perhaps I can allay them by taking you into the village and letting the good citizens make of you what they will. Make no mistake, you would end up in a prison cell by day's end." He kept his harsh glare trained on me. "Now listen carefully.

"We have been invited to visit Alexander Hoghton and his wife, and you will pass yourself off as their niece. My sister. I am, you see, their nephew. They've just employed young Will Shakespeare as schoolmaster, player, and musician." He spoke in short, clipped sentences, and I didn't dare interrupt him.

"Also in residence is a Jesuit priest. He wishes to claim Shakespeare for the priesthood. For obvious reasons, we cannot allow that to happen. Not only would his work be lost to history, but his very life may also be at risk."

He was talking so fast it was dizzying. Maybe my incredible trip through time was fogging my mind. I massaged my forehead, then cut off Stephen's "you will obey me" speech. "Wait a minute. We know Shakespeare became the world's greatest playwright. His work wasn't lost, and he lived into his fifties. Freakin' ancient. So what's the problem?"

"You would do well to trust me on this, mistress," came the sharp response.

"Ha! I should trust *you*, the man who kidnapped me and dragged me back to a different century? I don't think so."

"You do not have a choice, do you? In this time, I am your only friend and ally."

I wanted to smack that smug look off his face. "Pardon me if I have trouble seeing you that way."

He turned his back on me and put some distance between us.

For the longest time he stood there, hands on hips, as if he was thinking something over. *Maybe I should try to run again, while he isn't paying attention.* But I knew he was right. In this century, I could end up in a jail cell if the wrong people found me. I didn't exactly fit in. And there was no way I could get home without him.

He had swiveled around and was talking to me again. "All you need to know at present is that events in history may not always unfold the way in which they were meant to. It is my job to see that they do. For my sins."

He was completely serious. The intense gleam in his eyes proved it. "So you're like a time warden or something?"

"That's as good a way as any of describing it, I suppose."

"I still don't really get it."

"It is not necessary for you to understand everything right now. As we progress, I'll explain further."

"Let's say I actually believe you. Which I'm still not sure I do. What does all this have to do with me, anyway?" I flung my arms out to make sure he grasped the true level of my frustration.

"Your mission is to save Shakespeare from this foolishness. Convince him the life of a Jesuit brother is not one he wants."

"And how would I do that?"

"You're going to seduce him," Stephen said with a perfectly straight face.

Chapter Three

I SHOT TO MY FEET. "You're out of your mind!" I glowered at him, because now I could see amusement barely hiding itself in Stephen's eyes. "You got me here. Now get me back!" I lobbed the wet cloth at him, and to my extreme satisfaction, it hit him in the chest.

"I couldn't send you back, even if I wanted to," he said, juggling the cloth. "Certain limitations and restrictions exist. Even when conditions are ideal, it doesn't always work. Perhaps after your mission is complete, the time will be right for your return."

"What do you mean, 'perhaps'? There's a chance I could be stuck here?"

"Only a slim one."

"Perfect." I turned my back on him and howled with frustration. After a few seconds, I whirled around and said, "The seduction thing. That's my mission?" I figured I'd better play along. If this wasn't a reenactment, I had to be caught up in a joke, a dream, or a major misunderstanding. Shakespeare's work was a done deal, as far as I was concerned.

Stephen's lips quivered. "Yes."

Anger, outrage, even bashing him on the head hadn't worked. Maybe I needed a change of tactics. "Please, Stephen." I reached for his hand. "I'm scared. I want to go home."

"Your life in Boston seems to be on hold."

I dropped his hand. "What do you know about my life?" My temper flared again when I realized that he was changing tactics too. *Jerk.*

"I know how things stand between you and your mother."

"What's that supposed to mean?"

"And that you're thinking about giving up acting. A serious mistake, in my opinion."

"It's none of your business. You don't even know me! We barely had a conversation before last night."

Scowling, he said, "God save me from your prattle. You talk too much, mistress. I'll explain the rest later. Right now, we need to get on with it."

Crossing my arms, I leaned against the nearest tree to think things over. Stephen, cursing under his breath, walked away and kicked a pile of leaves before circling back. Unbelievable as it seemed, I had to admit that my instincts, as well as all my senses, were screaming the truth of my situation. I'd been transported to William Shakespeare's time. How could this have happened to me? Gradually it dawned on me that I had a bargaining chip.

Stephen was holding the cloth against his wound, watching me.

"All right. I'll do the seduction thing, although there's no guarantee it will work. But only if you show me how to get back."

"That's out of the question," he protested. "'Tis done by a powerful magic which you do not possess."

"And you *do*, I suppose."

"Aye, and I cannot bestow it upon you. Trust me; you wouldn't want it."

For a moment he looked exhausted, like maybe this powerful magic was wearing him down. And there was an indefinable sadness in his eyes, along with something else. Vulnerability. But I couldn't allow it to sway me, because this was my life we were talking about.

"Fine. You can't force me to seduce someone. I'll make myself so undesirable, Shakespeare won't come near me. In fact, I'll encourage him by telling him I'm thinking of becoming a nun."

"I was right," Stephen said. "You are peevish and quarrelsome, much like Katherine. And we don't have nuns in England anymore." He turned his back to me, muttered to himself, and then spun around and said, "What if I promise to get you home safely when this is done? Swear to you?"

"How do I know you won't change your mind? And I'm nothing like Katherine, by the way."

He smirked. "I swear by our Lord to do everything in my power to get you back unharmed. That is a binding oath, the best I can offer."

"That's not good enough. What if I got stranded here in this plague-infested time, when the king—"

"Queen."

"Right, queen. When she can chop off your head or throw you in the tower for no reason? And there're plenty of other diseases besides plague to worry about, like smallpox and typhoid and leprosy, and no cures for anything. You can't even get a flu shot, for God's sake!"

Stephen snorted. "Calm yourself, Miranda. There's no leprosy in England anymore. And you have immunity to most diseases, do you not? Because of vaccines?"

"I guess so," I grudgingly admitted.

"Do you not feel a duty to ensure that Shakespeare will make his way to London and compose his sonnets and plays? That the greatest writer in history will triumph?" He stepped forward, as though he might grab me by the shoulders. Apparently he decided not to, although he was close enough for me to see the pleading look in his eyes.

"I'm telling you he *does* triumph! You know it as well as I do. So what's the big deal?"

His voice was shot with intensity. "The threat is real. It may not seem so to you yet, but mark this well: If the priest has his way, the course of history may be irreparably broken."

Put in those terms, the whole situation sounded scary . . . and more believable. "I guess I have no choice but to accept your explanation. But why me?"

"You act in his plays. Your parents have made Shakespeare their life's work. It is in your blood."

"What about my family and friends? Do they think I was kidnapped, or simply disappeared with no explanation? My grandparents will be frantic! Will the police be out looking for me?"

"Nay. It does not happen that way," he said.

"Well, how does it happen, then?"

"'Tis as if time stops. It was roughly the same day and time when I returned to this century as when I left."

"But—"

"Do not ask me to explain, for I understand it no better than you."

"So, when I go home to Boston, I'll be dropped backstage, where I was when you found me? And it will still be Friday? March twenty-first?"

"Close enough. It may be sometime the following day. And it is more likely you will end up on the roof, where we found the portal." He sighed, sounding irritated. "We are wasting time, Miranda. My aunt and uncle are expecting us."

"There's one other little problem," I said.

He waited.

"I . . . uh, well, that is, I haven't, when it comes right down to it, ever seduced anybody before."

He had the good grace to look down, even though I could see his shoulders shaking and hear little gasps of laughter spurting out.

"Okay, that's it. I'm not doing this. Why should I give up my . . . virtue . . . to William Shakespeare? And this is absolutely not funny. You kidnapped me, but you can't make me do anything."

"Pray forgive me, Miranda. You are all innocence, eh?"

I didn't answer. He was laughing at some bizarre joke only he understood.

"You are a well-favored young lady, and I have no doubts about Master Will Shakespeare becoming smitten with you. There is much dancing, walking, riding, and eating together. Ample time for seduction."

He still didn't get it. Flirting, I could handle. It was more the actual physical aspect I wasn't well acquainted with. Which didn't really matter, since I wasn't about to have sex with William Shakespeare anyway. There had to be something else, some other way of keeping him away from the church. But I was too exhausted to argue any more, at least for now. I'd simply pretend to go along with whatever Stephen wanted if it would get me closer to going home.

"I expect you to keep your word—your oath. If you give me any reason not to trust you—"

"That will not happen. I swear it." He looked right at me, his gaze unflinching. I believed him, even if I didn't quite trust him.

I released a huge breath. "All right, then. So what do we do now?"

"Remember, I am the Hoghtons' nephew, and you will be masquerading as their niece. Their actual niece, my poor sister, has become rather conveniently ill. Temporarily. The two of us will arrive at Hoghton Tower right on schedule."

"I'm hardly dressed for the role of an Elizabethan teenager," I said, glancing down at my outfit. Jeans, T-shirt, green hoodie, Uggs.

"I borrowed some of my sister's apparel," Stephen said. "You are roughly of the same proportions." He walked over to a pile of leaves and, brushing them aside, pulled out a wooden trunk.

"Where was I when you were stealing your sister's clothes?"

"You were . . . sleeping. My dog Copernicus stood watch over you, so you were perfectly safe."

"Ha! I bet. And I don't see any dog."

"He's with the horses. Now, you must change before your arrival on horseback, accompanied by yours truly," he said, sweeping into a bow.

"Won't they know I'm a fake? They must be able to recognize their own niece."

"Our aunt and uncle—and you should begin to think of them as that—have not seen you for a few years, because of a quarrel between our families. You are the same age as my sister, and there is enough of a resemblance to satisfy them."

I nodded. That seemed plausible. "But if there's a quarrel going on, why would you be visiting?"

"My uncle has long been a student of husbandry—farming. I need his advice on certain practices such as drainage of land, surveying, enclosure. The visit serves as a gesture of reconciliation as well." He paused a moment, studying me. "Her name is Olivia."

"Whose name? Your aunt's?"

"Nay, my sister's."

Light dawned. "Now you're telling me I have to change my name?"

He shrugged. "'Tis the least of our worries. You will grow accustomed to it soon enough."

"'Tisn't the least of mine," I said. "You're not the one with a new name!"

He ignored me and reached for my pack, which I was still clutching against my chest. "Just out of curiosity," I asked, "what are the other reasons you chose me? Out of all the young women throughout time, why me?"

"Aside from what we've already discussed? Your parents once performed here, so you have a connection to the place. You're thoroughly grounded in Shakespeare's works, which gives you a glimpse into his mind. And you are a good enough actor to pull this off, Miranda, although you would never admit to it."

He thinks I'm a good actor. A warm feeling spread through me, and for the first time I thought maybe Stephen and I could be friends. But even so, I stood still a moment, making him wait, until he looked as if he might explode.

"Now, if we can put an end to these questions, you must change while I fetch the horses." He unzipped my backpack and began to sort through my things.

"What are you doing? You have no right to—"

"I must confiscate your keys, wallet, watch, and this, uh, instrument."

"It's an iPod," I said with a smirk. "It plays music. You listen to it through these things." I waved the earbuds in his face. "Didn't you wonder what everybody had stuck in their ears all the time?"

He looked vulnerable again, and I actually regretted my sarcastic comment. "I didn't want to ask," he said. "Give me the talking box . . . that instrument you talk into."

I shot him a horrified look.

"God's breath, Miranda! 'Tis of no use here. I'll keep everything in your pack. Do you have anything else that would arouse suspicion if someone happened to search your chamber?"

"No. You thought of everything," I said, glaring at him. "And I want all of that stuff back before I go home."

"You shall have it." Stephen opened the clasps of the trunk and fished out a rust-colored dress and cloak. "Wear this," he said, thrusting them at me. "It is a traveling costume." I grabbed them and waited for him to leave.

"One more thing. I need your clothes."

"What? You must be joking!"

"You cannot have modern apparel in your room because the

servants are sure to find it. I'll turn my back while you disrobe. I need your shirt, jeans, shoes, socks, undergarments. Everything." He turned and waited.

"But . . ." I started to argue but knew I'd never win. I tugged off my Uggs and threw them aside. Then I stripped, tossing everything so it all landed right beside him. He stuffed it into my backpack.

"Did you bring me any shoes?" I asked, trembling in the cool air.

"Nay. Wear your boots for now. There is a cupboard you can hide them in later today. Is that everything, then?"

"Sorry," I said, shivering. "You can't have my underwear . . . garments. That's where I draw the line."

"Then make sure you're wearing them at all times—or keep them well hidden." I thought I heard a snicker before he strode away.

"I'll return in ten minutes. Be ready," Stephen said, turning briefly to call over his shoulder.

Chapter Four

I WAITED BESIDE STEPHEN in the inner courtyard of the great stone house, the sleek hound Copernicus resting on his haunches next to me. My hand kept darting down to pat his silky, dark head. So far, he was the best thing about this century. A big, drooling baby, he'd taken to me immediately, smearing wet kisses all over my face when Stephen introduced us.

While we'd ridden on horseback up the long approach road, Stephen had tutored me on the names of people, buildings, household items, and other things I'd need to know. "You must call the Hoghtons Aunt and Uncle. They will expect it."

"What are their first names?"

"Alexander and Elizabeth, but no need to use them."

"What if they figure out I'm not Olivia? Then what?"

"If you play your part well, that will not happen."

Throughout his lecture, I was trying really hard not to fall off the horse. I'd never ridden in my life, and here I was, perched on a sidesaddle. Stephen had held the reins while I clutched the pommel with a death grip most of the way. I felt as if I were miles above good old terra firma. Dismounting near the stables, he passed the reins off to a young man and helped me down. We picked our way around dung, chickens, and even a pig or two before passing through an outer courtyard, at last reaching the place where we now stood.

A bearded older man hurried toward us, his dark hair ruffled by the breeze. Alexander Hoghton, no doubt. "Uncle," I managed to choke out, shocked and a little repulsed by his stained teeth and sickly-looking face.

"Olivia! We are so happy you have come."

I looked around for Olivia, suddenly overwhelmed and confused. In that brief moment, I felt Stephen's hand at the small of my back, steadying me. By the time the older man leaned in to kiss me, I'd snapped out of my haze and offered my cheek.

"Stephen, well met!" He plopped a kiss on Stephen's cheek too, then grasped my hand and pulled it through the crook of his arm. I assumed the lady standing nearer the house was his wife, Elizabeth. Stephen strode ahead of us, removed his hat, and embraced her. "Aunt, 'tis good to see you again."

"Welcome, Stephen." She clung to his arms, her eyes finding the wound on his head. "My dear boy, you've suffered an injury!"

"'Tis nothing," Stephen said in a rush. "An errant stone a boy threw at a pack of dogs hit me."

"We shall have the doctor look at it."

"Nay, Aunt, it is not worth the bother."

She pursed her lips. "As you say."

When she turned to me, Master Hoghton released my arm. I smiled and stepped forward to greet her.

"My dearest Olivia." She took my hands in hers, and her warm and friendly eyes studied me. "It is too long since we have last been together. You look . . ." I held my breath while she searched for the right word. "Different," she eventually said.

"And you look beautiful, Aunt." The words had slipped out, but it was true. Though she was no longer young, her style was anything but matronly. She wore a heavy outer gown, slashed in front so her skirt showed. The bodice was cut low, displaying an undergarment—maybe a chemise?—made from a delicate, gauzy material.

"You have not lost your sweet nature, I see." I couldn't help glancing at Stephen, but he'd ducked his head, probably trying not to laugh. "How fare your mother and father?" she asked.

"Well, um, they—"

Stephen jumped in. " 'Tis a most busy season for our father. He rides out every day to visit his tenants."

Master Hoghton stepped forward. "I am so pleased he and your mother allowed this visit. We have much to discuss, and 'tis time for this trouble between us to end."

A look of understanding passed between him and Stephen. We made our way into the house, entering through a drafty hallway and then climbing a flight of stairs.

"Bess will show you to your chambers," Stephen's aunt said. "When you are refreshed, come to the banqueting hall for the midday meal. No need for haste."

Bess, followed by a man carrying our things, led us through a passageway of sorts formed by the opened doors that led directly from one room to the next. Although similar to the doors in adjoining hotel rooms, these were much thicker and made of oak. The passageway glowed with sunlight streaming through tall windows. I grabbed Stephen's arm and darted a horrified look at him. How could I have any privacy with people trooping through my room? He quirked a brow and shrugged.

Our little procession stopped at the first room, and Bess told Stephen this was his chamber. We continued down the passageway through one more set of double doors, to my room. It was nearly identical to Stephen's, except the furnishings and colors were more feminine. Rose and pale gold instead of burgundy and black. I followed Bess inside, if you could call it "inside."

"Where would you like your trunk, mistress?"

"Over hence yonder . . . thence." I felt my face color. *Shut up, Miranda.* "There, if you please." I pointed toward one side of the room, and the male servant dropped it to the floor.

Bess gave me a tight smile and they both left.

I hurried back to Stephen. "What's up with these rooms? How am I supposed to dress, wash, and . . . ?"

"Use the chamber pot?" he finished for me.

"Exactly." I felt my cheeks grow warm and could see that Stephen once again was trying not to laugh.

"Let me explain how this works. The doors are closed at night, after ten o'clock, I believe. The servants open them around eight in the morning, and they are kept open during the daylight hours."

"Wonderful. In other words, during the day, I have absolutely no privacy."

"That's not quite true. If you need to be alone, close the door on your side. If someone's coming through the passage, they'll allow you a few moments. Much of the day you will not be in your chamber. And if you are, you will probably be sewing or reading, pursuits which do not require privacy."

I could think of dozens of reasons I needed to be by myself, but it was useless to argue since I had no control over my life right now. "Do you think they suspect anything?" I asked.

"You gave them no cause," he said. "Now you must change into a bodice and petticoats. Wear a smock underneath." He steered me gently back toward my room.

"I'm closing the doors," I said as I backed away. "And there's no way I'll be doing any sewing!"

"Mistress." Stephen bowed and a broad grin broke over his face. He closed the door on his side and I closed mine, at both ends of the chamber.

Before changing, I checked out my room. A high four-poster bed with a fringed, rose-colored canopy stood at one end. Other pieces of furniture were scattered around: a writing desk facing the windows and a wooden love seat—a settle, Stephen had said—in front of a fireplace. Against the back wall, there was a wardrobe, and next to it, a door. I tugged it open and found that it led onto a stone stairway. No time to explore now, though.

A washstand with a pitcher and bowl reminded me that I hadn't bathed since yesterday. I poured water and washed my hands and face with the perfumed soap provided, drying off with a linen towel. That felt so refreshing, I stripped naked—after making sure I didn't hear footsteps or voices—and washed all over as well as I could. Covered with goose bumps, I shivered in the chill air and hurriedly wiggled back into my underwear. At last it was time to open the trunk.

On the very top was a crimson gown. Trimmed with lace, it was probably meant for special occasions. I pictured myself wearing it, escorted by a handsome Renaissance gentleman. There were smocks, some made of silk, others of a delicate linen. I pulled one on. If someone decided to come through the passage, I didn't want to be caught sitting there in my underwear. Besides that, I was freezing. Thank God the smocks had long sleeves.

Digging deeper, I found a layer of plain-looking dresses I thought were called kirtles. Petticoats—skirts to a modern girl—were folded neatly beneath them. Next came a pile of bodices, blouselike garments worn on the upper body, a bit like a man's doublet. At least I knew what most of the clothing was called because of all my years of watching and studying Shakespeare's plays. Before, they had all just been costumes. Now they were my actual clothes.

When I reached the bottom layer—a wool cloak, several pairs of hose, and slippers—I heard a light tapping on the door at the back of the room, and Bess slipped through. "I thought you might need some help, mistress."

I smiled and stepped aside, more than willing for her to choose my outfit. She handed me a kirtle and petticoats and helped me pull them on and fasten them. Then she asked me to choose a bodice. When I'd been riffling through the trunk, I noticed a silk one in a brilliant red, embroidered with fine gold threads. Bess nodded approvingly, so I figured it would suit the occasion. After she'd laced it up the back, I realized I was standing there in my bare feet. She dug around in the trunk, as I had done, and found stockings, strips of cloth I assumed must be garters, and slippers. I drew the stockings on and tied the garters tightly, afterward slipping my feet into the shoes.

"Would you like me to brush your hair?"

That sounded wonderful. "Yes. I mean, aye." The long strokes of the brush relaxed me to the point of semiconsciousness. I hardly realized it when Bess spoke to me again.

"That's all we've time for now. Tonight, I'll arrange it special for you."

"Thank you, Bess."

"I'll put your things away later, mistress. In the press." She gestured vaguely toward the back wall.

The what? Oh. She must mean the wardrobe thing.

After she'd curtsied and left, I hurried next door to Stephen's chamber. He pulled me into the room and looked me up and down.

"What do you think? Will I pass as an Elizabethan teenager?"

"I have no qualms about that. You look lovely." His smile seemed warm and genuine.

He'd changed too, back into the velvet doublet, silk hose, and fancy boots from last night. He also wore a small ruff at his neck. That would take some getting used to.

"Allow me to escort you to the meal," he said, holding out his arm.

"Why do these shoes feel so weird?" I asked, hobbling along beside him.

"Because there's no left or right. The shoes will gradually mold themselves to your feet."

Oh, this just gets better and better. Until that happened, I'd have to walk as though my feet couldn't coordinate with my brain.

Along the staircase—different stairs than we'd used before—portraits of various family members lined the walls, their expressions either haughty or grim. In the lower hallway, Stephen said, "The chapel is hidden away down here somewhere, I believe."

"Hidden?"

"The Hoghtons are Catholic and cannot practice their faith openly."

"What's wrong with being Catholic?" I asked, lengthening my stride to match his.

"The queen and Privy Council—and an act of Parliament—have decreed that we must all be Church of England. Protestant."

"Are you saying it's against the law to be Catholic?"

"The queen, for the most part, is tolerant of Catholics."

"That didn't really answer my question."

He acted like he hadn't heard me. "For now, our concern is to identify the priest, the Jesuit attempting to recruit Shakespeare. He's disguised as . . . something else. We shall find out soon enough."

A soft grunt of irritation slipped out. "You still haven't explained how this is all supposed to work."

"We must find our bearings before taking any action. Shakespeare will be at the meal. It will be your first chance to meet him."

"William Shakespeare will be at lunch?" My voice rose an octave, and Stephen grinned.

"It would behoove you to study him. Notice whom he converses with and what he says. Discreetly, of course."

He couldn't resist bossing me around. "Too bad I don't have my laptop, or at least a spiral. I could take notes."

He raised an arrogant brow. "And whatever else you do, remember who—and where—you are."

I rolled my eyes at him. "No problem." *How could I forget?*

My heart pounded like a jackhammer as we entered the hall where the others were awaiting us. I inhaled deeply and followed Stephen. *Showtime.*

Chapter Five

THE CAVERNOUS ROOM DISTRACTED ME, which was what I needed. I marveled at its size and the rich textures of the wood covering its walls. The wood's darkness was offset by the light streaming through the tall, mullioned windows set in alcoves on either side of the room. Stephen led me to a long oak table on a dais, where several people were already seated. As we approached, the men rose.

After greeting us, Master Hoghton said, "Stephen and Olivia, may I have the honor of introducing you to some of the members of our household? Our cousin Jennet Hall has lately come from Clitheroe. And this young man is Master William Shakespeare, our new schoolmaster."

My breath caught. I'd forgotten Shakespeare would be my age. I'd been picturing someone older, with a receding hairline. This Shakespeare was a boy with a high forehead, chestnut hair, and a playful gleam in his eye. He stood, doffed his cap, and bowed. Jennet rose and curtsied, and I followed her example. My cheeks flamed. I knew my curtsy must look awkward and probably comical. No doubt I'd have lots of opportunities to perfect it in the coming days.

My uncle introduced three other men. The oldest was Peter Gillam, Master of the Revels. The youngest was his son, Fulke, who looked about Shakespeare's age. The remaining man, called Thomas Cook, was a scholar on his way to Oxford. "And now, Olivia, please be seated next to me," Master Hoghton said.

"It would be my honor, Uncle." A servant standing against the wall pulled out my chair for me. Stephen claimed the seat on my other side, next to his aunt. I was having a hard time thinking of the Hoghtons as my aunt and uncle. I only had one of each, and they lived in California. I rarely saw them. Since "Master Hoghton" was so formal, I decided to call him by his first name, Alexander. Only in my mind, of course. And I'd begin to think of his wife as Elizabeth.

A young boy walked around with a pitcher of water, a basin, and a towel, and everyone washed their hands. Then Alexander offered a prayer of thanks, which dragged on for so long I nearly dozed off. After the amen, he toasted Stephen and me.

"On this happy occasion, we honor our niece Olivia and nephew Stephen. May their company gladden us for many days."

I frowned at Stephen. *Not too many days.* Everyone raised their cups and drank, including me. It was beer or ale; I wasn't sure which. It was served at room temperature, but it was smooth and thirst-quenching.

Servants made the rounds, heaping food onto wooden dishes at each place. The first course was fish. I looked on as everyone else used a knife to lift the layer of meat from the bone. Once that was done, they used their fingers to eat. There was no knife by my plate, only a spoon, so I sat there waiting for someone to rescue me.

"Sister, have you forgotten your knife?" Stephen asked. "I shall help you." Deftly he deboned the fish and then laid the knife on the table between us.

"Thank you, Stephen. I can always depend on you." My tone was deadpan, but he raised a brow at me, looking amused. I realized I was ravenous. I never ate more than a snack before a performance, so I hadn't had a meal since lunch yesterday. I shoved morsels of fish into my mouth like a starving person, and when I finished, I broke off a piece of bread from a loaf at our end of the table and gobbled it down.

"This bread is totally good," I whispered to Stephen.

"It's called manchet."

"Right." I broke off another piece and stole a glance toward the other end of the table to see what Master Shakespeare was up to. Absorbed in conversation with the man introduced as an Oxford scholar, he didn't seem the least bit interested in the new arrivals.

After the fish, servants brought us little cakes of almond and sugar. Marchpane, Stephen quietly informed me. No sooner had I popped one into my mouth than the next course was served. More fish.

"Eel," Stephen mouthed.

Oh, yuck!

When Stephen and I went for the knife simultaneously, he politely deferred to me.

"What news from home, Stephen?" Alexander asked between bites. "You spoke of your father. How is my sister?"

"She is afflicted with toothache. Father nags her to have them pulled, but alas, she is too proud and would rather bear the pain."

"I am sorry to hear it. And what of yourself?"

"I am much busy with account keeping and helping Father manage the tenants."

"You are taking on more of your father's responsibilities. Good lad."

I leaned back in my chair so Stephen and Alexander could talk more easily. Meanwhile, the servers made room on the table for more sweets and a salad of lettuce, onion, and fragrant herbs. By this time I definitely had that stuffed feeling and wished there was some way to loosen my bodice. I turned to Stephen during a lull in the conversation and in a low voice asked, "Do all the meals take this long?" An arm darted between us, whisking my tankard away and refilling it. I drank deeply.

"Go easy on the ale, Miranda," Stephen said softly. "You're not used to it."

I rolled my eyes. "I drink sometimes."

He looked skeptical. "To answer your question, only the noon meal. Unless there is some festivity in the evening, as there will be tonight."

"I—" Apparently he wasn't interested in what I was about to say, because he resumed his conversation with his uncle.

My eyes roamed around the vast room while the remaining courses were served—cheese, apples, and fruit tarts. I washed down the food with lots of ale. In the center of the huge hall, a long table rested before a massive stone fireplace. At the far end, food was being passed to the servants through slats barely wide enough for the purpose. I heard my uncle speaking to me, and I shifted my attention to our table.

"And you, lass? What occupies your time?"

"Ahem. Uh, needlework, Uncle. And assisting my mother when she requires my help." That could cover just about anything, couldn't it?

He gave me a sly look. "Any proposals of marriage yet?"

Was he joking? "I am but seventeen, sir."

"I daresay many young ladies of your years are wed."

"I shall wed when the queen takes a husband," I said. *Where did that come from?*

The whole table roared with laughter. "Cheeky, is she not?" Stephen asked. My face burned, and I knew I would never have said such a thing if I hadn't been gulping ale.

"Have a care, Olivia," Alexander said. "The queen nearly married the Duke of Anjou a few years past." More laughter. *Ha ha. Very funny.* Embarrassed, I glanced down at my plate and shoved a piece of marchpane into my mouth.

Then a new voice entered the conversation, and I jerked to attention. It was Will Shakespeare.

"Our queen has never lacked suitors, if we're to believe all the gossip."

"'He speaks! O, speak again, bright—'" *Did I say that out loud?* Since Stephen's sharp elbow had jabbed me in the ribs, I assumed I had. I leaned forward so I could peer around him to get the optimal view of Shakespeare.

"But it seems she has always been more enamored of riches and power than of any man," he went on.

"Perhaps she's waiting for Venus to reward her with the fairest man in the kingdom," Stephen said. All eyes now turned toward him, so I pressed into the back of my chair, hoping I hadn't been caught staring.

"Yet if she delays too long, her charms may wither on the bough," Will said.

"If they haven't already," Stephen responded. He and Will guffawed, along with a few others. I wondered if in this year, 1581, the queen was old enough to be wearing that hideous white makeup. In the movies about her, it seemed like the older she got, the thicker she smeared it on.

Their comments had earned them a stern look from Elizabeth. Apparently she didn't approve of jokes at the queen's expense. Stephen and Will apologized, but I noticed a few people hiding smiles behind their napkins. The talk turned to politics. I finished off another tankard, which was quickly refilled, while the conversation droned on. Spain was at war with Portugal, whose king had died recently. Shakespeare asked what the queen might do. "Stay out of it, I hope," Stephen said.

Alexander plunked down his tankard. "It seems Her Majesty would make war with all of Catholic Europe."

"At the peril of her soul," Thomas Cook answered. That was a conversation stopper. Thomas's eyes glinted an unusually intense blue, and his gaze was deep and penetrating. I'd felt it myself a couple of times during the meal. Even though my brain was a little fuzzy because of the ale, it occurred to me that he might be the Jesuit.

I sneaked a glance around the table. Keeping her eyes cast down, Jennet seemed to be the only one uncomfortable with the turn the conversation had taken. Her dress was plain, a simple white bodice and black skirts. Maybe she was a Puritan, I thought.

We washed our hands, and without waiting to see what everyone else did, I stood. Stephen pulled me back down. I was feeling more than a little woozy, and I giggled when I saw what was happening. All around the table, people were picking their teeth. The ladies discreetly, with their free hands covering their mouths. Most of the men, however, picked away with abandon, including Stephen.

Ick.

"We'll have to see that you get your own knife and picks," he said when he could spare a moment.

"How exciting." I narrowed my eyes at him. "Picking your teeth in public is so . . . attractive."

When Alexander had finished, everyone put their picks away and rose. I swayed, the alcohol rushing to my head. The room spun, and Stephen grabbed my arm. "Whoa. Take care, Mir . . . Olivia."

"Olivia is tired from her long ride," Elizabeth said. "It is best she spends the afternoon resting."

"My thought exactly, Aunt," Stephen said.

Blah, blah, blah, whatever. Just get me out of here.

"Come, Olivia. I shall see you to your chamber."

"Mir-livia. Call me Mir-livia," I said drunkenly. "Thash my new name."

"Hush," Stephen said, a smile pasted on. "Someone will hear you." I clung to his arm to keep from keeling over.

Back upstairs, Copernicus greeted me with his sloppy kisses, and I knelt down to pet him. "Nice doggy," I said, stroking his long back. When he shifted position, I rolled right over onto the floor. Stephen hauled me to my feet and lifted me onto the opulent bed, where I hoped to sleep for the rest of the day.

Alas, it was not to be. He let me sleep for two hours, and then awakened me for dancing lessons. I opened my eyes and immediately squeezed them shut again.

"My head," I moaned. "Go away. Leave me alone."

"Nay, you must get up. You do not want to look foolish tonight, do you?"

"I don't think I can walk, let alone dance." I told him I'd learned country dances at school and seen them performed a zillion times in plays and at Renaissance fairs, but he still insisted.

"You try my patience, Miranda. Fresh air is what you need."

I staggered over to the washstand and splashed my face with water, cringing when I remembered the "Mir-livia" incident. As we headed outside I said, "I think you should call me Olivia all the time. It's too confusing for both of us if I have two names."

Stephen nodded. "Olivia it is, then." We circled the house, finally ending up in a rose garden full of bushes bearing tender buds.

He guided me through all the moves, called "double," "single," and "slip step" or "French slide." The dances always began and ended with an "honor," when the ladies and gentlemen bowed to each other. At first, I could barely coordinate my brain with my feet. "How do you people drink so much alcohol and still function?" I asked Stephen.

He shrugged. "Because we are accustomed to it, I suppose."

After a while, the fresh air revived me. All the dancing made my face grow warm and sweat trickle down my back. "I hope no one sees us. Wouldn't they think it was weird for a brother and sister to dance together?"

"They will think only that we are high-spirited youths free of parental restraints," he said. "Here, let's try a volta!"

Before I could react, Stephen had lifted me high and was twirling me around. "It is rumored that the queen loves this dance!"

I shrieked, afraid the spinning would make me nauseous. My stomach seemed okay, though, so I just laughed and grasped his shoulders. An elated feeling gripped me for a moment. I threw my head back and let it fill me up.

When Stephen put me down, I noticed a drape on one of the second-story windows open. In a flash, it fell quickly back into place. Someone had been watching us.

Chapter Six

DURING THE EVENING MEAL, Alexander announced that tomorrow, Maundy Thursday, we would ride to Preston to distribute
food and alms to the poor. "'Tis customary," Stephen whispered to
me. I could live with that, except for the "ride" part. I hoped Preston wasn't too far.

When the meal and all its rituals ended, Alexander stood and
said, "Let us have some dancing!"

While we waited for the servants to rearrange the furniture, I
stood off to the side, my mind clear and alert. I'd limited my ale
consumption at dinner to half a tankard. I was dressed in the
crimson gown I'd found in the trunk. After the dance rehearsal,
Bess had helped me wash and change, and she'd done my hair too.
I could get used to being waited on, I thought.

The hall looked beautiful. Hundreds of chandeliered candles
illuminated the room, casting a warm amber glow over everyone,
and the minstrels' gallery had been hung with greenery. Even

though I felt pretty confident about the dance steps, I didn't really know the order, which explained the uneasy feeling in the pit of my stomach.

Stephen strolled over to stand beside me. "That gown suits you, Olivia," he said, his eyes laughing. *Right.* It was difficult to read Stephen—I was never sure if he was teasing me or not.

"Sucking up to me won't help," I said. "I still don't want any part of your stupid little scheme." His eyes hardened, but he didn't comment. Too late, I wished I'd kept my mouth shut. The laughing-eyes Stephen was much better looking than the scowling one.

In a moment, music began to drift down from the gallery, and when I looked up, there stood Will Shakespeare plucking the strings of a lute. Fulke was playing a recorder, and a boy I hadn't seen before, fingering a strange-looking keyboard instrument, rounded out the ensemble.

The music had a familiar ring from plays and movies I'd seen, and yet at the same time it sounded completely foreign. It was, after all, some four hundred–plus years removed from modern music. "Who are all these people, by the way?" I asked, glancing around at women and girls wearing brightly colored gowns and men and boys in fancy doublets.

"Friends from the neighboring villages and manors and their sons and daughters. My uncle wanted this to be a festive occasion. Until Easter Sunday, there will be no more entertainment."

"So, how long do you think this seduction stuff will take?"

"Longer than you'll like if you don't find an opportunity to pass some time with Master Will."

"Difficult when he's up there and I'm down here," I pointed out.

"I'm sure you'll think of something." Stephen glanced toward the musicians, and I thought he was about to suggest a way for me and Shakespeare to get together. Instead he said, "Will you dance with me, Olivia?"

I sent him a cynical glance. "If I must."

Stephen laughed. "You provoke me, mistress." Looking around the room, he said, "I see Jennet Hall is not dancing. She is, I believe, from a strict Protestant family. Her father is a minister."

"Wait a second. I thought she was a cousin of the Hoghtons. Which would make her *your* cousin too."

"A distant one, on her mother's side. I've never met her, or even heard of her, so the connection must be rather tenuous."

"Protestants are not allowed to dance?"

"Not necessarily. But I believe they are Puritans. The so-called godly. They have rather extreme views about such things."

So I'd guessed right about Jennet's religion. "Why would she be staying with Catholics, then?"

"As I said, her mother was a Hoghton."

Stephen and I lined up for the next set with the other couples. *Don't screw this up, Miranda.* He took hold of my hand, as did the man on my other side, and we performed the honor. Then the dance began, and I concentrated on getting the moves right. All I had to do was repeat them endlessly until the music stopped. After a while, I was able to relax into the rhythm of the steps and even enjoy myself a little.

Somewhere in the middle of it, Stephen said, "You are a graceful dancer, Olivia."

Did he mean that, or was he teasing me again? I felt ridiculously pleased by the compliment. "Not really," I said, flustered. He didn't answer, but when I glanced up at him, he was grinning.

"Young ladies must learn to accept compliments graciously."

"So now you're my etiquette teacher?" His grin broadened, and my irritation grew.

After the dance, he offered to get us something to drink. "Wait right here." He returned quickly, thrusting a cup of wine at me, and then said he was going to speak to Shakespeare. Sipping the wine, I followed his progress up the stairs to the minstrels' gallery, where he whispered in Will's ear and then motioned toward me. Pretending not to notice, I pressed myself against the wall, dying for an escape route. A route back home, preferably.

Stephen accepted the lute from Shakespeare, who began to make his way down to the hall. Just then I noticed Jennet standing not too far away from me. Her eyes were riveted on Will, and I could tell as he drew closer that she was waiting for him to come to her, that she fully expected him to. When he passed her by with a slight nod and headed toward me, her face crumpled at first, but then her expression rapidly changed from disappointment to anger. Maybe even rage. Her eyes glittered, and I thought she might stomp over and grab Shakespeare away from me.

"Mistress Olivia, may I have the next dance?" Will bowed, and I didn't think about Jennet again until later. This was my first chance to get a really close-up look at Shakespeare, and I liked what I saw. His eyes, a pale gray, were unusual and captivating. No sign of the earring—that must come later, in London.

But the truth was, he could have looked like Godzilla. I wouldn't have minded. He was the great William Shakespeare, and I was about to dance with him.

"Mistress?"

With a shock, I realized I'd been standing there gaping at him like an idiot. "My pleasure," I murmured. I had no idea if people of this time said things like "my pleasure," but I thought it sounded right.

"Your brother offered to play so that I might have the honor of a dance." He gestured toward Stephen, who was turning out to be a man of many talents.

Will and I made our way to the dance floor. The dance was announced, an almain, which, I remembered from practicing with Stephen, had more complex moves. It began easily enough, doubling forward and backward a few times.

"'Tis lovely here, is it not?" Will asked.

"Aye, very fine," I said, trying to keep track of my footwork. Oops. I turned the wrong direction, and Will gently corrected me.

"And why are you here, Master Will? Are you also a distant cousin I've never met?"

He laughed. "Nay, I am schoolmaster to a bunch of unruly little beggars who do not care much for learning. They are the children of Master Hoghton's tenants."

"What do you teach them?" I had to wait for my answer since we were again facing away from each other.

"The youngest learn letters, the older, some Latin. When everyone grows bored, I tell stories and recite rhymes. Sometimes we sing or dance, on occasion even act." He smiled. "I disliked school as a young lad. The masters looked for reasons to whip us. I refuse to do that."

"Your stories and poems—are they of your own composition?"

Now we held hands and moved in a half circle. I clung to Will's hands, not realizing I was supposed to release them for the next move. "Pardon me, sir," I muttered when he pulled away from me. Shakespeare looked like he was trying not to laugh.

"Some of them are mine. I am fond of writing poetry. Do you think me odd?"

"Not at all. What kind of rhyme do you write?"

"Nothing worth anybody's notice. Sonnets and songs. Rhymes for the schoolroom. But someday I hope to be a real poet."

I nearly choked. "That is admirable, sir, for the world lacks great poetry."

"Do you think so? Have you not read Virgil and Ovid, then?"

My stomach lurched when I realized my blunder. I was no classics student and really didn't have a clue which poets Shakespeare would have read.

"You are right. I have not. Perhaps you could instruct me while I am here, help me to further my education." I smiled and raised my eyebrows, going for an alluring look.

"I would be delighted."

It had worked! I couldn't wait to tell Stephen.

After the honor at the end, I watched as Will snaked through the crowd and back toward the gallery. Jennet's arm reached out and latched onto his, and he stopped and leaned toward her. They spoke for a moment, and then, after a slight bow, he left her. I immediately strolled over to see what I could find out.

"Mistress Jennet, you do not dance?"

"Nay, I do not," she said. "My faith does not allow it." Rather than looking at me, she kept her nose pointed toward the dancing.

"And yet you are here."

"Aye. It seemed rude to simply retire for the evening."

"You have made a good friend of Master Will Shakespeare."

Now she turned toward me, anger flaring in her eyes. "Aye, and what of it? He is teaching me to read, and I help him with his scholars. I have two younger sisters and am accustomed to dealing with mischief."

I couldn't keep the shock from my voice. "You do not read?"

"Mayhap I have not had the advantages of your station in life." After a quick curtsy and a brusque "Good even, mistress," she scurried away.

That went well. I hadn't meant to make an enemy of Jennet. Nevertheless, I'd managed to embarrass her because she couldn't read, and worse yet, I had danced with the man she clearly admired and possibly even loved.

After Shakespeare returned to the minstrels' gallery, I noticed Stephen heading toward an outer door. I danced a few more times, once with Fulke and then with a boy who said he was a neighbor. Afterward, I wandered outside to look for Stephen. Cut adrift from all that was familiar, I felt a little lost when he wasn't around. I strolled through the courtyard, hoping to spot him. I thought I saw him, but when I called out, I realized I'd interrupted a man and woman kissing, locked in an embrace so tight they looked like one person. Mumbling an apology, I hurried on. By now I'd made it to the outer courtyard, where I could no longer hear music or voices.

It was so still and quiet here. No traffic noises and no artificial light. A solitary bird sang in the night, and a light breeze rustled through the vast forest. So different from my world, where absolute silence existed in very few places. Maybe above the Arctic Circle.

"Miranda?"

I jumped. "I wish you wouldn't call my name like that, just out of nowhere. And you're supposed to be calling me Olivia."

"A slip of the tongue," Stephen said. "Were you not looking for me?" He was seated on a stone bench, just beyond the outer court-yard. Reaching out, he grabbed my hand and pulled me down next to him. "Did you tire of the revelry so quickly?"

I snorted. "Time travel can be exhausting."

He gazed at me for a second but didn't comment. "This is the tilting green. The benches are provided for watching the jousts."

Briefly, I conjured up a vision of King Arthur and Lancelot. "Do you do that? Joust?"

"On occasion. I'm very poor at it and would far rather protect my own skin than gain the worshipful notice of the ladies. Tell me about your dance with Shakespeare."

"He offered to deepen my knowledge of poetry. I felt really special until Jennet informed me he was teaching her to read."

Stephen chuckled. "Aye, that would be part of it."

"Meaning what?"

"Jennet is here to learn how to manage a home and probably to continue her education—what little she may already have had. Her father most likely requested it, for Puritans are keen on every-one reading the Bible. In English, of course."

"I'm afraid I offended her."

"Indeed? How so?"

I related my comments to Jennet and her reaction.

"You must try to hide your modern views, Olivia! Many girls and women of this era cannot read, even those from wealthy homes. And it is best not to make an enemy of anyone." I could hear the disapproval in his little lecture, so I decided to tease him with my theory about Jennet.

"She has a major crush on Shakespeare, you know."

"A . . . what?"

"A crush." I thought for a second. "She fancies him."

"You've had one conversation with her and deduced this?"

"It's more than just from our talk. I've been watching her watch him."

"And what of Shakespeare? Does he fancy her?"

"I'm not sure. Maybe."

"Your job will be more difficult if he's already besotted with someone else."

Which would force me to stay here even longer! "If Will fell for Jennet, he wouldn't run off to become a priest, would he? Maybe you don't need me after all."

"Ah, but a Puritan girl will not allow any . . . physical demonstrations of affection, shall we say. In your time, young ladies have no such inhibitions."

"You mean we're willing to have sex with just anybody. Is that what you're saying?"

When he didn't answer, my temper flashed. "Well, you're wrong, Stephen! Not all of us are . . . experienced."

"Calm yourself, Olivia. I do not mean for you to slip under the coverlet with Will, at least not immediately. But there's no harm in letting him believe you might."

I seethed. I'd better set some limits on what I was willing to do, even to save the genius Shakespeare. "Well, if you think—"

"Soft! Someone could overhear us," he cautioned. Stephen reached for my hand, but I yanked it away. "Kate the Curst," I heard him mumble under his breath.

"Excuse me?"

"'Twas nothing." He looked up and said, "I missed the night sky when I was in your century. Even in moonlight, the stars glow passing bright here."

I relaxed a little. He was right. With no artificial light to dim their effect, the stars rocketed out of the darkness. I was spellbound until Stephen's voice called me back.

> "Come, gentle night, come, loving, black-browed
>   night,
> Give me my Romeo; and when he shall die,
> Take him and cut him out in little stars—"

Recognizing the lines from *Romeo and Juliet*, I joined in:

> "—And he will make the face of heaven so fine
> That all the world will be in love with night,
> And pay no worship to the garish sun."

"Have you played Juliet?" he asked.

"I wanted to audition for Juliet in last year's play, but my mother thought I was too inexperienced. Of course, she's played her dozens of times. Now she's too old. She dreads being relegated to roles like the nurse."

"But she is playing Cleopatra at present, is she not?"

"How did you know that?"

"I heard you talking to your friend Macy about it."

God, it was weird to think Stephen had eavesdropped on some of my conversations. "She *is* playing Cleopatra. Stage makeup does wonders for wrinkles. And of course, she's had work done."

"I do not understand—"

"In my time, doctors can surgically remove sags and bags and wrinkles. It's called a face-lift."

"Amazing. And which of Shakespeare's ladies is your mother most like?"

"Lady Macbeth," I blurted out.

Steven laughed. "You mean she would dash your brains out to further her career?"

"If that's what it took, probably. But she's always arranged things so that wouldn't be necessary. What would her fans think if she murdered her only child?"

"Surely you are too hard on her."

"You don't know what she's capable of," I insisted.

"Perhaps not."

Something was puzzling me. "How can you know Shakespeare's work well enough to quote from it? How do you even know it's worth saving?"

"'Tis a long story."

I looked straight at him. "I have all night."

He sighed, probably wanting to keep his secrets. "I had to gauge the authenticity of the information I'd gleaned about Shakespeare. I spent many months in your time studying the plays, watching performances, and—as you already know—acting. It was no easy task passing myself off as a modern youth, years younger than my true age of twenty. But it was essential to my . . . work."

I hadn't guessed Stephen's age, although I knew by now he had to be older. Hiding my surprise, I said, "How did you get away with it?"

"By cowering in my lodgings whenever I was not in a library or school or at a performance. Distancing myself from everyone. In truth, I did not venture out except to purchase food, and of course clothing when I first arrived."

"And you lived . . . where?"

"Cheap inns. It makes no difference."

"How did you get money?"

"I was able to acquire some of your currency with gold coins."

I had a sudden vision of Stephen hurrying off after every rehearsal, always making an excuse when the rest of us were going out for pizza. "You must have been lonely."

"Aye, very, but I couldn't risk too much exposure. My ignorance of modern society was all too obvious."

"Just as my ignorance of Elizabethan society is."

Amusement flashed in his eyes. "But you have me to assist you."

"There is that."

Rising, he said, "Let's go in. We'll need to be up early tomorrow."

I could see I wasn't going to get any more out of him tonight, so I followed him toward our chambers, where we wished each other an awkward and rather formal good night.

Chapter Seven

IN A LIGHT DRIZZLE, Stephen helped me onto my small horse, which he called a palfrey. We were out beyond the stables, and no one else had joined us yet. This morning we would ride to the town of Preston, five miles from Hoghton Tower. It wasn't long before the grooms were leading the other horses out, walking them around while waiting for their riders. The air was redolent with dung, dampness, and the unique odor I was beginning to associate with riding.

"This is a smaller horse, good for ladies," Stephen said. "You can rest your feet on the planchette." He pointed to the footrest hanging down on the horse's side. "Or you can place one knee over the pommel and turn yourself toward the front. Try it."

"What's her name?" I asked, easing my right leg up and hooking it over the pommel. My left foot stayed on the planchette. Awkward, but I thought I'd feel more in control if I was facing forward.

"Peg." I felt Stephen's hand wrap around my foot. "Where are the pattens I gave you this morning?"

I grimaced. "I forgot all about them." Earlier, he'd given me some very weird-looking wooden overshoes. They had slightly raised heels, and according to him, were supposed to prevent your slippers from getting wet and muddy. Leather straps held them in place.

"Your feet will be wet and cold without them."

I hated to admit it, but he was right. "I'll run and get them."

"I'll walk you in."

"Oh, don't bother. I'll be fine."

I found my way with no trouble. After strapping the pattens on, I hurried down the stairs and came face to face with Master Thomas Cook. Without any hesitation, he offered his arm. "May I have the honor?"

I nodded and we strolled back toward the horses. "'Tis a pity about the weather," I said.

"'Tis indeed."

My turn. "How long before you travel to Oxford, sir?"

He looked down at me with those piercing blue eyes and a hint of a smile. Maybe I shouldn't have asked. Perhaps he thought it was none of my business. I felt my cheeks growing warm.

But he answered me easily enough. "I am in no hurry. Master Hoghton has a fine library and has allowed me the use of it for my studies. I do not need to be at Oxford until Trinity term begins."

Whenever that was. "And what do you study, Master Cook?"

"I am a teacher of religion and philosophy. Latin, too." He smiled kindly. "How long will you and your brother remain with your aunt and uncle?"

"I am not certain," I demurred. "It is for Stephen—and my father, of course—to decide. A month or so, I suppose."

"Much time for enjoyment. We never lack for pastimes here at Hoghton Tower."

Will Shakespeare, astride his own horse, waited beside mine. Master Cook inclined his head slightly toward me before handing me over to him. A groom helped me remount the little horse. "I would be honored to escort you to Preston, Mistress Olivia," Will said, taking hold of my horse's reins.

"Good. Excellent. Thank you, sir." Will looked like he might laugh. Oh my God, why couldn't I just stick with short answers?

When Jennet appeared, she glowered at me. As one of the grooms helped her up, Stephen guided his horse over to her and stayed by her side. I wondered how he'd maneuvered this, me with Will and himself with Jennet, who obviously would have preferred Shakespeare as her escort. Stephen said something to her, and I caught her smiling, so she must have adjusted pretty quickly. Well, it was fine by me. I'd much rather chat with Will than deal with Stephen's sarcasm and big-brother attitude.

Everyone was mounted and ready, clustered together talking. We were a small group, Masters Hoghton and Cook, Fulke, Will, Jennet, Stephen, and me. When our procession finally got under way, I felt like one of the stars of a movie about Queen Elizabeth or her mother, Anne Boleyn. As hooves clattered over the cobbled outer courtyard, Hoghton liveried men, dressed in black doublets with white trim, assumed their places at both the front and rear of our group.

For the outing, I'd worn the russet travel outfit and wrapped myself up in a heavy wool cloak with a hood. Before long, the rain had soaked into my cloak, which now hung cold and sodden on my body, and my hands were freezing. No wonder people in these times caught every disease in existence.

I hoped the long ride down the approach road counted as at least one of the five miles to Preston. Will had been riding a little ahead of me, but now he slowed his horse so we were side by side. "How do you fare, mistress?"

"Not well, I fear. I am cold and wet." He'd probably think I was a whiner.

"I see a clearing sky yonder," he said, pointing. Ahead, the clouds were separating, and the sun broke through in gauzy rays. "We shall be dry before too long, I think."

"I hope you are right." Not only was I wet, but with every step Peg took, mud shot up onto the hem of my skirt. I could have killed Stephen for getting me into this. Maybe I'd catch pneumonia and die. Then what would he do?

Take a deep breath, Miranda. "Where is your home, Master Will?"

"I come from Stratford, upon the Avon River. 'Tis a fair-sized market town south of here."

"And your family?"

"My father is a glove maker, and I sometimes assist him. But I don't wish to follow him. 'Tis not for me, the glover's trade."

"I would give anything for a pair of gloves right now!" I said. "My hands are frozen."

He gave me a questioning look, probably wondering why I wasn't wearing any.

"And what would you like to do? Besides write poetry?"

"You will not approve," he said, his eyes sparkling. "I hope to make my way to London to be a player."

"You wish to perform?"

"Aye. Do you care for the stage, mistress?"

"Very much."

"Then you have seen the Corpus Christi and Passion plays?"

"Uh—" Luckily I was spared having to bluff my way through a response, because Thomas Cook conveniently rode up and drew Will's attention away from me. From the names, I could tell the plays were religious, but I knew I'd better get more specifics from Stephen in case the subject came up again.

Master Cook rode off after a few minutes, and Will turned back to me. "He seems a fine gentleman," I said.

"Thomas? He is a most learned man," Will said fervently. His expression, as well as his words, suggested great respect, maybe even devotion, I thought.

After a few more miles, the drizzle stopped completely and the fog lifted. The countryside gave way to the outskirts of a town. We passed some thatch-roofed huts, and the children who lived in them chased after us, running barefooted and calling out. I realized this visit from the local gentry was not only expected, but much anticipated. No wonder Alexander had filled the carts to the brim with meat pies, cakes, sweets, loaves of bread, and kegs of ale.

Our horses' hooves clip-clopped over a stone bridge spanning the River Ribble, letting the town know we'd arrived. Preston looked like a medieval village, with one main street, a market square with a large stone cross, a church, and a few other buildings, some of them abandoned and in ruins. I could see men hauling wood near the square. An open gutter, filled with garbage and human waste, ran down the middle of the narrow street, and I nearly gagged at the stench. When we reached the church, a man stepped out to greet us. He wore clerical garb, including a square cap; I assumed he was the local minister.

"Good morrow to you, Master Devin," Alexander called.

Master Devin tipped his head. "And to you and your party, sir."

Will helped me dismount. When my feet touched the ground, I had to grab his arm or I would have fallen.

"Are you unwell, Mistress Olivia?"

"Nay, sir. Only, my legs feel a bit stiff." I also had the odd feeling that the earth was actually swaying beneath me, but after a few more steps it passed.

Master Devin was trying to organize the people who had gathered. By now, the news of our arrival had spread. Men, women, and children of all ages stood before us with watchful eyes. Several older boys elbowed their way to the front, nearly trampling the smaller ones. Alexander signaled with his hand, and the crowd settled down.

"Good people of Preston," he began. "We have come on this Holy Thursday to reward your sacrifices during the Lenten season. We bring gifts of food and drink for your Easter celebration. There is enough for all. My young friends will pass out our gifts to those who patiently wait."

Each of us lugged a basket. Mine, filled with meat pies, weighed a ton. I'd already decided to situate myself under a giant tree, its branches spreading like tentacles. As I made my way there, Stephen appeared beside me.

"Need some help with that?" He grasped the handle and I gladly let go.

"Whew!" I said. "Thanks. It's much heavier than I expected."

By the time we reached the tree, several women, most of them with thin faces and missing teeth, were already crowding around, waiting. Hands darted out and grabbed the pies as fast as we could get them out of the basket. The women wore white caps on their heads and aprons over their skirts. Many of them had bare arms despite the cold, and the hands that grasped the pies were red and rough. Their days must be filled with an endless round of hard work, I realized. When I had a chance to look, I noticed the children flocking around those who had baskets of sweets, and men lining up at the ale kegs, holding flagons in their hands.

I glanced up at the sound of riders approaching. A wave of excitement rippled through the crowd. Clutching their gifts, parents gathered their children and dispersed quickly. Stephen and I locked eyes, both of us wondering what was going on.

About half a dozen men rode up to the church, and when Master Devin came bustling out, they alighted from their horses. They wore swords at their sides, and the leader had some sort of symbol emblazoned on his doublet.

"Bring out the prisoner," he said to Master Devin.

"Gladly, Sheriff," Devin responded. He scurried back into the church.

I grabbed hold of Stephen's arm. "What's happening?"

"Let's find out."

Alexander approached the sheriff, our group at his heels. "Good sir, who is this man and what is his crime?"

He gazed at us with contempt. "The prisoner is a Jesuit, discovered hiding in the home of a gentleman. He is to be burned."

I gasped and tightened my hold on Stephen.

"That is hardly a burning offense," Alexander said. "In these cases, the offenders are most often put in prison for a few months."

He smiled, and I could see he was trying to ingratiate himself with the sheriff.

"He was tried and found guilty as a traitor, for attempting to persuade citizens to leave the Church of England for the Church of Rome."

"And that is treason?"

"It is, sir, by an act of Parliament."

"But it is Eastertime! Surely you can show some mercy."

"You would be well advised to look to your own actions, sir. Mayhap you have something to hide?"

"Indeed I do not." Which, from what Stephen had told me, was not exactly true.

"Then stand aside, sir. I have an execution to carry out."

Alexander bowed curtly and strode toward us.

This cannot be happening. My mouth had gone dry. Stephen patted my hand, and I was stunned when he pried my fingers off his arm. When he started to walk away, I shouted, "Where are you going?"

"Do not move from that spot," he said, his eyes boring into mine.

As if.

Now I understood the activity around the market square. They'd been building the platform . . . pyre, whatever it was called. Fear spiraled through me, and all I wanted was for us to get out of this town as fast as we could.

Alexander, looking shaken, walked over to speak to us. "I will not allow you to witness such a vile act. Wait until the prisoner is brought out, when the sheriff's attention is diverted. Stand near your horses." I noticed Stephen speaking to one of his uncle's liveried men, probably about our need for a hasty departure.

The townspeople, who had returned to their wagons or homes to safeguard their gifts, now streamed back into the town toward the market square. In a moment, the prisoner was brought out in a cart. Hands tied behind his back, he shifted from foot to foot to keep his balance. He'd obviously been tortured. A torn and blood-stained shirt hung on his gaunt body, and his face was scratched and bleeding. When the cart began to move, he fell against the side and cried out. For a brief moment, his gaze latched on to mine. I stared at him in horror. His eyes shone with a brilliant despera-tion, and I gasped and looked away. When the cart jolted on, I felt like a coward. I should have said something comforting, or tried to reach out to him. The touch of another person might have let him know he wasn't completely without friends.

"Now!" Alexander shouted, gesturing toward the horses.

I tore my gaze from the prisoner and looked around for Peg. Just when I began to panic, Stephen rode up. "You will ride with me."

"But Peg—"

"One of the men will lead her." He leaned down. "Put your foot on mine in the stirrup and I'll pull you up." Grasping his hand, I did as he said and tumbled awkwardly into the saddle in front of him. I fumbled for something to grip.

"Do not worry. I will hold on to you," Stephen said.

I kept looking back toward the prisoner, surrounded by the sheriff and his men. Our horse pranced and shook his head, as if he could sense the unrest. Stephen leaned around me, patting his neck and talking softly to him until he calmed. The crowd was growing unruly, and a few people shouted at the prisoner as the cart passed them.

"Evil papist!"

"Antichrist!"

The prisoner, who had righted himself, ignored the taunts. He seemed to have retreated into a different reality.

"Let's go," Alexander said.

We kept our horses at a walk, probably so we wouldn't attract attention. But in a moment I heard hoofbeats, and suddenly three of the sheriff's men surrounded us.

"Where are you going, sir?" one of them asked.

"We have no stomach for this," Alexander said.

"The sheriff wishes you to be present. As witnesses."

"I shall stay if I must, but please let these young people return home. You have many witnesses." Alexander motioned to the crowd.

"You must all stay. The sheriff commands it, and it would be unwise to disobey his order."

"I beg you, sir, to allow—"

"To the square, now!" Obviously, there would be no further argument. The sheriff's man turned his horse, expecting us to go ahead of him.

White-faced, Alexander said, "We must do as he says or risk arrest."

And in a moment we found ourselves part of the crowd spread out in the town square, encircling the pyre. The cart holding the prisoner rolled over the cobbles, with the sheriff and Master Devin following closely behind. Between gulps of ale from their flagons, a few rough-looking men continued to jeer and shout at the prisoner. Although it seemed loud, I realized they were the only ones actually taunting the poor man. Most people looked as solemn as we did.

Soon the sheriff and his men were hauling their captive up

onto the raised planks that held the pyre. Then Master Devin stepped forward and started reading from the Bible.

The condemned man shouted over him, his voice breaking. "I am innocent of treason. I love my queen and country, and want only to minister to my people. If that is a sin, then may God forgive me!"

The sheriff's men stepped forward and dragged him to the pyre. They chained him to a stake, which seemed completely unnecessary.

Stephen had put his arm around me, and I turned and buried my face against him. My chest felt tight, and my breathing was shallow. Glancing up briefly, I wondered what had become of Thomas Cook. "Do you see Thomas?" I asked, suddenly fearful for his safety.

"Nay. Perhaps he was able to slip away."

Two men with torches stepped forward and lit the fire. "Oh, no!" I looked up at Stephen. "Can't we do anything?"

"I fear it is too late. Do not watch." Gently, he pushed my head against his shoulder.

"May God have mercy on your souls!" the man shouted. "I am innocent! I have done nothing wrong!"

The flames crackled and the wind fed them. They grew higher and now the prisoner's garment caught fire. He continued to shout, but I could no longer make out the words. And then the keening began, quickly followed by prolonged screams as the heat seared his flesh. I covered my ears, not moving from Stephen's side. Right before I closed my eyes, I'd glanced over at Jennet and Will, standing together. His wide, sorrowful eyes met mine for an instant before he lowered his head. It was Jennet's manner that shocked me. Arms crossed in front of her chest, she watched intently, seemingly composed. Perhaps she'd seen this many times and was inured to the horror. I didn't know what to think.

Stephen pressed his cheek against my head. I opened my eyes long enough to see that his were squeezed shut. Smoke now hung thick in the air, stinging my nose, and there was another smell as well. I understood that it must be burned flesh. The screams kept on. "Please, Stephen, can't we leave?" I begged.

We began backing away, and then he released me. "Run to the horses!"

Before long all of our party except Thomas had gathered and mounted. I noticed Jennet was now riding with Will. Alexander gave the signal to move out.

"Sir!" Will shouted. "What about Thomas?"

"Thomas is safe. Do not concern yourself." Alexander whipped his horse into a gallop, and the rest of us followed. Stephen held me tightly, and his strength was the only thing that kept me from hysterics. Tears streamed down my cheeks and little sobs burst out, even though I tried to hold them in.

We didn't break our silence until we'd ridden about halfway home and finally slowed our pace. When I felt enough in control of my emotions I said, "If Shakespeare becomes a priest—a Jesuit—could this happen to him?"

"I do not doubt that it could. The Jesuits are willing and prepared to make the ultimate sacrifice, which would place Will Shakespeare at grave risk if he joined their ranks."

For the first time, I understood the danger to Shakespeare and the urgency Stephen felt. I recognized the zeal in the prisoner's eyes, and understood that a young and sensitive boy could be influenced by such fanaticism. I knew and accepted that we had to act while there was still time.

I twisted around toward Stephen. I wanted to make sure he could hear every word I was about to say. "I know I've been hesitant about saving Shakespeare. But after this, I'm in. You can count on me to do whatever it takes."

He pressed his mouth to my ear. "Thank you, Olivia. You will not be sorry."

I'd have to take a wait-and-see attitude on that.

Chapter Eight

AFTER WHAT WE'D WITNESSED IN TOWN, the mood at Hoghton Tower was grim. When Alexander told his wife the news, her manner remained calm, but the serene expression in her eyes changed to wariness, and maybe fear, I thought. Conversation at supper was subdued. Thomas, who had mysteriously reappeared at the side of the road on our way home, was not present. The rest of us picked at our food, and I was relieved when the master and mistress stood, marking the end of the meal.

I hurried upstairs to my room and threw myself on my bed. My limbs felt heavy and rigid. Despite my determined effort to block them out, visions of the prisoner tormented me. I heard his screams, saw his tortured body, and stared once again into his hopeless eyes. After a while I must have dozed off. A hand on my shoulder and a voice whispering my name awakened me.

I twisted my head around. "See what I mean about the lack of privacy?"

"Are you unwell?" Stephen asked from his perch on the side of my bed.

"How could I not be? I watched a man burn to death today!"

"I am full of sorrow for you, that you had to see something so monstrous."

When I didn't respond, Stephen squeezed my hand. "Olivia?"

I rolled over onto my back. "Stephen, I'm scared to death! What could anyone have done to deserve such a horrifying end?"

With a sigh, he released my hand. "Nothing. Nothing at all." For a moment, he studied my face, and I forced myself to look right back.

"The time has come for you to know more. I had hoped that the religious discord wouldn't involve you, but I see now that was foolish of me."

"So start explaining," I said, scooting into a sitting position. I needed to look into Stephen's eyes. I wanted to know how much truth he was telling me.

"Since the pope excommunicated the queen, matters have become worse for Catholics."

"When was that?"

He waved his hand through the air. "I don't remember exactly. Sometime in the 1570s. For keeping or sheltering priests, as the Hoghtons and many others are doing, there are fines, even imprisonment. People suffer the same consequences for recusancy."

"I don't know what that means."

"Recusancy? Not attending Protestant services."

"Do your aunt and uncle attend?"

"For a time, they did. In recent months they have given it up as hypocritical. That is what our families quarreled about."

"Your family *does* attend, even though they're Catholic?"

"My father feels it is the safest course. They go to Protestant services, and when there's a priest about the neighborhood, they come home and hear Mass."

I nodded. "Okay. Go on."

"For the priests themselves . . . some have been tortured and executed, as you witnessed today. Especially the Jesuit missionaries."

I shuddered involuntarily. "That poor man—do you think he was a Jesuit?"

"The sheriff said as much, and it is they the Privy Council are after. Especially a priest named Edmund Campion."

"I've never heard of him. Why are they afraid of him in particular?"

"Campion is a brilliant thinker, a natural leader. He is much loved by the people, even Protestants. Wherever he goes, Catholics arrive in droves to say their confessions to him and hear him preach."

"Thomas disappeared before the burning. What was that about?"

"I do not know for certain, but I think Master Cook is our Jesuit priest. He dared not linger, in case the prisoner recognized him. When Thomas met us along the road, his face was pale and he said not a word."

"So he's not an Oxford professor after all."

"He was probably educated at Oxford, as were many of the priests who left England. No, I believe that is the role he plays while here. We'll find out for certain at Mass on Easter morning."

"Are the Jesuits really so dangerous to the government?"

"The members of the Privy Council believe they're in league with Spain to overthrow the government and put Mary, the Scots queen, on the throne. Treasonous acts. The Jesuits swear they come only to minister to their neglected flock."

"Who do you believe?"

"I think the truth lies somewhere in between," Stephen said, "as it so often does."

My contempt for this era rose to the surface. "I guess your rulers don't believe in freedom of religion."

"Religious freedom is not a concept embraced by the queen and her Privy Council. One state, one religion. Things are different in these times. You know that."

"Why is this Privy Council so powerful?"

"The council members are the queen's closest advisors. Most are from the nobility."

"So the Privy Council is after the Jesuits, and we have one living right here. Wonderful."

In a soothing voice Stephen said, "Try not to worry. You must concentrate on your mission, which is to keep Will Shakespeare out of the clutches of the church. Let me worry about all the rest."

He reached up and smoothed my hair away from my face. I ducked my head, feeling unexpectedly shy, and he swiftly withdrew his hand. When I looked up, there was a softness in his eyes I hadn't seen before. I believed he'd told me the truth, as much of it as he himself knew.

"All right," I said, feeling some of the pressure in my chest ease. "I'll try."

Good Friday was marked by eating hot cross buns for breakfast. Spiced with cloves and filled with currants, each round bun had a cross carved in its top. Bess brought me a basket of four; I scarfed down two and saved the rest for later. She told me it was customary for all the meals to be served in our rooms because it was such a solemn day.

I was restless, fidgety, so I decided to walk up and down the passage. All the sets of double doors were standing open. Although I saw no sign of Stephen, Copernicus loped over and joined me in pacing up and back. His claws made a soft clicking sound on the wood floors. "So, what would you do in my place, Cop?" He raised his head as though he was thinking it over.

"Should I go on with this crazy scheme, or try to get out of it somehow?" I could pretend to be sick. If Stephen thought my life was threatened, he'd send me back, I was sure. When we reached the staircase at the end of the passage, Copernicus halted. I turned; he stood where he was, whimpering. I walked back to him. "Yeah, I know this is crazy, boy, but I'm afraid it's the only exercise we'll be getting today."

"Mistress Olivia," a disembodied voice said.

I jumped and whirled around to see Will Shakespeare standing there. He must have come from his room at the far end of the passage. God, I hoped he hadn't heard me.

"Master Will! I didn't think anyone else was about."

"Pray forgive me for startling you. I thought you would hear me approaching."

"Nay, I did not." *Probably because I was having a fascinating conversation with a dog.*

Will was holding a small, oblong parcel, which he now handed to me. "This is for you, mistress."

I frowned, puzzled. "For me?"

"Aye. Open it, pray."

I untied the string. The paper fell away to reveal a pair of leather gloves. "Oh! They're beautiful, Will." I smiled ruefully. "But I can't possibly accept them." I didn't think an Elizabethan girl would accept such a personal gift, and I didn't want to break any rules.

"Will you not even try them on?" he asked.

What could it hurt? "Very well." I tugged one on, then the other. They fit perfectly, and I couldn't help grinning up at him. "They're so soft." I stretched my fingers out and then fisted them, getting a feel for the shape and fit.

"You will do me a great service by keeping them."

"But sir—"

He held up a hand. "Hear me out. My father, as I told you, is a glove maker. He bade me give these to Mistress Hoghton, though I made them myself."

I was horrified. "Well, then, that's even more reason why I can't possibly keep them." I started tugging them off.

"Have you noticed her hands?" When I shook my head, he went on. "They're large and long fingered. This pair would never do for her. That's why I want you to have them. That, and the fact that your hands were freezing yesterday."

I stammered a little in my reply. "I-I'm very forgetful, I fear. I did not think to bring gloves with me, as the weather was fine when we set out." I held out my hands and studied them. As gloves went, they were more serviceable than elegant, fashioned of brown leather, with a stamped fleur-de-lis at each wrist. One of them was a little crooked, proof that Will's talents lay elsewhere. I decided there was no harm in accepting them if they wouldn't fit Elizabeth.

"Thank you, Master Will. I confess my hands have been rather cold since I arrived here."

"'Tis chilly inside these stone manor houses." He took a step closer to me, and my heart sped up a little. Grasping one of my hands in his, he slowly smoothed the leather over each finger, sending a chill up my spine. Then he did the same with the other hand.

"*Oh, that I were a glove upon that hand, that I might touch that cheek.*" The line from *Romeo and Juliet* jumped into my brain, and I wondered if any poet besides a glover's son would have written it. I stared at him in awe, and dropped my gaze when he caught me.

"I thought you did not share your father's work."

"I grew up with the trade, watching my father, and when I was old enough, helping. As a young boy, I put tools and materials away and swept. Later I progressed to cutting tranks, and after many years was permitted to do everything from designing to sewing. I suppose it is how I knew I could not spend my life in such work."

"Pardon me, but what are tranks?"

"I forget you will not be familiar with glover's terms. Tranks are the forms one cuts from leather to make the gloves." He lifted one of my hands again. "These are made of kidskin. Very supple, are they not?"

"Aye. I'm very grateful." I felt weird. Under his spell. Something about the way he said "supple" . . . if not sensuous, it was definitely flirtatious. I brought my hand to his face and caressed his cheek. Wasn't this exactly what I was supposed to be doing?

He smiled, eyes catching mine playfully, and leaned his head toward me. Just as he was about to kiss me, footsteps sounded behind us and I heard Stephen's voice calling out. *Great timing, Langford.*

Will and I leaped apart. I quickly pulled the gloves off and held them at my side, and Will balled up the wrappings.

"Well met, Olivia, Will," Stephen said when he reached us.

"Where were you?" I asked.

"Mass. 'Tis a strictly observed holy day. As you know," he said, quickly covering up the fact that I actually didn't know.

"All morning?"

"I broke my fast with our aunt and uncle afterward."

"I should have attended," I said.

"I did not want to wake you. After yesterday I thought you needed some extra rest."

We all looked at each other in dismay, silently acknowledging the horror of what had happened, but knowing we didn't want to discuss it.

"You were missed, Will. Thomas Cook asked after you."

Shakespeare winced. "I'm afraid I fell so deeply into Ovid's poetry, I lost all track of time. Until I heard Mistress Olivia." He glanced at me. "Which reminds me, mistress. We must arrange a time for me to instruct you in the classics."

"Indeed," I said. "I am most eager to learn."

Stephen had a funny look on his face. "I hope 'tis the *Metamorphoses* and not the *Amores* or *Ars Amatoria* from which you will be instructing my sister."

"Oh, I promise to choose only the most moral and allegorical verses."

Ugh. That sounded boring. I'd much rather hear the love poetry. I had a feeling Will was needling Stephen with his innocent act.

"I shall hold you to that," Stephen said, giving him a sidelong glance. "Do you care to go for a gallop with Fulke and me, Will?"

"Aye! Let me change. Shall I meet you at the stables?" Stephen nodded, and Will hurried toward his room.

I must have looked pathetic, because Stephen said, "Would you like to come, Olivia?"

I knew he was simply being kind. "No thanks. It sounds like a guy thing."

He squeezed my shoulder. "As you say, then. Maybe you'll find an opportunity to spend time with Shakespeare tomorrow. If not, most surely on Easter. I shall look for you after the ride. We can share a meal." He turned and strode off.

"Right." I didn't mention he'd interrupted Will and me as we were about to kiss. If he was so eager for me to seduce Shakespeare, why had he acted so weird about the love poetry?

I strolled over to the windows and looked out onto the courtyard. I glimpsed Stephen as he emerged from the house, on his way to the stables. He seemed very single-minded in his purpose, and yet I sensed protectiveness toward me too. Like he cared for me a little, in a brotherly way, even if he did think I was promiscuous.

Maybe losing my virginity to Will Shakespeare wouldn't be a bad thing. After all, it had to happen sometime. Why not with Will? He was definitely cute, and he liked me. Even if I didn't love him, I loved the sonnets and plays. Those were a part of him, and would forever be a part of me, too.

I smiled, thinking about how hooking up with Will would really give me one up on my mother. Not that she'd ever know about it.

Chapter Nine

I WOKE UP FAMISHED on Saturday morning, only to find out from Bess that the day before Easter was a strictly observed fast day. The only food and drink in my near future was a slice or two of coarse brown bread and a tankard of ale. Lucky for me, I had one hot cross bun left from yesterday. I'd save it for later, though. By evening I'd probably be half dead from hunger. I felt restless, like I might start screaming if I didn't find someone to talk to or something to do. Since I'd been trapped inside yesterday, a walk around the grounds sounded appealing. I couldn't find Stephen, so I headed downstairs by myself.

On the lower level, I passed the library, backed up, and decided to peek in for a quick look around. The door stood partially open, and I heard voices, which I recognized as belonging to Will and Thomas Cook. After scoping out the hallway to make sure no one else was around, I pressed my back against the wall, as close to the door as I could get without being discovered.

"You are shaken about what you witnessed yesterday," Thomas Cook was saying.

"In truth, I never thought to see something so evil. I have not found my heart's ease since, I confess."

"I am sorry, Will."

"You are not to blame. Did you know the poor man?"

"In Rome, but I did not know he had been sent to England. 'Tis a lonely and fearful life we lead here."

So Stephen had been right about Cook being the Jesuit. The events in Preston must have been horrific for him.

"Your life could be in danger too, Father Thomas!"

"I have made my peace with God, Will. I do not fear death, although I would not like my life to end so soon."

"Indeed, no."

"Prayer offers great comfort after such as we saw yesterday," Thomas said.

"I—I have tried to pray, but each time, the image of the man burning leaps into my mind. All I see are his haunted eyes."

"I find at times like these, solitude and quiet enable me to find God's peace."

"Aye," Will said. He sounded depressed.

Maybe to lift Will's spirits, Thomas changed the subject. "Have you given thought to further education?"

"It was my wish, and my father's, too, that I be educated at Oxford. But Father fell into debt, and so here I am, a lowly country schoolmaster." There was a slight pause, and then he said, "Do not mistake me, sir; I am grateful to have this post."

"But mayhap there is another path you could take."

"What do you mean?"

"The one I chose. The priesthood and the Society of Jesus." I could hear the passion in his voice, could imagine him leaning close to Will, his eyes gleaming. I stepped away from the door. I had to tell Stephen about this. But Thomas kept talking, so I kept listening.

"You could leave England for the Continent. Rome, perhaps, or the Low Countries. You'd be in the company of many Englishmen, and could remain there until things are more settled here." Thomas Cook's voice was made for the theater. It was deep and resonant, almost hypnotic, and he spoke with perfect diction. Mr. Finley, my annoying drama teacher, would love him.

"I don't know if I want that life, sir. With all due respect, one gives up much to become a priest. And after yesterday . . . I fear I am too cowardly to submit to torture and burning."

"Not all are asked to make such a sacrifice. That does not mean you are not suited to the priesthood."

"I will think on it," Will said.

He didn't sound at all convinced. Should I interrupt, say I was looking for someone to walk with? I hesitated. The sound of footsteps heading my way decided me. I didn't want to be caught listening at the door, so I pushed it open and strolled in.

"Oh! Pardon me. I was looking for Stephen."

Both men turned toward me. Master Cook, whose face fell when he saw me, stood near the fireplace. Will was on the settle.

"I believe Fulke and your brother are practicing with the longbow," he said.

"'Tis such a lovely day, now that the rain has stopped. I thought a walk about the grounds would be pleasant. Would either of you like to join me?"

Will took the bait, practically leaping off the settle. "I would," he said. Bowing briefly to Master Cook, he offered me his arm. Thomas tilted his head a fraction, and I curtsied. Outside in the hallway, we found Jennet studying a tapestry. Had she been eavesdropping too? More likely, she'd heard Will's voice and was waiting for him to emerge.

"Mistress Jennet, come walking with us," Will said.

A glow suffused her face at his words. Jennet really was attractive, which had slowly been dawning on me. She was one of those lucky girls whose hair grew thick and wavy, and its tawny color framed a fair complexion and brilliant green eyes. Her teeth were still white and even, which was pretty amazing, because dental work, or the lack of it, was definitely a problem in these times. Missing and decayed teeth seemed pretty common.

Jennet held Will's other arm. Outdoors, although the grass was wet, the sun shone strong and bright. We headed toward the tilting green, where Will said the shooting was taking place.

"Pray go ahead of me," I said. Once we'd left the outer courtyard and stepped into the garth—Stephen's word for the stable yard—dodging puddles and dung was easier to do by myself. I did manage to listen in on Will and Jennet's conversation, though. I was turning into a first-class snoop.

"I thought you were leaving us this morning," Will said.

"My father will presently arrive to escort me home for Easter Sunday. I wanted to take my leave of you first."

Will smiled down at Jennet. "I am glad that you did. When do you return?"

"On Monday morning." Jennet gave him a dazzling smile, and then abruptly changed the subject. "What were you and Master Cook discussing?"

"My education," Will answered. "He believes I should continue my studies."

"And will you?"

"I have no plans to do so at present." His answer seemed guarded. He mentioned nothing about the priesthood idea.

Maybe Thomas Cook faced a real challenge in recruiting Will, who, at least for now, didn't seem that interested in becoming a Jesuit. If that were the case, Stephen wouldn't need me, and I could go home.

We heard Stephen and Fulke before they came into view. "Friend, do you wish to become more indebted to me, or shall we just shoot for the sport?" Stephen asked.

Fulke hooted. "Lady Luck has favored you, Langford."

"And your bragging is more skilled than your shooting," Stephen shot back, extracting arrows from the target. As he pivoted toward the shooting line, he spotted us.

"Good morrow, ladies," he said, bowing. "Master Will, some archery practice?"

"Would you mind?" Before Jennet or I could answer, Will pulled away from us and accepted the bow from Stephen.

"May I walk with you, ladies?" Stephen asked.

"I shall stay here and watch the archery," Jennet said. "Go on without me."

"As you wish," Stephen said. He whistled, and Copernicus came galumphing over and walked along beside us.

"So, you're an archer and a musician, as well as a time traveler," I said. "What other talents do you possess that haven't revealed themselves yet?"

"Mind your tongue, Olivia. You could be overheard." He glanced quickly around. "To answer your question, only skills all lads of my class are taught, so that one day we can provide for our wives and children." He turned sober for a moment, his eyes darkening and revealing that wounded look. Something was troubling him. Something besides the Shakespeare mission.

"Social class, you mean? I assumed you were a knight or something."

Stephen chuckled. "No, I am merely a gentleman, the same as my uncle." He took my arm. "Let's walk to the rose garden." Once there, he led me to a stone bench warmed by the sun, and Copernicus plunked down at our feet.

"Why did you name your dog Copernicus?" Hearing his name, Cop rose and rested his head in my lap. I scratched behind his ears, and he gave an appreciative whimper.

"Because I am interested in Copernicus's cosmological theories, especially that the Earth revolves around the sun."

I gulped. "I hope you didn't mention that to anyone when you were—"

"I am not slow witted, Olivia. I knew enough not to speak of scientific matters." He scowled at me before asking if I'd had a chance to talk to Shakespeare.

"Not alone. But I overheard a conversation between him and Thomas Cook." I told Stephen what I'd heard the two discussing.

"So it is Cook! He is a man of great intellect and persuasive power. I could see Will easily falling under his spell." He rested a hand on my shoulder and squeezed. "Nicely done, Olivia. Now that we know for certain what we're up against, we—you—can concentrate on the real work," he said, with a meaningful lift of one brow.

This seemed as good a time as any to speak my mind. "Stephen, I don't think this plan of yours makes sense."

"I beg your pardon?"

I smirked. "You heard me. My sleeping with Will won't be enough to prevent him from becoming a priest. Don't lots of priests have mistresses, even wives?"

"Indeed. But your . . . liaison . . . would, mayhap, be enough to convince him that his interests are more worldly."

"I told you, Stephen, I'm not worldly. Not experienced."

He looked like a man who wasn't sure what he was about to say was a good idea. After hesitating a few seconds, he spoke. "The youth who played Petruchio in *The Taming of the Shrew*. John. He's your lover, is he not? I saw the two of you embrace."

Oh, God. Macy was right—he had been watching me, and not just at rehearsals. "What, you were following me around?"

He shrugged. "Sometimes."

Well, at least he wasn't lying about it. "We were dating, but we never slept together."

"So he hasn't bedded you?"

I ground my teeth, hard. "Of course not. I don't even like him that much."

"That would be a problem?"

Breathe deeply, Miranda. "It would be for me."

"So you've never slept with a man?"

"No!" I repeated. "How many times do I have to say it?"

He looked skeptical, and I was pretty sure he still didn't believe me. "While in your time I viewed some plays on the TV device. All the young ladies were bedded by their gentlemen friends."

"What shows were you watching?"

Stephen leaned forward and propped his chin in his hands. "Let me see if I can recall. One was *Gossip* something."

I was incredulous. "*Gossip Girl?*"

"The very one."

"And you believed all that? You think that's how girls in my century behave?"

"It wasn't that alone. The colorful quartos in the shops. So many near-naked wenches with their bodies draped around their young swains."

"What, you were hanging out in 7-Eleven reading *People* and *Us Weekly?*" I couldn't help myself; I laughed out loud.

He looked so guilty that I smothered my laughter. "Stephen, the TV shows are exaggerated so more kids will watch them, and the ratings . . . Oh, never mind. The magazines—they're just trash. Not about normal people."

"Ah. So I was deceived." He grinned sheepishly.

"I'm afraid so."

"Soundly gulled, eh? And yet there must be a kernel of truth there. I took note of couples at the school, how they kiss and hold each other in public. And the young ladies dress provocatively."

He had me there. No denying lots of couples were big on PDA, and girls went around in tight, low-cut tops and shorts as skimpy as panties. "Yes. But not me."

He watched me for a long moment, and then reached out and grasped my hand. "Have you already put aside the vow you made yesterday?"

"Of course not. I'm just not convinced seduction will be enough."

"It will be enough for now. We have an immediate need, and seduction would be an immediate help."

"What if I can't pull it off? Jennet's gorgeous. She's always hitting on him, but has Will even noticed? He treats her like a friend. If she can't tempt him, I don't stand a chance." Without warning, I felt on the verge of tears. *Idiot! Don't cry.*

"Olivia." Stephen gently pressed my hand. "Have you looked at yourself in a glass lately?" My lips were trembling a little, so I didn't answer.

"Do not look down; look at me," he said. "You are lovely. Beautiful."

I didn't want to raise my head, because I knew my tears would overflow. But Stephen forced me to by cupping my chin with his hand. "No. I'm ordinary looking, Stephen. Maybe your idea of beauty is different from mine." I blinked, and the tears rolled down my cheeks. I didn't even know why I was crying.

"Do not cry, Olivia," he said, rubbing his thumbs across my face. Of course, that just made the tears flow faster.

Get a grip, for God's sake. I didn't speak for a minute. Stephen produced a handkerchief from somewhere and handed it to me. I blotted my face and finally felt enough in control to go on.

"Besides, we may not even have a problem. I just heard Will tell Thomas that he was too 'cowardly' to . . . martyr himself. And he didn't seem at all interested in the priestly life. Maybe there's nothing to worry about."

"If that were so, we—you—would not be here. I brought you here for a reason."

"I'm never alone with Will, even to speak to him. What do you expect me to do? Sneak into his chamber after everyone's gone to bed?"

"If necessary. But I believe the coming days will afford you more opportunity. Tomorrow is Easter, a feast day with much celebrating. Mayhap you could lure him away for a time."

I rolled my eyes. "Oh, that should be easy," I said, giving him back his handkerchief.

"Enough of this for now," he said. "Come, let's walk."

We headed back to the path toward the front of the house. Rounding the corner, I noticed a stable boy holding the reins of a couple of horses. As we walked under the keep and into the garth, Jennet and a man I'd never seen before were walking toward us from the outer courtyard. She hurried to keep up with him.

"That must be Jennet's father," Stephen said.

Master Hall was dressed all in black, with a modest white ruff around his neck. He wore a square hat similar to the one the minister in Preston had worn. Although he obviously intended to pass us without a greeting of any kind, Stephen practically jumped into his path.

"Good morrow, sir," he said, bowing. "I am Stephen Langford, Master Hoghton's nephew. May I present my sister, Mistress Olivia Langford."

I curtsied, and he bowed brusquely, removing his hat. "Matthew Hall. I am Jennet's father."

Master Hall had a broad face with a square jaw. His bushy eyebrows arched above hard eyes. Before replacing his hat, he ran a hand through his thick, dark hair. Jennet, who looked completely miserable, must have taken her coloring from her mother's side, I thought.

"I've come to fetch the girl home for Easter," he said, nodding toward Jennet. "Come along, Daughter. We must make haste to be home by supper."

Jennet's face colored. Her eyes darted toward us, then quickly away as she mutely followed her father toward the horses.

"He's scary," I said. "And he seems awfully cold to Jennet."

"Puritan minister," Stephen said, scorn in his voice.

"Is that bad?" I asked. "Puritans founded the Massachusetts Bay Colony, you know."

"That is in the future."

I must have looked bewildered, because he said, "It has not occurred yet, Olivia."

Of course it hasn't. "Well. It's near Boston. The Puritans left, will leave England, because they were persecuted."

"They make their own trouble. Nothing is pure or godly enough to suit them. They aren't content with the dismantling of churches and monasteries, and abolishing the Catholic faith. Even the Book of Common Prayer is too papist for them."

"But they have a right to their beliefs."

"Certainly they do. But they do not have a right to force everyone else to believe the same, which is what they would like to do."

As soon as he said that, I remembered learning about the Salem Witch Trials in American History. Stephen was right. The Puritans had been pretty extreme in their views, and more than a little judgmental.

Stephen's voice smacked of bitterness. "In truth, nobody knows how to worship anymore. After Henry VIII died, his son Edward forced a rigid Protestantism on the citizens. Then Mary, who reigned after Edward, went back to Catholicism. She was a zealot—burned hundreds at the stake. And now, under Elizabeth, we must all be Protestant again."

"I just don't understand this time," I said.

"Is it really so different from your own?"

I thought about it. Al Qaeda and 9/11. Palestinians versus Israelis. In America, conservatives against liberals. Not waging war, though. But overall, I saw his point. "I guess not," I reluctantly admitted.

That afternoon, I glanced out the window and noticed dozens of people milling around in the courtyard. Curious, I took Copernicus outside to play fetch. I threw sticks and he dashed after them, dropping them at my feet. I knelt down to pet him and looked into his kind, trusting eyes. Impulsively, I grabbed him and pulled him close. He nestled his head against me, and I thought how good it felt. *I'm hugging a dog. How pathetic is that?* I shot to my feet, brushing off my petticoats. Recognizing one of the servants, I walked over and gestured to the crowd.

"Who are all these people, Andrew?"

"They are come to . . . that is . . . they are here for—"

"Never mind," I said, because I caught a glimpse of Thomas Cook at one of the doors. He was dressed like a monk, in a brown, wool robe. Someone was leaving, and Thomas gripped his shoulder and said something to him. I couldn't hear the words, but they'd brought a smile to the listener's face. A woman stepped forward and followed Thomas Cook through the door. Thomas, it seemed, had many followers.

I whistled to Copernicus and headed back to the house. Tomorrow was Easter, and I figured I'd find out a lot more about Master Cook.

Chapter Ten

I awoke to a tapping on the passage door. When I rolled over, there was Stephen, holding a candle and wearing a smock nearly identical to the one I slept in. I had to fight down a giggle.

"Olivia, 'tis time to rise. You must prepare for Mass." He lighted the taper on a table near my bed with his own.

"What time is it? It's still dark."

"Near dawn," he said. "Pray ready yourself quickly."

I groaned. Once he'd gone, I hopped out of bed onto a small rush mat, shivering in the cool air. Bess had set out my clothes last night. After dressing hastily, I stepped over to the basin and pitcher. The water was warm, and I realized she must have brought it in when I was still asleep. I'd found out that the door in my back wall led to the servants' work area, so Bess—or anyone else who wanted to—could sneak in that way.

I splashed my face, washed my hands, and rubbed at my teeth with a cloth and the icky goop that passed for toothpaste. From the scent, I figured out it was herbal, with something abrasive mixed in. It tasted evil, whatever it was. After brushing my hair, I covered it with a fancy headpiece called a French hood. Then I grabbed my cloak and met Stephen in his room.

We walked down the back staircase into the passage that led to the banqueting hall. "I think the chapel is through here somewhere," Stephen said when we'd reached the far end of the hall.

"You must have been in it before." I was definitely annoyed at being awakened before dawn.

"Not since I was a child, and then I would have been guided by my father."

After descending a few steps, we continued down a darkened hallway. At the end of the hall, a heavy door swung open, and we entered the chapel. Lots of people, crammed together awkwardly, stood or knelt on the hard stone floor. *Where were the pews? I had to stand for a whole hour?*

The room was alight with dozens of tapers, illuminating statues of the saints, paintings of the Virgin Mary and the Christ Child, and religious regalia. Deep reds, silver and gold, the blue of the Virgin's robes, merged into a panoply of colors and movement. Before an altar at the front, Father Thomas Cook, today dressed in a plain white robe, knelt with his head bowed. Stephen had told me that when I'd seen Thomas yesterday, he was probably hearing confessions. That would explain why so many people had been waiting in the courtyard.

Stephen led me into the room and we found a place to squeeze in. He crossed himself, and I did the same. Immediately, Fulke Gillam threaded his way to the front and began to sing in a haunting, high-pitched voice. His face looked sweet, almost angelic. The music reminded me of a medieval chant, the sound echoing off the walls and filling me with a mystical sensation. To know that we were worshiping in secret, maybe risking our lives, made my stomach clench.

When Fulke's song ended, the Mass began. Thomas Cook turned to face the worshipers.

"*In nomine Patris, et Filii, et Spiritus Sancti. Amen.*"

"Amen," I whispered. I glanced around to see who else was in attendance. Alexander and his wife, of course. Next to Fulke and his father stood Will Shakespeare. Bess, and some other servants I recognized but couldn't name, clustered together. A few people who'd been at the dance my first night at Hoghton Tower were there too. Just then I felt fingers biting into my arm, Stephen's customary way of getting my attention. Everyone had dropped to their knees, so I followed suit.

I'd been to Mass a few times with friends, but this was in Latin and harder to follow. Fulke sang a few more times, Thomas read from the Gospels, and finally there was a long set of prayers and responses leading up to Communion. I had to participate, even though I felt like God might strike me down since I wasn't a Catholic. Receiving Communion under false pretenses must be a major sin.

When it was my turn, I imitated what I saw the others doing. Opening my mouth, I stuck my tongue out a little and accepted the bread, keeping my eyes lowered. But Thomas Cook's powerful gaze drew my face up and compelled me to meet his eyes. It was as if he knew me, knew the truth, and saw through the whole ruse Stephen had so carefully planned. No man could have that kind of power. I blinked, and he passed on to the next person.

Easter was a huge celebration in Elizabethan England. We were to have a great feast, and there were games planned for this afternoon. I started salivating as I neared the banqueting hall, inhaling the scent of roasting meats wafting through the passageways. We sat, and the servants began bringing overflowing platters of meats. Roast beef, veal, and legs of mutton. Later came turkeys and chickens, and other, smaller birds I couldn't identify.

"Eat heartily, my friends," Master Hoghton exhorted after the blessing. "The end of Lent and fasting; the beginning of spring and feasting!" He raised his glass, and the rest of us joined in. Thomas was in his usual place, having shed his priest's outfit for a doublet and hose.

Between the meat courses, we were served a rich array of vegetables. Artichokes, turnips, peas, cucumbers, and salads, too, some with violets peeking through the delicate lettuces. By the time dessert showed up, my bodice lacings felt uncomfortably tight. So I resisted the temptations of pies, fruit and nut tarts, and cheese, instead nibbling on strawberries and cream and sipping my wine. What I really craved was some H_2O. Bottled water. Tap water. Any water, but it was never offered. Stephen had told me it was not safe to drink.

What with eating, drinking, talking, and teeth picking, it was after two o'clock before anyone got up from the table. "I will help ready the games," Stephen said to me. "'Tis customary for the ladies to rest for an hour or so before coming outside."

I nodded. A short nap would feel good.

Later, I jerked awake, hoping the festivities hadn't started without me. I hated not having my watch. While I was splashing water on my face, Bess cracked open the door in the back wall. "Mistress?"

"Come in, Bess," I said. "I know, 'tis time for me to dress."

"And I will arrange your hair for you." She eyed my sleep-tousled locks.

When Bess's back was turned—I didn't want her to see my underwear—I slipped into a fresh smock. Then she helped me dress in a green wool bodice and petticoats, proper apparel for the games, according to her. When I was all put together, she sat me down at the dressing table and began to brush my hair.

"Shall I fix braids around your head, mistress?" she asked.

"Sure. Er, that is, I would be pleased if you would."

Bess's gentle hands began to work their magic, and when she spoke, her words didn't register right away. "Has Stephen courted anyone else since Mary Swindon died?" she asked. "We all felt so sad when we heard the news."

Stunned, I couldn't think of a sensible reply. Stephen had courted someone who died? Maybe that explained the sadness that sometimes showed in his eyes. The vulnerability.

"Nay, he has not had the heart for it." I had no idea, of course, but I suspected I was right.

Before leaving, I glanced at my reflection in the glass. My hair looked pretty with the braid. I was beginning to resemble, if not quite feel, like a girl of this century.

Let the games begin, I muttered to myself as I hurried outside.

At first, I felt like I was at a Renaissance fair. The grassy area out back had been transformed, and a crowd was already gathering. Canopies covered tables of refreshments, and playing fields had been marked off with stakes. I noticed several boys and men heading toward the archery range with bows and quivers of arrows. An uneasy feeling in the pit of my stomach reminded me I was supposed to find a way to spend some one-on-one time with Shakespeare. I was committed to it, though, so I'd have to get control of my jitters.

I wandered around and watched the various competitions. A game a lot like soccer was in progress, except there didn't seem to be any rules. I noticed Stephen in the thick of it, doublet and hose covered with mud and sweat dripping off his face. The most important part of the game seemed to be subtly tripping members of the opposing team. I waved to Stephen, but he didn't see me.

I drifted on, threading my way through merrymakers, strolling musicians, and servants carrying food and drink. At last I found Will and Fulke playing a game that looked like bocce, but I knew was called bowls. It involved throwing balls at a target, with the goal of having your ball end up closest. If I walked over to the refreshment tables right now, I could be waiting with something for Will to drink when the game was over. Arriving back at the bowls area just as Will and Fulke's match was ending, I held out two tankards of ale and smiled.

"Ah, mistress, you are an angel," Fulke proclaimed. He drank his ale in one long gulp and excused himself. "I'm off to the archery butts."

Will looked at me and offered his arm. "Come. Let's stroll awhile. I see the football is done."

"Do you play?"

"Aye. 'Tis a common pastime in Stratford, where I grew up, when there is free time to be had."

Stephen and one of the other footballers rushed up. "Are you ready for barley-break?" I couldn't imagine why he wanted to play something else, since he was still breathless from the football game. He eyed Will and me with a mischievous grin. "The two of you can be the couple in hell."

Will snorted, and I pretended to know what Stephen was talking about. I gave a feeble laugh. *Couple in hell? How appropriate.*

"Over here. The court is already staked." Stephen motioned and we followed. "Wait while Henry and I find partners."

"Barley-break is a good excuse for hand holding," Will said, grinning. He grabbed mine and led me to the square in the middle, which I guessed must be "hell." Two long rectangles led off from either side of the square.

"Aye. But I don't mind." I tried to look modest but tempting, and figured I was probably succeeding in looking like a moron.

Stephen and Henry returned, each with a girl in tow, and joined hands with their respective partners. Each couple stood in one of the rectangles. For the next half hour or so, Will and I, without letting go of each other's hands, tried to tag the other couples as they ran through the center square. They were allowed to drop hands when necessary to get away, but we were not. It took forever for us to finally tag someone, one of the girls.

What had started as a game with six people morphed into something else. By the end, lots of couples had joined in, and the rules had seemed to change. When someone was tagged they joined the end of the line in the center square, which had taken on a life of its own. Those who hadn't been tagged still had more freedom, but the long line of people could swing around and trap them. It was a little like playing crack the whip. This was the most fun I'd had since my enforced stay in this era began, and I couldn't stop giggling. I sneaked glances at Will whenever I had the chance, and when he looked back at me, his eyes glowed good-naturedly. The game grew more physical as we tried to catch the two remaining players, Stephen being one of them.

When the great long line swung around to capture them, I felt a ripple of overpowering momentum. I was thrown to the ground, piling on top of the heap of bodies already there. I knew somewhere at the bottom, Stephen had been caught at last.

Someone fell on me, and then grasped me around the waist and flung me over. It was Will, and his face was only inches away. His lips brushed mine for just a second, and I thought I should take advantage of the opportunity. I grabbed him and pulled him closer, putting everything I had into the kiss. His lips were soft and sweet, and the kiss lingering. My pulse raced when I realized I was kissing Will Shakespeare, the man I idolized. When we finally split apart, he looked surprised, but then smiled. I glimpsed other couples stealing kisses and figured this must be the traditional ending of the game.

When at last we'd all rolled off of Stephen, he lay there, eyes closed, not moving. A tremor raced through me. "Stephen?" I said, shaking him. "Are you all right?" He burst out laughing.

Will leaned over and locked wrists with him, pulling him to his feet. "In truth," Stephen said. "I feared you would crush me."

The games were ending, and exhausted competitors were now making their way to the food and drink tables. I wandered over with Stephen.

"Well?" he said, latching on to my arm. "Anything to report?"

His words, his tone of voice, made me unaccountably and irrationally angry. I said nothing.

"Olivia? Did anything happen?"

I fingered back a few stray locks of hair and pretended to think. "Let's see," I said, "we held sweaty hands for what seemed like hours during that stupid barley game, and at the end, we all fell on top of each other. Are you satisfied?" I hurried off ahead of him.

Stephen caught up with me, grabbed my arm, and spun me around. "Something's amiss. Tell me." His eyes looked confused, and his words seemed sincere. But I was still ticked off.

"Nothing. I'm going in. Have a pleasant evening." I turned and stalked off toward the house.

"Olivia!"

I kept walking, hoping he'd be distracted by the food and drink. Which I guessed he was, since he didn't come after me or call out again. If I could find Bess, I'd ask her if I could have some extra basins of water brought in. Apparently actual bathtubs hadn't been invented yet, or else people of this time didn't care about smelling bad, because lots of them did. After running around, I was hot and sweaty and really wanted to bathe.

In the upstairs hall, I looked for Bess. I'd noticed her outside a few times during the games, but she must have come in by now. She'd probably enter through the servants' door soon. Meanwhile, I sprawled on my bed and thought about why I was so angry with Stephen. Instead of this stressed-out feeling, with my guts churning, I should be feeling ecstatic. I'd kissed Shakespeare. It was the second time we'd had a fairly intimate encounter, which was what this little trip to the past was all about.

Deep down, though, I knew why I was upset. Stephen still thought I was promiscuous, and that really got under my skin. He considered me a wanton. That whole conversation we'd had yesterday, about sex and nearly naked girls and horny guys ... he'd never talk that way to an Elizabethan girl. To the girl he was mourning, Mary what's-her-name. It totally pissed me off that he didn't care if he was using me, or if I got hurt in the process.

And yet, sometimes he showed genuine concern for me. He'd proved that by the way he acted after the burning in Preston—insisting I ride with him, and then holding me close the whole way home. Checking on me that evening to make sure I was all right, and explaining everything to me. Yesterday, when I'd cried, he very tenderly brushed my tears away.

But the reality was, Stephen was so focused on this job of ours he was prickly with me more often than he was tender. Saving Shakespeare. That was what I was here to do, and I'd just have to get on with it so I could go home. I couldn't worry about what Stephen thought of me. What did it matter? *Good girl, Olivia. Stick to your guns.* Oh my God. Now I was talking to myself using my new name, as though I'd actually *become* Olivia. In some ways, I guessed I had.

I rolled over and right onto a folded piece of paper. It was cream colored, like the coverlet, so I hadn't noticed it before. I unfolded it and read the one line written there:

I know you are not who you say you are.

I had to really concentrate to decipher the strange writing, but I finally got it. The message was curt and its meaning unmistakable.

A shiver of fear unfurled inside, like a wisp of smoke. Bess knocked and came in, and I jumped.

"Pardon me, mistress. Did I frighten you?"

"Nay." I looked at the words once more before I threw the paper aside. "Would it be possible for me to have some extra water brought in?" I asked.

Later, I heard Stephen in his room. After giving him a few minutes, I hurried over and rapped on our adjoining door. When he hollered "Enter!" I opened it and found him standing right inside as though he'd been waiting for me.

"What ails you, mistress?" he asked, looking irritated. "Why so peevish this afternoon?"

I didn't answer, only held the note out. He quickly read it. "God's breath! Where did you find this?"

"It was on my bed when I came in from the games."

"Who could have done this? And what does it mean?"

I shrugged. "Anyone could have written it. During the games, someone could have sneaked inside, thrown it on the bed, and run back out. We wouldn't have noticed."

"Or someone who didn't attend the games." I stood there stiffly. "Be seated," he said, gesturing toward the settle by the fireplace.

I sank down, glad my back was to him. In a minute, I heard him pouring water into the basin, and then some energetic splashing. I risked a glance and saw that he'd stripped to the waist. *Whoa!* Stephen was the owner of an amazing set of pecs. He looked like a modern guy who was into some serious lifting, but I was pretty sure his lifting was confined to things like saddles, farm implements, and hay bales. As though he felt my eyes on him, he turned his head to the side and looked right at me. *Oh, shit!* My cheeks burned, and I spun back around.

After another minute, Stephen sauntered over and plopped down beside me, still wiping off with the towel. He had put on a clean, sleeveless doublet. "Whoever left the note cannot know the truth about your . . . origins. I think we may assume that much. So what, then, does it mean?"

"I have no idea." I stared at the fire, resisting the powerful urge to gaze at him straight on.

"You are still in a foul mood, I see. Will you not even look at me? In truth, I know not what I did wrong."

Should I tell him? Would he even understand or care? I sucked in a breath. "I don't like that you're using me. Even though I agreed to it, it still feels wrong." And then I did look at him directly. "It really irritates me that despite my telling you over and over I'm a virgin, you still think I sleep around."

"Well," he said. "Well." The second "well" came out more softly than the first. He looked stunned, and after a minute he rose and paced around the room. "Pray forgive me, Olivia," he said, circling back to face me. "You are a maid, then, and must lose your maidenhead to Shakespeare in this scheme. No wonder you are angry."

"Well, now you know. So let me do this in my own time and in my own way. Don't ask me every five minutes what happened between Will and me. I'm committed to this; in a weird sort of way I'm even looking forward to it—sleeping with the greatest writer of all time—but I don't want you to hassle me about it."

"*Hassle.* I am not familiar with that word, although I take your meaning. But we do not have forever." He said it kindly, so I couldn't be too annoyed.

"Also"—he grimaced when he realized I wasn't done—"I'd appreciate it if you treated me with a little respect. Like you might treat an Elizabethan girl of your class."

"What brought this on?"

"Our conversation yesterday. Would you have said those things to a girl of this time and place? And just now, would you have been over there half-naked and washing in front of, say, your betrothed?"

If the reference to his dead fiancée pained him, he hid it well. "Most assuredly not. My betrothed would not be in my chamber. But you are different. You are more worldly—"

"Stephen!"

He plunked back down beside me. "Sorry. 'Tis hard to think of you as belonging to this time. I will, starting now, treat you with the respect you deserve. But we must sometimes speak of the seduction, you know."

"Of course."

He eyed me, almost as though he was seeing me in a new light.

"You look passing lovely with your hair arranged thus."

Oh, puh-leeze. Was this what he thought I wanted? Phony compliments? I jerked my eyes away from him. "The note. Someone thinks I'm not Olivia Langford. Why do they think so, and what do they intend to do about it?"

"'Tis a threat of some kind. But do they mean to expose you?" He leaned forward and ran a hand through his hair. "Who here could mean you harm?"

"My guess would be Jennet. She's jealous of me and Will. Not that she has anything to be jealous of—yet—but that's probably not the way she sees it."

"Isn't she away at present?"

"She may have returned; we were outside at the games, so how would we have known? But she can't read, so she couldn't have written the note, anyway." We went through the list of other possibilities, but nothing made sense. "Maybe it's someone we don't know. A spy," I said.

"If there is a spy about, he would be after Thomas Cook, not you."

After tossing ideas around for a few more minutes, we gave up.

"I'll think on it," Stephen said, "and you do the same. And be watchful. We may discover something."

I nodded. "I'll hide the note somewhere in my room."

"Nay, we must burn it. Someone else could find it." He thrust it into the fire and we watched as the flames devoured it.

"I'm going to bed," I said, rising. "Oh, just so you know: Will kissed me. And I kissed him back."

"And was it so bad, kissing Master Will?"

"Not at all." I headed for the door, but Stephen grabbed my hand.

"So you enjoyed it, then?"

I shrugged. "He's a good kisser."

Stephen dropped my hand, his eyes dark and unreadable. "Then mayhap seducing him will not be so difficult."

What could I say to that? Before he had time to utter another word, I fled into the passage, toward the safety of my room.

Chapter Eleven

THE WEEK AFTER EASTER, everyone resumed their usual routines. Will spent his time in the classroom. Jennet returned from her visit home and continued learning how to manage a staff. Occasionally I spotted her trailing through the house in Elizabeth's wake. From conversations with her at meals, I knew she was also studying the ancient arts of spinning, dyeing, and herbal healing.

Although Stephen and I had been ill at ease with each other since Sunday, he had quit pestering me about how I was getting on with Will. He spent most days with his uncle, riding out to survey fields and learn about enclosure and drainage systems. Sometimes, he went hunting or hawking with the other men, and I wished he'd take me along. Hadn't Anne Boleyn accompanied King Henry when he'd hunted and hawked? I was sure I remembered that from a movie or a miniseries. I blamed Stephen for my boredom.

So one afternoon I sneaked into Alexander's library. Thomas

studied there every morning, but I knew he took a break after the midday meal. After a few moments of browsing, I discovered that I needed a lesson in reading the print. I could make sense of some of the words, but others completely tripped me up. It might as well have been written in code. Giving up in frustration, I grabbed a translation of Ovid's *Metamorphoses*—at least, that was what I thought it was—to take back to my room. It looked like several volumes from the Ovid section were missing. Probably Thomas or Will had them.

I couldn't resist looking for the love poetry, even though I wouldn't be able to read it. I was sure Will would approve if he caught me reading one of the ancient poets. Leaning in as close as I could, I tried to decipher the writing on the spines of the books.

"Ahem."

Busted! I spun around fast, making myself dizzy. It was only Will, standing there watching me. Thank God it wasn't Thomas Cook or, worse yet, Alexander. "Good day to you, Master Will," I said.

"Well met, Mistress Olivia. You are borrowing a book, I see."

"Aye. Am I allowed . . . that is, would my uncle approve?"

He smiled sheepishly. "I've a whole stack of them in my chamber. What have you chosen?" He walked toward me, holding out his hand, and I passed the book to him. Before I could answer, he said, "Ovid! My favorite poet."

"Then I chose well."

"The *Metamorphoses*. Have you read the stories?"

"Nay. I was hoping you might have time to help me with them."

"My students are dismissed for the day," he said. "If you can spare the time, why not begin now?"

"Aye, I do have time." *You have no idea how much.*

He motioned to a long oak table. It reminded me of the tables in some of our modern libraries, except it had benches instead of chairs. I thought Will would sit across from me, but instead, he plunked down beside me. "What do you know of our esteemed poet?"

"Very little. That is why I need your guidance."

He propped an elbow on the table and rested his head against his hand, staring suggestively at me. "Did you know much of Ovid's work is considered wanton and highly erotic?"

Gulp. "Nay, I did not," I choked out.

"That is why your brother cautioned me against using the *Amores* or *Ars Amatoria* in my instruction." He lifted his head and inclined it in my direction, moving a little closer to me. "Mayhap he's forgotten that the *Metamorphoses* can be just as amorous as Ovid's other work."

I played naïve. Easy, since I'd never read *any* Ovid. "Truly?"

"Oh, aye," he said. "You are coloring, mistress. I am embarrassing you."

"A little."

"You look quite lovely with your cheeks pink and your eyes a bit glazed."

Excuse me, my eyes are not glazed. He couldn't even see my eyes, since I wasn't looking at him. I was staring straight ahead, too self-conscious to look at his face. I was beginning to suspect that Will was a first-class flirt.

His voice came in a low whisper. "May I steal a kiss, Olivia?"

I turned toward him then, and he took that as a yes. Bending down, he pressed his lips to mine and kissed me sweetly. I felt his fingers tangling in my hair, then caressing my scalp. *Ah. I'm kissing Shakespeare, my hero. My idol.* I opened my eyes and looked straight into his gray ones. That shocked me back to reality. Full-blown making out in the library wasn't appropriate, at least not in this century. I pulled away.

"Ovid. We should begin, sir."

Will laughed. "Aye." He practically leaped off the bench and began prowling around the room, all the time lecturing about the great Latin poet. His life, his work, how he got in trouble with the emperor Augustus and was banished to some far-off port city, where he ended up spending the remainder of his life, pretty much a broken man.

"What caused the trouble?" I asked, when I could get a word in.

Will gave me a sensual grin. "The *Ars Amatoria.* The *Art of Love.*" He strode back over to me and brushed his fingers down my cheek. "You see, it is a manual of seduction."

"Oh." *I could use a copy.*

"Augustus was attempting moral reforms, and he was not pleased. There was no doubt more to it than that, but the *Ars* played a part in Ovid's downfall."

I thought we needed to move on. "Which are your favorites of *these* stories?" I asked, holding up the *Metamorphoses.*

"I am fond of them all." He let out a sharp breath. "They are not happy stories, yet somehow they please me. The characters make mistakes. They do not choose well, and must suffer the consequences. 'Tis an interesting time to study the human character, is it not?"

"You mean when we are in turmoil over something?"

"Aye. Sometimes we destroy the thing we want the most or love the best."

A funny little whimper burst out on a rush of breath. *Othello. Lear. Hamlet.* Even some of the comedies. "Will you read me one?"

"I'll read you the story of Apollo and Daphne, from the first book. Do you know it?"

I shook my head. Of course, I knew they were part of Greek mythology—I just wasn't sure what part, exactly. This time, Will seated himself across from me. He read and I listened, mesmerized by his voice, the characters, and the simple fact that it was Shakespeare reading to me.

A god named Apollo falls for Daphne, a nymph. She doesn't love him back; in fact, his declaration of love creeps her out. The more she resists him, the more he wants her. A big turn-on for him, apparently. One day he literally chases her, hoping to get her to change her mind, but instead he scares her senseless. *Proving that guys, even gods, have always been idiots.*

Daphne runs, her glorious hair streaming out behind her. She calls to her father, a river god, to save her, and on the spot he transforms her into a laurel tree. Apollo, when he catches up to her, places his hand on the trunk and feels her heart still beating. He's crushed. *At least he doesn't have to be a tree for all eternity.*

Will finished, and the room was still. "Couldn't he see how frightened she was?" I asked.

"He knew it, but was powerless to stop. He let himself believe he could win her, despite all evidence to the contrary."

"But if he'd just approached her in a reasonable way, maybe she would have changed her mind."

"Do you not see he was incapable of doing so?"

"He was an idiot. A fool," I said, maybe a tad too loud.

"Perhaps. But his foolish actions make a powerful story, eh?"

Chasing someone until she's forced to morph into a tree just seemed downright depressing to me. But I was looking for the happy ending. Will, on some level, was delving into human emotion and laying the groundwork for his future role as the world's greatest storyteller. I could almost see the pinwheels spinning inside his head. "Read me another," I said.

So he did. Pyramus and Thisbe, the classical version of *Romeo and Juliet*; and Ceres and Proserpina, featuring another lovesick god who kidnaps the woman he lusts after.

By then it was late afternoon. Bess would be wondering where I was, I knew, since it was time to dress for dinner. "Thank you, Will. This has been most . . . instructive."

He gave me his arm and we walked upstairs together. "I hope we can do it again."

"I would be disappointed if we did not." I gave him what I hoped was a teasing smile and turned off into my chamber. But he pulled me back, bending over and kissing my fingers. I kept my eyes fixed somewhere above his head, and I sensed rather than heard his soft laugh.

The next morning, when I was trying to decipher Ovid in the ladies' withdrawing room, Elizabeth approached me, a kindly look on her face.

"Olivia, dear, I am so pleased to see you reading." Her hands were folded in front of her skirts, as they usually were. "Ovid, I see. 'Tis always good to study the classics."

"I, ah—"

Apparently a response wasn't required. "Sadly, our cousin Jennet does not know how to read. She lately confessed this to me when I called upon her to read a passage from the Bible. I have asked Master Will to teach her."

"Aye, she told me."

"You did not bring any needlework with you?"

I felt my cheeks flush. "Nay, Aunt, I—I forgot it."

"Come, I have chosen a project for you." She led me to the chest where she kept her embroidery threads and fabrics. "A lady's hands must never be idle. While I am happy to see you improve your mind by reading, I fear you neglect other skills." Speaking of hands, I noticed that Will had been right about hers. They were definitely a few sizes larger than mine, with long, tapered fingers.

I forced a smile, even though I felt sick inside. I'd never embroidered—or even sewn anything—in my life, and I didn't think I could fake it. "What would you like me to do?"

"An altar cloth is always needed, and you would honor our Lord with your work." She handed me a basket. In it was a length of soft fabric of some sort, threads, needles, scissors, a thimble, and a frame. "Now you will be able to spend part of each day plying the needle."

"Thank you, Aunt. I'll begin this afternoon."

She smiled benevolently at me. "I am glad we are in accord." She paused a moment, as though gathering her thoughts. "I shall be leaving for a time, my dear. My brother's wife is gravely ill, and he has summoned me to help care for her."

"I hope she will recover, Aunt."

"I fear not. She had influenza, and it has gone to her lungs. But mayhap I can help ease her passing."

"Safe journey to you, then," I said, stepping forward to kiss her. There would be no antibiotic and no doctor who knew how to treat this poor woman's disease. But Elizabeth would be there to do all she could. Caring for the sick and dying must have been a major part of a woman's life in this time. Elizabeth seemed to bear it stoically.

After lunch, I decided to prowl the passageways and check out some of the rooms I'd yet to see. Elizabeth was supervising Jennet in the stillroom, Will was with his students, and I had no idea where Stephen was.

I heard a faint clacking noise and followed the sound to a room down the hall from the minstrels' gallery. When I glanced in, I found Stephen bent over a table, lining up a cue with a ball, ready to take his shot. So this was the billiard room. It also must have functioned as an office, since a desk and a chair were nestled together at one end and bookshelves held tall volumes that looked as if they might be account books.

The billiard balls were wooden, and the table, covered with felt, seemed about the same size as one in modern times. Stephen's ball missed its target, and I heard him mutter his favorite curse, "God's breath!"

He circled the table, scoping out his next shot. When he glanced up I blinked, catching my breath. He'd shaved his beard and mustache. Flashing a mischievous smile, he looked more like a teenager than a twenty-year-old. *And totally hot.*

"What do you think?" He rubbed his bare chin.

"I—I approve. Very much so. Do you mind if I stay? I can continue my exploring if you'd rather be alone."

"Do keep me company, pray. I've asked for some spiced ale to be brought up."

I stepped closer to the table and only then noticed there were no pockets. "How do you play this game?"

He handed me the cue. "Aim for the cue ball. The idea is to strike one of the other balls in such a way that the cue ball will bounce against the side and rebound into another ball."

I bent over the table, concentrating. I'd played pool a couple of times at friends' houses, but had never been any good. I drew the cue back and rammed it willy-nilly into the ball, with no thought of where it would go or what other ball it might strike.

"Well done, Olivia!" Stephen exclaimed when it slammed into another ball, caromed off the side, and rolled back, smashing into yet a different ball.

I curtsied. "I'm very skilled, I assure you." We both laughed. Stephen's eyes were warm, and I thought maybe we could patch up our relationship. "I need help with something," I blurted out. "Actually with two things, but you can only help with one of them." Somehow, I didn't think Stephen would be much good with the needlework emergency.

He lifted a brow. "You know I will do whatever I can."

"I can't read the script in the printed books in the library. With Shakespeare instructing me in the classics, I should learn. And since I'm practically dying of boredom . . . will you teach me?"

Moving around the table, cue in hand, he answered. "Certainly, I will teach you. What about handwriting?"

"I read the mysterious note, but that was less than ten words. I probably need help with that, too."

"I had difficulty with both in your time," he said, smiling sheepishly. "I understand how you must be feeling." After taking a shot he added, "What else do you need help with?"

I told him about Elizabeth and the embroidery project.

"Mayhap you should approach Mistress Jennet about that. It may provide a good opportunity to learn more about her."

"Good idea."

Just then, a servant entered the room with a tray holding a pewter jug and tankard. Stephen took the tray and I followed him to the window seat, where he set it down between us. An aroma, a little like pumpkin pie baking, drifted my way as Stephen poured. "We'll have to share, unless you want me to send for another tankard."

"I don't mind sharing." I accepted the mug from his outstretched hand and swallowed a giant sip. Big mistake. The pungent drink burned my throat, and it tasted like Satan had dreamed up the recipe. "Oh God, this stuff is horrible!" I thrust it back into Stephen's hands and jumped to my feet, coughing so hard, my eyes watered. When he held out a handkerchief, I grabbed it and dabbed at my eyes and nose.

Stephen rose. "Are you well, Olivia?" he said, his mouth quivering.

"Oh, go ahead and laugh. You know you want to." He did, but restrained himself from being totally obnoxious about it.

"You knew that would happen," I said. Croaked, really.

"Pray pardon me for laughing. Only you cannot know the number of times the same thing happened to me when I was in your time. Especially when I tasted your Coca-Cola drink."

Stephen took a long sip of the evil brew while I got myself under control. He offered it to me. "You're joking," I said. Every time we looked at each other, we cracked up.

"You resemble your mother, do you not?"

I quit laughing abruptly. Why did he have to ruin things by bringing up my mom? And how did he know what she looked like? Maybe he'd seen photographs of her when he was in the present.

"Some people think I do, I guess."

He peered at me over the rim of the cup. "Your hair is dark like hers? Your eyes a deep blue, your nose straight, and your mouth is . . ."

"Is what?"

He studied me for a moment, his eyes settling on my lips and making me squirm.

"Just say it. Big. Isn't that what you mean?"

"Olivia, do not be so sensitive. Your mouth is lovely and expressive. I would never make sport of your mouth."

"Ha!" I said, feeling stupid. "I may look like my mother, but I'm not *like* her at all. She has an ego the size of . . . of the Earth. Which she thinks revolves around her."

"Is she that bad?"

I sighed, feeling on the edge of a major freak-out. I hated talking about my mom. Our relationship was complicated, and sometimes, I felt, hopeless. "I hate her."

"Nay. You do not."

"I love my mother, but . . ." Stephen looked smug until I finished the thought. "But she hates me." Now, after all the laughing, I felt like something had grabbed hold of my heart and twisted.

"Surely you are mistaken. Hasn't she taught you her craft, trained you, encouraged you?"

"Sometimes. But other times, I'm convinced she wants me to

fail. She doesn't want me to be a better actor than she is." I gave a choked laugh. "No worries there. I'll never be as good, let alone better."

"What has she done to make you think this?"

I thought a minute. "Every summer, she and my father hold a workshop with young actors on Cape Cod. Until recently, she wouldn't even let me go." I remembered last year, when she and my grandfather had gotten into a huge fight because of it. In his view, a young girl who was separated from her parents as much as I was should be included in any summer plans. He prevailed, and I got to go.

"Continue," Stephen prodded.

"She let me come along, but only to help with props, wardrobe, and that kind of thing. I begged her to let me have a small part—it was *A Midsummer Night's Dream*, so there were plenty to go around—but she wouldn't allow it."

"And what reason did she give?"

"I wasn't ready, I didn't have enough experience, I'd embarrass myself and her. Whatever. It didn't really matter."

"Maybe she was right. Have you ever considered the possibility?"

Anger pressed against my chest, but I fought it down. I didn't want to lose it with Stephen. "She could have let me understudy! Or I could have acted in some of the rehearsals. Something special, just for me."

"Perhaps she is afraid for you. Afraid you might not succeed."

I glowered at him. "The great Caroline Graham? Those feelings are beneath her. She just wants to control me and my acting career. And keep me in my place."

"Then you must not allow it to be so," he said, reaching out for my hand. "You are not a child any longer, but a young woman, capable of thinking for herself and deciding her future."

"And that's why I decided to quit acting. It's her thing, not mine."

"Are you certain this decision was not made to spite her? To spite both your parents?"

"I knew you wouldn't understand." My anger had dissolved, disappointment taking its place.

"Olivia—"

Before the tears could come, I hurried into the corridor. Not caring who saw me, I ran through the passageways back to my room.

Chapter Twelve

I COULDN'T STOP THINKING about what Stephen had said, although it was making me crazy. Was he right? Did I want to quit acting to spite my parents? That was definitely part of it. There was no doubt they'd be disappointed and hurt. But if I believed that, wasn't it contradictory to believe my mother was jealous of me?

Something else about that conversation kept flickering around the corners of my mind. Stephen's kindness. The way he'd taken my hand and reassured me. I was positive he'd been sincere and not just trying to get on my good side. He had looked at me with soft eyes, his mouth gently curving around his comforting words. I was touched by his concern, even though in the end he'd infuriated me with his statements about my mother.

By bedtime, so many competing thoughts were spinning in my head that I had trouble falling asleep. I spent a restless night, never relaxing into a deep sleep, and woke up groggy and irritable. When

I heard Bess's quiet footsteps, I threw the coverlet over my head and groaned.

"I've brought your breakfast, mistress. You'll want to eat it while it's hot." With a little more prodding, I dragged myself out of bed, splashed water on my face, and plopped down on the settle by the fireplace. I ran a hand through my tangled hair while Bess covered my shoulders with my wool cloak and spread a blanket over my lap. Distracted, I began to spoon bites of pottage into my mouth. Didn't they ever eat anything else for breakfast? This stuff was something we'd eat for dinner. What I wouldn't give for a bowl of cornflakes.

"Mistress? Pray, what are these strange garments?"

With a sinking feeling, I spun around, nearly dropping my bowl. An odd look on her face, Bess was holding out my Victoria's Secret bra and panties. *Oh, shit!*

For a crazy moment, I thought about making up some ridiculous story about what they were. Putting the bra on my head, cups over my ears, and pretending it was some kind of hat.

"Mistress?"

I blinked and slowly got to my feet, still not sure what to say. Walking toward her, I reached out and took the raspberry-colored lingerie from her outstretched hands. "I'll show you, Bess. Turn around, pray."

I slipped into the panties; then, after removing my smock, I put on the bra. In truth, I hadn't been wearing either of them much. I'd hidden them under a stack of bodices, but Bess's sharp eyes had spotted them.

"You may look now," I said. I suppressed a smile, thinking that Macy would howl with laughter if she could see this.

Bess whirled around and stared. "Jesu! I've never seen such apparel before." She circled around me, getting a view from all angles. Tentatively, she reached out and touched the fabric at the back. I didn't move a muscle, just allowed her to examine and marvel. Meanwhile, I was starting to shiver.

"These, ah, garments were brought back from the Indies by a . . . a female relative." *How to explain synthetics?* "The cloth is a special kind made only there, and the stretchy parts are rubber, which comes from trees." Bess didn't say anything. "This garment"—I gestured at the bra—"supports and lifts your, um, breasts." God, I felt like I was in a commercial or something.

"Aye, so it does," she said.

"I'm freezing, Bess. I wish to dress now." Just as I reached for my smock, the doors between Stephen's and my chamber banged open. He walked into the room, head down, mumbling something to himself.

"Stephen!"

His head jerked up. Eyes widening, he gawked unabashedly until I covered up with my smock. "I'm dressing. Get out!"

"Pray forgive me." I noticed a spark in his eyes, and his lips definitely twitched right before he spun on his heel and exited. *Damn him!* I heard Bess snickering behind me.

She didn't question my explanation for the "strange garments." After helping me dress, she grabbed my breakfast tray and departed through the servants' door.

Alone at last, I perched on the edge of my bed and pondered my situation. Maybe my awful night's sleep was to blame, but foremost in my mind was one simple fact: *I wanted to go home.* I missed my friends, my grandfather, my parents. Okay, just my dad. And to get home, I knew what I had to do.

So what had I accomplished so far? I was making some progress with Will, but I needed something to help move things along more quickly. A plan of my own, one I could put into action by myself, without Stephen's involvement. For starters, I should push Will toward writing and acting. As I'd tried to tell Stephen, I was convinced seduction alone wouldn't work. If I persuaded Will to read me some of his writing, from there it would be easy to talk to him about the stage and his dream of becoming an actor. And I should make another date with him for more instruction in the classics.

Will seemed intent on gaining more than just my friendship, what with giving me the gloves and kissing me during our session in the library, and I'd do whatever I could to encourage him. And even though part of me felt like a pawn in some game Stephen was playing, I was committed to going through with the seduction program. I suspected Will would prove to be a gentle and patient lover.

I knew I should definitely keep close tabs on his relationship with Thomas Cook. Find out how far Will was leaning toward the religious life. Perhaps I'd have to search both their rooms, and when the opportunity arose, follow them and listen in on more of their conversations.

Although I couldn't pinpoint it, there was something suspicious about Jennet. I remembered her anger with me the first night, and her cool demeanor during the burning. She had an irrational possessiveness regarding Will. And I still hadn't ruled her out as the writer of the note. Even if she couldn't read or write, she could easily have asked someone else to write it, since she'd been away most of the weekend. My suspicions of her had nothing to do with Will becoming a Jesuit, but nevertheless, she bore watching.

I mulled everything over until hunger pangs alerted me it must be time for the midday meal.

Stephen had presented me with my own knife and a set of ivory toothpicks in an enameled case, so it was no longer necessary for us to sit next to each other at every meal. But at lunch he plopped right down next to me, gave me a wicked grin, and watched me blush. I wondered how much mileage he'd try to get out of seeing me in my underwear.

"How did you explain your . . . attire . . . to Bess?" he asked.

"Don't even go there. I'm not telling you anything about it."

He laughed out loud.

"Oh, just shut up," I hissed. Since Will, on my other side, was talking to someone else, I faked a sudden and profound interest in my surroundings. Eventually my gaze settled on the long table in the center of the hall. Three people were eating there today, two women and a man. A rather extraordinary-looking man, stout, with a ruddy face and ginger hair and beard. Momentarily forgetting my determination not to talk to Stephen, I turned and said, "Who's the funny little man over there?"

"At the long table? 'Tis Joseph, the cunning man."

"So what exactly does that mean?"

"People believe him to possess certain powers, and he does what he can to encourage that belief."

"Such as?"

"They come to him with their troubles, like losing a lover, or needing to know if the cereal crop will thrive this year, and he performs such rituals as persuade people he has some control over these situations. For coin."

"In other words, he's a con man."

"By that you mean he gulls people out of their money?"

I nodded. A servant passing a platter of carved roast interrupted us. I helped myself to a portion, and Stephen did the same. After the servant moved on, I resumed my questioning. "Does he live here on the manor?"

"Nay, in one of the villages. But he visits here often, I believe. My uncle does not like it, but the tenants and workers would complain if he forbade it."

I glanced around quickly before speaking. "Does everybody believe in this kind of thing?"

He narrowed his eyes at me. "In magic? You can certainly count me among those who do."

I smirked at him, until I realized he wasn't joking. "You do?"

"Given my situation, all you know about me, would you expect me not to?"

I had to smile at that. "Yet you admit Joseph is gulling people."

He cocked his head at me. "Aye. His brand of magic is not for me, but if it gives comfort to others, so be it."

My face must have registered confusion. He leaned in close and spoke softly. "Remember where you are. There are forces at work in the world that learned men cannot explain. How are we to account for diseases, monstrous births, and other such oddities?"

"Germs. Poor nutrition. Poverty," I shot back.

"But we do not have your advanced scientific knowledge. It will be centuries before we do." He rubbed at the stubble on his chin. "The church once performed such rituals as casting out demons, and purifying and blessing. But the Protestant clergy does not allow such practices. What is left for the common folk but to turn to magic?"

Grudgingly, I agreed. "Point taken." Stephen began stabbing pieces of roast with his knife and shoving them in his mouth, so I took the opportunity to speak to Will. His conversation at an end, he'd been concentrating on his meal while Stephen and I were . . . discussing. I hoped he hadn't overheard us. Even if he'd tried, he couldn't have caught more than snatches of our talk.

"Master Will, may I visit your schoolroom this afternoon?"

He looked surprised, but answered without any hesitation. "I would be honored."

After enough time had elapsed for lessons to resume after lunch, I followed the directions Will had given me to the east wing. In a few minutes, I heard the buzz of young voices, sounding a lot like children in a modern classroom. I paused in the doorway to check things out. The room was long and narrow, with tall windows on one side. In the far corner, a door opened onto an outdoor staircase. The children didn't have to navigate the maze of passages inside the house to find their schoolroom.

The older students, all boys, perched on stools at four tables. A group of the youngest children sat cross-legged on the floor, each one holding a slate with a long handle. They were reciting their letters to each other. I was surprised to see a few girls in the bunch. Will Shakespeare and Jennet were seated at a separate table and seemed to be engrossed in what I assumed was a reading lesson. I'd been hoping to put my plan into action, but that couldn't happen with Jennet here.

One of the children spotted me and hollered, "Look! Mistress has come to visit!"

Will and Jennet looked up, Will with his usual sweet smile. He got to his feet and came over to greet me. Jennet's jaw tightened as she reined in the glare about to burst out on her face.

"Mistress Olivia, welcome," Will said.

"Good day, Will. I hope I am not disturbing you."

"Nay. I was helping Jennet with her reading. Come, meet my students."

Jennet rose, and we curtsied to each other.

Then Will introduced me to the older boys, who stood and bowed. "What are you studying?" I asked.

"Latin grammar," one said. "Conjugating verbs."

"*Amo, amas, amat*," I recited, scrunching up my nose, and they all laughed. I knelt down before the little kids. Apple cheeked and well scrubbed, they surrounded me, some stroking my embroidered bodice or my hair, others bending in for a kiss. They were adorable. "Are you being good children today?"

"Aye, mistress," they assured me.

"Robby hit me with his hornbook," one boy said. Obviously the class tattletale.

Will stopped to have a word with the shame-faced culprit, and I wandered over to Jennet.

"Mistress, how do you get on with your reading?"

"Well enough."

"Master Will is a good teacher?"

"Aye."

Okay, then. She didn't want to talk to me. I had turned for the door when I heard her voice, so low I almost missed it.

"Do not mistake me, mistress. I will have Master Shakespeare for my own."

"I beg your pardon?"

She laughed, her green eyes glittering. "You heard me."

I returned her stare for a moment and then wandered over to the door to wait for Will. It wasn't my place to tell her that particular plan wouldn't work out. Myself aside, there was Anne Hathaway in Will's very near future if all went well.

Before Will walked over to join me, I heard him ask Jennet to mind the children while he spoke to me. Boldly, I grasped his arm and pulled him into the passage. "Master Will, I know you are occupied with your duties, but I wondered when we might . . . you might . . . spare the time to continue my classical education. If you still wish to enlighten me, that is."

Eyes gleaming playfully, he said, "Oh, I do. I will always make time for you, Mistress Olivia." He thought for a moment. "Hock Monday and Tuesday are next week, so there will be no school. If it suits you, come either morning. I shall be here."

I pictured boys racing around with hockey sticks out on the tilting green. "Oh, I forgot about Hock Day, er, that is, Days. I'll come on Monday."

"I shall look forward to it, mistress."

Before he could get away, I said, "I would very much like to talk to you about your writing and act—playing, too."

"You would?" He seemed genuinely surprised.

"Aye. Perhaps I should come both days."

He grinned at me. "It would be my pleasure, Mistress Olivia."

Chapter Thirteen

THAT NIGHT, I TOLD STEPHEN about Jennet's "I will have Master Shakespeare for my own" comment. After the evening meal, the two of us had sneaked off to the library for some privacy.

"I wonder if she wishes to wed him," he said. "Maybe to escape her controlling father."

"Wed him? He's Catholic! Her father would never allow it . . . would he?"

Stephen gave a curt laugh. "Nay, you are right about that. But mayhap she is more willing to lose her virtue to him than I originally thought."

"But you said a Puritan girl would never do that! That's why you needed me."

"Do not look so vexed. She may have hidden motives we do not know about."

I sighed in frustration. "For whatever reason, she was warning me off."

He looked thoughtful. "'Tis almost as if she were throwing down the gauntlet."

"You mean challenging me? She doesn't scare me. I'm the one Shakespeare was reading Ovid's love poetry to a few days ago." I knew I sounded smug, but I was pretty confident of Will's interest in me.

"Instructing you in the art of love, was he? You did not mention it. And how did he get on?" Stephen's voice dripped sarcasm, confusing me. Wasn't this what he wanted me to be doing with Will?

"None of your business. Remember? You're not supposed to ask. And why are you acting all mad about it?"

Impatiently, he waved off my question. "What were you doing in a schoolroom, with Jennet and a passel of brats present?" he asked, and began pacing around the room with his hands on his hips. "Nothing can be accomplished under those circumstances."

"I had business with Will," I said, glaring at him. "And if you must know, I went to the schoolroom to arrange a time to meet privately with Will. I also told him I'm very interested in his writing, which is the truth. He seemed thrilled."

When Stephen shot me a skeptical glance, I said, near tears, "Why are you acting like this? What did I do wrong?"

He was at my side in an instant. "You did nothing wrong, Olivia. Pray forgive me," he said. "I'm a brute."

This made me laugh and brought me back to my senses. I wandered over to the grate, its flames dying. "Maybe if I had a better understanding of why I'm here, it would help," I said, huddling in front of the settle to soak up whatever warmth remained. "The plays are so much a part of my life. Shakespeare's revered in my century. He's practically a god! I know he dedicated his life to writing and acting, so why do you even need me?"

"I daresay you will carp at me until I explain further."

"Count on it."

"Where should I start?" he whispered.

I thought he was talking to himself, but I answered anyway. "Tell me how you knew about Shakespeare."

Stephen cursed under his breath and looked as if he might protest. Then he shrugged. "We may as well be warm while we talk." After heaving another log onto the fire, he sank down next to me.

"I can see the future," he said, finally breaking the silence. "Brief flashes of it."

A cynical grunt burst out of me. "Right." I lifted a brow at him.

"Mayhap I should not have used those words. I have visions. They come upon me; I do not summon them, and would rather not be burdened with them, to confess the truth."

"Then why don't you just ignore them?"

"They haunt me until I take action."

"So you're a wizard or something?"

"I prefer the term you used before. 'Time warden.'" He glanced at me quickly, and then his eyes darted away.

"Go on."

"'Tis a power I inherited, one that has been in my family for centuries. One person in each generation has the visions. When he reaches maturity, the astrolabe is bestowed upon him."

"How long since the job was passed to you?"

"I was seventeen. My uncle preceded me."

"Alexander? No way!"

Grinning, he said, "Nay, an uncle on my father's side taught me. When he knew his days were numbered."

"Does your family know?"

"Only my father." He leaned forward and rested his arms on his thighs. "This is difficult. . . . I never speak of it to anyone."

"The astrolabe—that's the instrument you had when we were on the school roof, isn't it?" After he nodded, I went on. "What's the point? Does it always involve time travel, and somehow preserving the future?"

"My family's duty is to protect Britain's destiny. Not to change it, but to preserve it."

I was about to laugh until I caught his deadly serious expression. He wasn't joking. "That's, well, amazing. Too much for one man." Tentatively, I ran my hand across his back in a comforting gesture.

"Aye," he said, looking at me with an ironic grin. "The visions set things in motion, and usually I must travel to the future to discover the actual truth. When I return, I take action."

I squeezed my eyes shut, trying to understand. "So you had a vision about Shakespeare. Had you met him yet?"

"Nay, the visions came first. But then my father told me Alexander had employed a young lad named Shakespeare as schoolmaster here, and it all began to make sense."

"What was in your visions, if you don't mind my asking?" He probably did, but was in too deep now to refuse to tell me.

"Fragments of the plays passed through my head. . . . Will Shakespeare appeared again and again. Writing and acting. Then, imaginings of plays I knew were being performed in the distant future. Plays he composed, clear indications of his genius."

"And that was why you came to my century, to figure out if the visions about Shakespeare were true. If he was really as great as he seemed."

He nodded. "It was not until I journeyed to your time that I understood the scope of Shakespeare's genius. Only then did I learn exactly what you and others had made of his work."

When he paused for a breath, I said, "So how are you able to time travel?"

"The astrolabe holds the magic that makes passage through time possible. And saying the right words."

"You mean the 'From this age' thing you said right before we—"

"Precisely."

I struggled to get my head around everything he'd told me and realized some parts still didn't make sense.

"But if you hadn't even met Will yet, how did you know he was in danger?"

"I learned that from the visions, although I did not discover the particulars until we came to Hoghton Tower. Some of the visions provide only a feeling, in this case one of dread. As in a dream, when you know something awful is about to occur, but you are powerless to stop it."

"Yet you told me on my first day there was a Jesuit here who had his eye on Shakespeare."

"I did not yet know who it was, nor did I perceive the true extent of the threat. 'Twas only after the burning I fully understood."

I couldn't help myself. I had to ask. "Did you see me in your visions?"

"I did."

I squirmed around so I was facing him directly. "So then you found me in the future and decided I was the one?"

He stared at me for a long time before answering; so long I had to look away from the intense scrutiny. But not before I noticed the look in his eyes. Longing, regret, and need, all mixed up together, and aimed directly at me.

"None other would do. You were the right age and sex, and because of your acting skills, you could pass yourself off as a young lady of this time. Given your parentage, and your own interest in Shakespeare and acting, it had to be you."

"Oh." A lame response, but I couldn't think of anything else to say.

Still with that intensity in his eyes, he went on. "Your purpose here is real. If we are unsuccessful in carrying out our mission, Shakespeare's work may be lost for all time. Indeed, there may never *be* any plays, poems, or sonnets, because he will not have composed them."

"Wow," I said softly and mostly to myself.

"Are you satisfied, then?"

I wasn't exactly clear on all he'd told me, but I'd absorbed about as much as I could for now. "I have more questions, but I'll save the rest for later. For now, one last thing. Why seduction? Was *that* in the visions?"

"That was of my own devising."

My jaw dropped and I stared, incredulous. "You thought that part up on your own? Oh, my God! You're no different from a modern guy with too much testosterone."

He raised his brows. "Pray, what does that mean?" In the darkened room, Stephen's eyes were almost black.

"You think sex is the answer to everything!"

"Nay, I do not," he protested. "I've spoken of this before—we have an urgent problem. 'Tis the quickest way to avert disaster."

That said, he got to his feet and walked over to the windows, his back to me.

Maybe I was being too hard on him. If everything he'd told me was true, he *was* grappling with a major problem and had no choice but to find an immediate solution. I followed him over to the windows and touched him lightly on the shoulder. "I'm sorry, Stephen."

Without looking at me he said, "And I apologize for my excess of, what was it? *Testosterone?*"

I groaned inwardly at his sarcasm. There would be no more communication between us tonight. We'd reached our limit of trying to understand each other. Passed it, in fact. "Good night then, Stephen."

He didn't respond, so I crept quietly out the door. When I reached my passageway, I glanced out the tall windows facing the courtyard. Night was falling, but I could make out two figures walking briskly toward the front of the manor. I recognized Shakespeare and Thomas Cook. Wasting no time, I detoured into my room for my cloak. Copernicus dozed by the fire, chin on paws, and didn't rouse himself to greet me. Just as well, since I didn't have time to play with him. I flew down the staircase in pursuit of the two men.

I made my way through the inner and outer courtyards, walking by the stables and passing beneath the great keep. No sign of Will and Thomas, but they couldn't be too far ahead of me. It was deep twilight, the first stars brilliantly awakening and a waning crescent moon curving in the sky. A profound peace and stillness gripped the night air. Nothing but some plaintive birdcalls broke the silence.

After a few minutes, when I was approaching the rose garden, the sound of voices drifted toward me. Stepping back, I huddled against a large shrub, wishing I could be an ordinary girl again. Not someone who skulked around listening in on other people's conversations.

"What drives you to this life?" Will asked. "To be pent up here like a prisoner?"

"I'm no prisoner, Will. My work is here for the present. I am free to come and go, when and as I must."

"Do you not miss the more worldly life? Do you never long for a wife and children?"

"I gave up those things for God."

"I do not know if I have such strength as you, to be so devout."

"Mayhap you would never be a missionary. But think of the pleasures of learning! Latin, Greek, history, logic, science. Studying the church fathers. Writing verse."

I covered my mouth before a laugh could burst out. Will would learn *that* well enough to please even Thomas.

Will said nothing.

"Your father has already signed his spiritual testament," Thomas continued.

"Aye. He sent me north with the priest who witnessed it."

"You are gifted, Will. You would adapt easily to the priestly life."

"I would love to study the classics. Such as I have already learned is but a trifle compared to your learning." Will sounded excited, eager. My mind spun out a fantasy of what might have happened if he had gone to university and become a brilliant scholar. Perhaps he would have been content with a scholarly life, but I didn't think so. The plays shone with too much vitality and spirit.

"'Tis getting late," Thomas said. "Promise me you will think on all we've discussed."

I didn't wait around for Will's answer, because I had to get away before they discovered me cowering in the bushes. But it sounded like Thomas was beginning to gain some ground.

Chapter Fourteen

A FEW DAYS CRAWLED PAST. It rained, not a gentle rain, but thick sheets streaming from the sky. I stayed indoors, trapped by the deluge, and saw Stephen mainly at meals. Things had stayed awkward between us, and I hated that.

One morning after I'd eaten breakfast and dressed, I walked through the passage to his chamber, clutching the volume of Ovid. At first, I couldn't see him. It was another dreary day, a veil of mist and clouds shrouding the landscape, and not much light found its way into our rooms. He must have already gone out, I thought, although I couldn't imagine what he'd be doing in this weather.

But after a minute of staring into the room, I sensed a dark shape hovering near the back wall. An uneasy feeling rippled through me. If it was Stephen, why hadn't he called out to me, invited me in? And then I heard a piercing moan, so startling I lost my grip on the book and it slammed to the floor. The dark figure made a sudden movement into the light. It *was* Stephen.

He continued to moan, softer now, but still an eerie and

primitive sound. I approached him slowly, not wanting to frighten him. He was in a trancelike state, and I knew beyond a doubt he must be in the throes of a vision. Although he was looking right at me, he didn't speak or acknowledge my presence. Whatever was playing out in his head, I didn't want to mess with it. So I continued to stand silently, keeping watch. If he got so loud someone else might hear, or seemed to be in pain, I'd intervene. Unless that happened, it was probably best to leave him alone until it was over.

After a short time, he moved toward the bed and collapsed sideways onto it, becoming so still it scared me. I rushed over and nudged him with my hip, whispering his name. Once, then again. He moved, rolling onto his back, and opened his eyes. He blinked at me and said, "Olivia, what are you doing in here?"

"Are you all right? I think you just had a vision."

"God's breath! Did you witness it?"

"Just the last few minutes. How long do they usually last?"

"According to my father and uncle, not much longer than that. You must have seen most of it. Was I moaning?"

"I guess you could call it that. I—I was frightened at first."

"Can you help me sit up?"

Positioning myself behind him, I slid my arms underneath his shoulders. His body felt slack in my grip. "Ready?" He nodded, and with my help, he managed to raise himself up. He swung his feet over the edge of the bed and gave me an apologetic glance. "I'm sorry you had to see that."

"Don't be. I'm glad. I wanted to know what it was like."

He grasped my hand and pulled me down beside him. "What do you wish to know? I can tell you are curious."

I hadn't expected him to be so open to my questions. "What was in the vision, obviously."

"It was not one of my clearer visions. More fleeting, and the feeling of dread I mentioned to you was pronounced." He paused and rubbed his hands over his face. "You will not like to hear this, but I saw the sheriff."

"Oh God, not him. What was he doing?"

"He was sitting at a table with another man. One I did not recognize. They were studying a map. I could see it was of the north of England, and Hoghton Tower was marked on it. They seemed to be plotting or scheming, but I couldn't hear their words. Suddenly, the sheriff looked up and fixed his icy stare on me, as if he were a hunter and I, the prey. That must have been when I felt the fear in my belly and began keening."

"That's bad!" I practically shouted. "I'm terrified of that man. He's evil."

"Hush, now." Stephen squeezed my hand. "No need to be alarmed. Sometimes it takes me a few days to sort out the meaning of a vision. I remember things I could not recall at first. It will come clearer, and we will understand more fully."

I nodded, wanting to believe him, but I knew I'd stress about it until he figured out exactly what the vision had been telling him. Giving him a sidelong glance, I noticed beads of perspiration on his forehead. I rose and went to the washstand, where I dipped a fresh cloth into the bowl of water. I hurried back to Stephen and pressed it to his head. I thought he'd bat my hand away, but he let me take care of him.

"Is it painful? When you have the visions?"

He looked at me in surprise. "Not painful. Only the sweating and sometimes a slight headache."

I lowered myself back down beside him. "The first day I was here, when you told me about . . . steering history in the right direction, you used the phrase, 'for my sins.' Did you mean that literally?"

Half-laughing, he said, "'Tis only an expression. But sometimes it seems I must have done something very wicked in the past, or mayhap an ancestor did, and now I must atone for it."

"Is it so bad, what you do?"

"I suppose some men would find it exciting. But I would far rather live a normal life—farm, marry, and raise a family—than deal with magic, visions, and hurtling through time."

"You sound like a real homebody," I said.

"Is that bad?"

"No. Not bad. Just surprising for someone your age."

"You do remember what century you are currently residing in?" he said, quirking his mouth at me.

I laughed. "It's amazing how different it is now. In my time, a young man your age would probably rather hurl himself off the Empire State Building than get married."

"That is one of your wondrous constructions?" He shrugged. "We don't live as long in this era, and so must get on with our lives."

"Don't say that."

"Why not? It is the truth. Disease is rampant, and nothing to be done for it."

"I don't like thinking about it." I swallowed hard.

He stared at me for a moment, looking confused, and then said, "We shall not talk of it, then. I see you brought a book with you."

"Oh, damn, I dropped it! I hope I didn't damage it." I walked over and picked it up. "I wanted to remind you about teaching me to read Elizabethan script. You probably don't feel up to it now, though."

"On the contrary, it will do me good to think about something else."

"It's the translation of Ovid. Will it work for teaching me?" I handed it to him and looked at his handsome face, now grown so familiar. Crazy, but for a moment I had the strongest urge to ask him to hold me. I wanted to feel his arms around me and beg him to forgive me for doubting his visions. Now that I'd seen him having one, I was convinced they were genuine. It seemed scary and surreal to me—so what must it be like for him? And then afterward, he had to figure out what it all meant. It must take an emotional toll, even if Stephen wouldn't admit it.

"Olivia? Are you unwell?"

I blinked back to reality. "No, of course not. I'm sorry, I was distracted, that's all."

"Let's work in the library, at the table."

"Won't Thomas be there?"

"He rode out earlier to administer last rites. I do not believe he's returned."

In a few minutes, we were seated at the oak library table, where Will had tutored me in Ovid. The smell of leather-bound books and beeswax candles drifted through the air. Stephen found a piece of foolscap—which is what they called sheets of paper—and began writing.

I rested my elbow on the table and propped my chin in my hand. "What are you doing?"

"Writing the alphabet. You must learn to recognize how each letter is formed. Printed books look much the same."

"Oh." I stared, mesmerized by the elegant script forming on the page. He slid the paper over to me and handed me the quill.

"You try."

I dipped the quill in the ink jar and attempted to copy the letters as he'd written them. "This feels so awkward," I said, glancing at him. I flashed back to second grade, when I'd learned cursive, always hopeful for a sticker on my paper. But I didn't write cursive anymore. Hardly anybody did, except for older people.

I wrote, crossed out, and sighed with frustration. Stephen curved his fingers over mine, so we were tracing each letter together. His touch sent an electric shock through me. I felt his breath on my cheek, could smell his shaving soap. When I looked goofily up at him and laughed, the quill slipped and slashed a long black stroke against the page.

My cheeks burned. What was the matter with me?

"You're hopeless," Stephen said.

I shot him a toxic look and tried again, finally making it through the lowercase letters. While I worked, Stephen had written capitals on another sheet, which he now scooted over to me. I groaned and said, "Slave driver."

It wasn't so difficult, only different, with a lot of curving, swirly lines. Extra loops and marks that looked as if they didn't belong. After a while, we moved to the settle and Stephen examined the book. "This will serve." He handed it to me. "Can you read any of it?"

I studied it for a few minutes. He rose, and I heard him at the desk moving objects and papers around. He came back over and handed me a magnifying glass. "This might help."

It did, but only marginally. Even enlarged, some of the words remained a complete mystery. Many were easily identifiable, and others I could guess at. Eventually I tossed the book aside, feeling a headache coming on.

Stephen laughed. "Do not give up. I felt exactly the same when trying to decipher your script. You'll catch on after a time."

"Absolutely. Just in time for my return to the present."

He narrowed his eyes at me.

"Sorry," I said quickly. I didn't want to ruin our tenuous peace. "And I nearly forgot to tell you. . . . I followed Shakespeare and Thomas Cook the other night after I left you. I overheard a very interesting conversation."

"Go on."

"Thomas spoke to Will about furthering his education, and ended by urging him—again—to think about becoming a Jesuit. Will promised he would. Think about it, I mean."

Stephen looked worried. "If we don't set the plan in motion, it may be too late."

"I told you I arranged a meeting with Will. Two meetings, actually. That should lead to something."

Stephen sent me an accusing look, which totally irritated me.

I folded my arms across my chest. "Don't worry. I'm looking forward to making love with Will. I can't imagine anything more exciting."

He muttered a curse under his breath. "Truly, mistress? I am glad the idea is no longer so loathsome to you as it once was."

He didn't look glad. He looked kind of miserable. That feeling I'd had earlier of wanting to be held reared up again, and suddenly my heart was in my throat. It had to be homesickness. What else could it be? Stephen took one look at me and must have seen the despair written on my face. He pulled me into his arms, and I clung to him. "Forgive me for pushing you. 'Tis not easy, I know."

I curled myself into his embrace for a minute. "I think I'm homesick," I said, drawing back. My voice trembled, my throat so tight I could barely speak.

"I am always here if you need me." He kissed the top of my head.

"Yes, I know. I'm being idiotic." I stepped away and inhaled a huge breath.

"Better?"

I nodded.

"We'll speak of this another time. Come, let's go to lunch."

Although my mind was on Stephen, I chatted pleasantly with Fulke and his father. "We may have a visit from Lord Strange's Men," Master Gillam told me between chewing bits of pheasant. He sounded excited, so I knew this must be something big.

"Ah. When do you expect them?" I had no idea who Lord Strange was, but I suspected his "men" must be a group of actors.

"Within a fortnight," he said, "and the Earl of Derby as well!"

"How . . . thrilling." I clumsily sliced off pieces of meat with my knife, popped them into my mouth, and washed them down with ale.

"Aye. Preparing for their arrival will mean extra work for the whole household. Then too, it is costly when an earl visits." He laughed and leaned in close. "Especially this earl, who fancies himself royalty."

"Father, what play are Strange's men to perform?" Fulke asked.

"*Orlando Furioso*, mayhap, or *Beauty and Housewifery*."

This was good news! A performance would definitely engage Shakespeare and help further my secondary plan. I glanced at Will and Thomas across the table, engaged in a discussion about, if I overheard correctly, the *Aeneid*.

"Virgil celebrates the majesty of Rome," Thomas was saying.

"The Roman Empire?" Will asked.

"Aye. But 'tis nothing compared to the holy church of Rome. The kingdom of Christ."

Can't they have a normal conversation? I gripped the sides of my chair in frustration. Darting another glance at Will, I caught him looking right at me. Maybe it was only a muscle twitch, but I swear to God he winked at me. Which made me wonder if he was taking Thomas Cook seriously and whether or not he was really on board with the religious program.

Fulke and his dad went on discussing the earl's visit. Stephen was talking to his uncle about sheep and pastures and other farming-related things, from what I could hear. Bored, I'd turned to scan the room when a man approaching our table caught my eye. If I wasn't mistaken, he was Alexander's steward. He leaned over and whispered in his boss's ear.

In a flash, Alexander was on his feet. "Thomas!"

Thomas wiped his mouth and walked over to Alexander. They had a whispered conversation, with lots of gesturing and frantic looks passing back and forth. Among the rest of us, talk ceased, knives dropped to the table, and everyone stared. The mood had quickly changed from jolly to fearful. Thomas and the steward eventually hurried out of the hall, and Alexander sat down. After a few tense moments, I heard pounding feet approaching through the courtyard. The door flew open and a troop of men barged in, led by the sheriff.

Seeing that man again made my stomach lurch, especially now that I knew he'd been in Stephen's vision.

"What is the meaning of this?" Alexander stood and glared at them.

"Sir, I am arresting you in the name of Her Majesty, Queen Elizabeth," the sheriff said.

"And may I know what offense I have committed, sir?"

"'Tis one I believe you are well aware of. You have not attended Sunday services for many weeks, in violation of the Act of Uniformity. Nor have you paid your fines."

The other men seized Alexander's arms. He didn't resist, nor did anyone make a move on his behalf.

"Can't you do something?" I asked Stephen, tugging on his sleeve.

"My lord sheriff," Stephen said, rising. "Would it not suffice for my uncle to pay the money owed?"

"Who are you, sir?"

"Stephen Langford, nephew to Master Hoghton." He gave a curt bow.

"Well, Master Langford, if you do not wish to end up in a cell with your uncle, stay out of this. It is not your affair."

"Indeed, this is too harsh," Stephen said, stepping forward, really getting in the sheriff's face. I admired his courage, but in this situation, fear trumped admiration.

"Stephen!" I hissed.

The sheriff's hand dropped to the hilt of his sword, and two of his men drew theirs. Stephen's hand flew to his side, and he blanched when he remembered he had no weapon. Still, he didn't back off.

"Stand aside, Nephew," Alexander said. "Pray see to the others." Two of the men led Alexander out to the courtyard while the rest of us watched, helpless. The sheriff turned his cruel gaze on us, and we waited for him to speak.

Chapter Fifteen

THE SHERIFF RETREATED SLIGHTLY from Stephen, who was at least half a head taller than him. "Where is Mistress Hoghton?" he asked.

"She is not here at present," Stephen replied. "Her sister-in-law is ill, and she was summoned to Clitheroe to help with her care."

The sheriff grunted. "We have learned there is a Jesuit hiding here. Before we leave, we intend to find him. Family members, and all others who live in the house, come with me. You will guide us in our search."

No one denied the accusation or argued. Coward that I was, I didn't say a word. We all followed him out the door into the courtyard, and from there to the main entrance. I clung to Stephen's arm, and Jennet, I noticed, stayed close to Will. Fulke and his father, and then the servants who lived and worked in the house, brought up the rear. Fear for Thomas coiled in my stomach, and I hoped he'd found a good hiding place.

"What else is here besides the entry?" the sheriff asked.

In the absence of his aunt and uncle, Stephen took the lead. "Nothing of any importance, sir. It is exactly what you see. An entryway." Stephen returned his severe look steadily, never dropping his eyes. The sheriff signaled a couple of his men to search the small storage rooms off to the sides.

The rest of us trooped upstairs, moving from passage to passage, room to room. The sheriff's minions scrutinized everything, including fireplaces, paneling, and cupboards. They pounded walls and stuck arms up chimneys. On hands and knees, they searched under beds and inspected shadowed alcoves. With only a few candles for light, I didn't know how they expected to see much of anything.

Meanwhile, the sheriff shot questions at Stephen. "Where have you concealed the Jesuit?" "How long has he stayed with you?" and "To what family does he go next?" Stephen deflected the questions skillfully, shrugging, shaking his head, or saying something noncommittal, like, "Sir, you have been misinformed." He seemed unflappable.

By now we'd marched back through the hall, finally reaching the passageway with the chapel. When one of the sheriff's men swung open the huge door, my heart went into overdrive. Thomas could be hiding there. What would happen if they found him? Would we all be arrested and thrown in the Tower? To my amazement, the room had been completely transformed. It no longer looked remotely like a chapel. No religious objects or paintings were in sight.

A particularly nasty-looking guy ran up to the sheriff. "The back wall is suspicious," he said, rapping his knuckles on it to make his point. "It sounds hollow. 'Tis not as thick as it should be."

"Look for a hidden latch."

While we waited, Stephen draped his arm around my shoulder and I leaned into him. When no one was looking, I whispered, "Were any of these other men in your vision?"

He shook his head.

"Where's Thomas?"

"I'll tell you later," he said.

After spending a long time examining, pounding, and rapping on the wall, the sheriff let out a roar of frustration. "Zounds!"

I'd never actually heard anybody but Shakespearean actors say "Zounds." I felt like I was in some kind of drama, so it seemed appropriate.

"Separate them," the sheriff said to his men. "Peter, take those two." He pointed at Will and Jennet, still standing together.

"Wh-where shall I t-take them, sir?"

"You have dozens of rooms to choose from, fool!" Next, he pointed to Fulke and his dad. "Simon, take this boy and his father to the library." Simon was the nasty-looking guy. A scruffy black beard sprouted from his square chin, and a fearsome scar curved from one corner of his eye down to his mouth, like a warning.

"I shall deal with Master Langford and his sister," the sheriff said, glowering at us. He directed the remaining two men to question the servants.

"Back to the hall with you," the sheriff said to us. "You lead, Langford."

Stephen squeezed my hand as we dashed off ahead of the sheriff. He set a fast pace and I had to hurry to keep up.

"Olivia," Stephen whispered, slowing a little. "Keep walking, but listen. No matter what happens, do not tell him anything."

"What do you mean, 'no matter what happens'?"

"Do not worry, only remember what I said. You must not reveal anything, under any circumstances. Agreed?"

"I don't like the sound of this."

"I beg you, do as I ask."

"All right!"

"Silence!" the sheriff yelled.

When we arrived in the banqueting hall, he motioned us to the table, still littered with platters, half-eaten meals, and tankards. He remained standing and made a show of rattling his saber. And I'd always thought that was just an expression.

"You are papists, like your aunt and uncle?" he began.

I'd let Stephen get that one.

"We were at one time, aye. Our parents grew up with the old faith, sir."

"Just as I thought. Traitors."

"That is an unfounded accusation!"

The sheriff continued as though Stephen hadn't spoken. "How long have you been staying at Hoghton Tower?"

"A few weeks."

"You, mistress," the sheriff said, suddenly turning his hard eyes on me. "Have you been to Mass here?" He was in my face now, so close I could see the broken veins spreading out at the end of his bulbous nose. His breath smelled of raw onions and ale.

"Nay! We do not attend Mass."

He reached down and grabbed my bodice, jerking me up in one swift motion. "You are lying, mistress." His voice was low and menacing.

Stephen leaped to his feet. "Let her go. She's telling the truth."

So fast it registered only as a blur, the sheriff let go of me and shoved Stephen backward onto the table, rattling the trenchers and spilling ale. As he pulled himself up, brushing bits of food off his doublet, I stole a glance at him. *Please, give me a signal! What should I do?* But all I saw was a cold glint in his eyes. I turned back to the sheriff.

"Please, sir, I know nothing of what you speak. 'Tis against the law to attend Mass." I barely got the words out, because my mouth had completely dried up.

"What do you know of young Shakespeare?"

Where did that come from?

"We only made his acquaintance since our arrival here," Stephen said. "We know nothing about him other than he is teaching the children of my uncle's tenants."

"What of his relationship to the Jesuit?"

"There is no Jesuit."

The sheriff blanched and moved an intimidating step closer to us. Then he hesitated a moment, like he was thinking things over. "Stay here," he said, and strode out of the hall. When he was out of hearing range, I rushed over to Stephen. "Are you okay?"

"Aye, for the moment. Did he hurt you?"

"He scared me a little," I lied. I'd never been so terrified in my life. "Why do you think he asked about Will?"

"It puzzles me. I've no idea."

"Do you know where Thomas is? Is he safe?"

"These homes have hiding places. Priest holes, they're called. I imagine he's safely hidden in one of them."

I nodded, relieved. "Stephen, why don't we hide? Let's make a dash for it. They can't search every chamber in this house!"

" 'Twould be cowardly. Things would go worse for the others. Besides, there's no time; I hear them approaching already." He took my hands in his. "Remember what I said. Reveal nothing, no matter what."

I knew something awful was about to happen, and I must have looked panicked. "Please, Olivia. All will be well," Stephen said, giving my hands a squeeze before dropping them.

Why didn't I believe him?

The sheriff returned with some of his men, who must have finished questioning Will and the others. He quickly turned his attention to me. "Your brother will pay for every lie you tell me," he said in a cold and calm voice.

"Wh-what do you mean?"

Simon, the one who'd been sent to question Fulke and his father, seized Stephen and yanked him to his feet. "Is there a priest living here?" the sheriff asked me.

I risked a glance at Stephen, who stared straight ahead and would not make eye contact with me. "Nay, sir. There is not."

While two men restrained Stephen, Simon punched him in the gut. With a grunt, he doubled over. They jerked him back up as he gasped for breath.

Horrified, I recoiled under the sheriff's threatening gaze. "Now, mistress. The Jesuit. Where is he?"

"I do not know of any such person," I said, my voice shaking.

One of the men holding Stephen grabbed a fistful of his hair and jerked his head up, while Simon, with his huge, hairy fist, bloodied Stephen's nose and gave him another punch to the stomach for good measure.

"I beg you, stop!" I lunged forward, but the sheriff yanked me back. Stephen was choking, trying to get a breath. He sounded awful.

"Where is the chapel? The vestments? The sacred vessels?"

"We do not have such things, sir! Not that I am aware of."

The sheriff said nothing, merely nodding to Simon.

This time it was a blow to Stephen's eye. I stared at him, hoping he'd signal me that I could confess all, but still he wouldn't look at me. Blood trickled out of his nose, which seemed a little off kilter. A cut had opened up above one brow and was oozing blood.

"Sir, I know nothing that could be of any help to you. You're going to kill him!"

They ignored me, instead delivering more blows when I refused to answer, or didn't give the answer they wanted. I'd always thought the sounds in staged fights in the movies or on TV were exaggerated. But not anymore. The sound of knuckles striking flesh and bone was appalling. And Stephen, poor Stephen, with no way to fight back or block the punches.

"You care not for your brother, mistress," the sheriff said derisively, "or you would cease your lying."

Eyes streaming tears, nose running, I felt nearly incoherent by this time. I glanced at Stephen's face, a bloody, bruised mask. He no longer seemed able to hold his head up, and I didn't think he could take much more. Wiping my own face with trembling hands, I didn't think I could either.

I inhaled a shaky breath. Pulling myself together, I looked at the sheriff straight on. "You're wrong, sir, I care deeply for my brother. But he is a stubborn man. You're wasting your time."

The sheriff looked like he might pop a blood vessel, and for a moment I thought he would hit me. Instead he turned to his men and, with a sharp glance at Stephen, said, "Let him go." They did, and he collapsed. Before following the sheriff out of the room, Simon kicked Stephen in the ribs, putting all of his viciousness into it.

"That's what we think of you lying papists," he said.

I rushed to Stephen. Kneeling beside him, I gently turned him over. "Stephen!" He tried to open his eyes, but his face was so swollen, all I could see were little slits. His breathing was ragged, and I knew the pain must be acute.

Where was everybody? *Somebody, please help me!* Then I screamed out loud. "Help!"

I shook with frustration when no one came running. Grabbing a napkin, I looked around for water and found the bowl used for hand washing. I dipped the napkin in it and dabbed at Stephen's face. I was able to soak up some of the blood, but that was about all. The cut above his eye should be stitched, and he would need ice for the swelling. If only I had my backpack! I always kept a small bottle of Advil tucked inside one of the compartments in case of cramps. And I seriously doubted there was any ice around here.

There was nothing more I could do until someone showed up to help me. I rested on my heels and grasped Stephen's wrist, trying to find a pulse. It throbbed, steady but faint. Hoping he might sense my presence and not feel completely alone, I clutched his hand tightly.

Chapter Sixteen

STEPHEN'S CHAMBER LAY SHROUDED in darkness, except for the soft light from one candle burning in a wall sconce. I had pulled the settle close to the bed, keeping watch over him through the night. Servants kept the fire going, and Bess draped a coverlet around my shoulders. Every time he stirred, I jumped up to see if his eyes were open. I worried about more than his visible bruises. What about internal injuries, those that no one in these times could even diagnose, let alone treat?

When the sheriff and his men had finally trooped out for good, a servant raised the alarm and soon Will, Jennet, Fulke, and his father found me, still crouched on the floor next to Stephen.

"God have mercy!" Jennet said when she saw him. "Is he awake?"

I shook my head, and hesitated before speaking. Should I ask about ice, or would they all think I was crazy? But I had to try to do what was best for Stephen. "Is there any chance . . . Do we have any ice?" I finally blurted out.

"Ice? Whatever for?" Master Gillam asked.

"Our healing woman recommends it for swelling and bruises."

"I shall ask one of the servants to check the underground cellars. I believe there were some large blocks cut last winter." He turned to a young man and gave some instructions.

"Pray, let's remove him to his chamber," I said, glancing at Fulke and Will. "Jennet, can you prepare a . . . some kind of medicinal potion? Something to ease the pain?"

She nodded and hurried away.

When a servant had brought the ice, I asked that it be broken into small pieces. I wrapped some in a clean cloth and placed it over Stephen's eyes and nose, catching a few strange looks from those still in the room. Jennet had delivered an infusion of willow bark, which was meant to relieve pain, for Stephen to drink. But so far he hadn't been awake enough to swallow anything.

Now, curled up on the settle, I had time to think things over. I didn't understand why Stephen was so set on saving Thomas Cook, when our purpose was to save Will Shakespeare. Not that I wanted the poor man to die or anything. But with Thomas out of the picture, wouldn't our problem be solved? Shakespeare, free of his influence, could go on his merry way to London and transform himself into the Bard—with a detour to Stratford to marry Anne Hathaway.

Stephen shifted and moaned. I removed the sodden cloth from his face, found a clean one, and wrapped it around some fresh ice. After repositioning the ice pack, I jiggled his arm, hoping he'd wake enough to let me know he would be all right. But nothing. No response. I lowered myself back onto the settle. My eyelids grew heavy and I dozed.

Someone was shaking me, and I jerked awake. Looking up, I glimpsed Bess, her face scrunched into worry lines. It was morning, and an army of people was crowding around Stephen's bed.

"Mistress, you must go to your chamber. The physician has come to see Stephen."

The doctor, a short, balding man, turned to me. "Did he drink the infusion?"

My mind was fuzzy, but I remembered that much. "He did not awake enough to drink anything," I said, shielding my eyes from the morning light.

"The ice did its work, I see. The swelling has eased. I am surprised, mistress, that you knew of such a treatment." He eyed me suspiciously. Probably thought I was a witch.

Bess gently grasped my arm. "Come now and rest, Mistress Olivia." She half lifted me off the settle and pointed me toward my room. "I'll help you wash and change."

I nodded and glanced toward the bed where the doctor and his assistants were already undressing Stephen. One of the helpers was laying out rags and instruments, and—oh my God—knives. That could only mean one thing.

"Please do not bleed Stephen! He is weak already."

"Do not worry yourself, my dear," the doctor said. "'A bleeding in spring is Physik for a King.' You must allow me to decide how to balance this young man's humors."

Near the bed, an assistant stood holding the bowl for catching the blood. The physician thumbed the knife's edge, which probably hadn't been washed after the last bleeding, let alone sterilized. I stood silently as he lifted Stephen's arm and looked for a vein. And then I screamed. "No!"

"Remove that young lady!" the doctor shouted.

Damn them! They'll probably kill him. Two of the assistants grabbed my arms and unceremoniously escorted me next door, Bess on their heels.

"Mistress," one of them said as he led me to my bed. As soon as they left, the floodgates opened.

"Oh, poor thing!" Bess said. She held me while I sobbed for Stephen, for Alexander, who must be locked up in some dank cell, and, okay, for my pathetic and weak self.

"There, now, mistress. You had a hard time of it last night, you and your poor brother. That wicked sheriff! Lord knows what's happened to the master. But the doctor will look after Master Stephen."

Right. He'll probably bleed to death, or catch some terrible infection from the filthy knife. And there was absolutely nothing I could do about it.

Bess helped me wash and change into fresh clothing. "You can rest now, Mistress Olivia. Or I can bring you something to eat and drink."

"Nay, I do not wish to rest, and I'm not hungry. I want to see my brother."

I pushed past her into Stephen's room as the doctor and his entourage streamed out toward the stairs.

"Sir!" I cried. The doctor turned and gave me a snooty look.

"May I sit with my brother?"

"He is not to be disturbed, mistress."

I couldn't help it. My eyes filled with tears.

His expression softened. "Do not fret yourself, child. I believe he will make a full recovery."

"Thank you!" I said, even though I believed it would be in spite of, not because of, the doctor's care.

Bess led me away. Back in my room, a young servant girl was setting a tray by the settle, in front of the fireplace.

"I thought you might change your mind about eating, mistress," Bess said.

I *was* hungry, I realized. So I ate the pottage and drank some of the ale. Afterward, my stomach comfortably full, I stretched out on the bed intending to sleep. But something—someone, actually—was on my mind. *Stephen.* He'd been incredibly brave, taking all those blows without once begging for mercy or revealing anything. And it wasn't even to protect Shakespeare; it was all for Thomas Cook.

I rolled onto my side, closed my eyes, and pictured Stephen's face, pre-beating. Hazel eyes shadowed by dark brows. Brown hair curling at his neck. His overlapping tooth, which somehow made him even more attractive. In my mind I traced the contour of his face with my finger, beginning at his jaw. Up over his cheekbone . . . no, wait, how about over his lips and . . . *Oh, God, get a grip, Olivia!*

This was not supposed to happen. I wasn't supposed to fall for Stephen, but the truth was, I'd felt it coming on for days. I'd known him for three months at home; had acted with him, seen him every day. I had felt nothing for him during that whole time, except a vague curiosity and the certain affinity actors develop for each other during a play. So what had happened?

I'd become a part of his world, his time. I'd been thrown together with him, and he'd turned out to be charming, handsome, and mysterious. It wasn't those qualities alone, though, that had tipped me over the edge. His personality combined an often maddening mix of cockiness, vulnerability, and kindness. He could be endearing; he could be infuriating. He was sweetly protective of me. Sometimes he seemed like a tortured soul I wanted to wrap my arms around and heal.

Not that I wasn't captivated by Will's personality—his lovable nature, his flirtatiousness. And the totally heart-stopping idea that I, Miranda Graham, had been privileged enough to make the acquaintance of the most renowned playwright the world would ever know. I had a connection to Will because of what he would become. He wasn't there yet, of course, and I wouldn't have been able to explain it to him if I tried.

Kissing Shakespeare had been sweet, no denying that. But the thought of kissing Stephen left me breathless. As exciting as that prospect was, in a few weeks' time, I'd no longer be a part of his world. Once I was back in Boston, I'd never see him again. So what was the point of getting all worked up over him?

Was it possible that he felt the same way about me? Of course he didn't. He'd brought me here to do a job for him; that was all. I had to get my feelings for him under control. At home, I rarely allowed boys to get close. There was no time for it. Always, I'd devoted myself to acting and school, so I could get into Yale. And frenetic runs around Boston, just to ease the tension. I'd had crushes on guys, of course, and a few nonserious boyfriends, but a real relationship had never been on my radar. Now, for the first time, I was experiencing a dizzy, floating giddiness. All because of Stephen. I could keep my feelings for him at bay, just as I'd done with most of the guys who'd ever shown an interest in me. And I reminded myself that I had to. I didn't have a choice, really, because I'd be leaving.

After a while, sleep claimed me. I dreamed someone was chasing me, calling my name. I was running so fast, my body seemed weightless. My hair fluttered out behind me. I wasn't scared; I knew it was a game of some kind. When I turned to see who my pursuer was, I fell right into Stephen's arms.

I woke up reluctantly. Not wanting the dream to end, I burrowed into my bed until reality sank in. Stephen had been beaten up, and instead of mooning over him, I should be finding out how he was doing. I called out for Bess. My hair needed some serious work.

After Bess repaired my hair, I tiptoed over to Stephen's chamber. I didn't see any change in him at all. Eyes still closed, face heavily bruised, already beginning to scab over in some places. What did I expect? The sheriff's men had used him as a punching bag.

I lowered myself onto the settle and thought I should probably try talking to him. Hearing my voice might rouse him. "Well, Stephen," I began. It felt so awkward, speaking to someone who was unconscious, but I pressed on. "I'm sorry the sheriff beat you up because I didn't give him the answers he wanted. Please forgive me—I was crazy with fear by the end. I know you probably can't hear me—"

"Olivia." His voice was weak, but perfectly clear.

I flew to the edge of the bed. "You're awake! I was so worried."

"The doctor pronounced me curable, so you need not worry. And how are you, sweeting?"

I looked more closely at his face. Maybe his eyes weren't focusing properly. Did he think I was someone else? The mysterious Mary, perhaps?

"Stephen, it's me, Olivia. Are you okay?"

He smiled, and then grimaced. "I know who you are. I heard what you said to the sheriff, so I thought perhaps you would allow me an endearment."

What was he talking about? Did he have a head injury? "I don't understand."

He snorted and then groaned. "Do not make me laugh, pray. 'Tis painful. You told the sheriff you loved me. Do you not remember?"

My face turned hot, especially given my newly awakened feelings, and I tried to recall exactly what I'd said to the sheriff. "I did not! I said I cared for you. And that was as your sister!" I hoped I didn't look as rattled as I felt.

"'Cared deeply.' That is what you said. 'Cared deeply,'" he whispered softly.

I didn't want to argue with him. Maybe he was delirious or something. "Whatever."

"I think they might have beat me to death—"

"Really? Maybe I should have let them."

"—were it not for your insistence that I am a stubborn man. I think after that they gave up."

"Because you give new meaning to 'stubborn.' And nothing I said made much of an impression anyway. If they'd wanted to kill you, they would have. We've seen what they're capable of."

Stephen closed his eyes briefly before he said more. When he opened them again, he looked up at me. "You were very brave, Olivia."

"You're wrong. I cried and whimpered and begged them to stop hurting you."

"But you told them nothing. I am proud of you."

"Why'd you do it, Stephen? Why didn't you tell them what they wanted to know?"

"And betray Thomas? My uncle will be locked up for a few days, pay his fines, and be sent home. Thomas, I fear, would have a much different end. Would you want him to suffer like that poor priest they burned in Preston?"

"Of course not! Maybe they would have deported him, or thrown him in jail, and he could have come home with your uncle. It's just . . . well, we want to get rid of him, don't we?"

"Deported him? He may have spent time elsewhere, but he's an Englishman! Do not be so naïve, Olivia. We will find another way. We *have* another way, if only we could set it in motion." Despite his bruises, he managed to send me an evil look.

I sighed. "I'm working on it. I'll let you know when I have something to report." He probably thought I was making it up to appease him. "I've been worrying about the sheriff asking us about Will. Do you think he has some reason for going after him?"

"His family are known Catholics, but so are many others."

"That last conversation I overheard between Will and Thomas—I forgot to tell you one part of it. Now it seems maybe it's important."

"Pray do not keep me in suspense," Stephen said with a slight groan.

"Sorry." I related what Thomas had said about Will's father

making his "spiritual testament." "Do you know what that is? Will said he came north with the priest who witnessed it."

"I've heard a rumor that some of the Jesuits have been traveling around, holding covert meetings and urging people to sign a document promising loyalty to the Catholic Church. 'Tis possible Shakespeare's father signed such a thing."

"And could something like that make the situation more dangerous for Will and his family than for other Catholics?"

"I know not, but 'tis all the more reason to move things along."

"I was thinking maybe the sheriff knows about Mr.—Master—Shakespeare signing the spiritual testament. That could explain his interest in Will."

"It is of no great import. A Jesuit about is a far greater threat."

"Shh. Someone's coming," I said.

Thomas Cook entered the room, with Will close behind. "Mistress Olivia," Thomas said. "Is he—"

"I shall be fine," Stephen broke in. "I do not feel so bad as I must appear." Thomas strode over to the bed.

"Please, be seated," I said, rising and gesturing toward the settle.

Thomas shook his head, so I reclaimed my seat. "Master Langford, how can I ever thank you for what you did? You saved me, so that I might continue God's work. I am most grateful, sir."

"You would have done the same were our positions reversed." Stephen glanced at me. "Olivia did her part as well. She bore the sheriff's bullying bravely and never gave in, though he questioned her harshly."

Master Cook turned to me. "If that is the case, I owe both of you my gratitude."

Stephen spoke to Will. "How did you fare in your session with the sheriff's men? Were you hurt?"

Will stepped closer to us and shook his head. "In truth, the man who questioned Jennet and me seemed quite disinterested in the whole matter. Especially after Jennet told him she was a Protestant, and her father a minister. Soon afterward, our interrogator was called away and we were told to stay put."

He was "called away" to help beat Stephen to a bloody pulp.

"Neither Fulke nor his father was harmed. 'Twas the two of you who suffered the brunt of the sheriff's wrath," Thomas said. "And Master Hoghton, of course."

"Master Cook, may I ask a favor of you?" Stephen said, trying to sit up. He made it about halfway.

"Anything," Thomas answered.

"My aunt. We must summon her home. Would you speak to the steward?"

Will caught my eye and motioned to me while they were talking. Taking my hand, he led me toward the passage. He leaned so close to me I could feel his breath on my cheek. "I am sorry for your brother, but I am most happy that the sheriff and his men did not harm you, sweet Olivia." He pressed my hand before releasing it.

Hmm. I wished Stephen could have overheard that little exchange. Maybe then he wouldn't be so hard on me.

When I overheard Thomas talking about death, my head snapped around and I walked back to the bed.

His face sober, he removed his cap and sighed from deep within. "I am prepared to die, expect to die in this great cause. But I do not believe the time is right. There is more work to be done."

I was horrified. "How will you know when it is the right time? In truth, 'tis never the right time to submit yourself to . . . to arrest and torture, in my opinion, that is." *Shut up, Olivia. You're babbling like an idiot.*

They all stared at me like I was some clueless girl. Which I was.

"I know it is coming," Thomas said. "Yet I do not care to leave this life until I am confident the true church is restored in England."

"Thomas, you have traveled about and given people the courage to practice their true faith again. Do you wish to continue in this way?" Stephen asked.

The passion so often reflected in Thomas's expressions leaped out at us, and I heard it in his voice too. "I want to save the queen herself," he said. "And her privy councilors. Her court. I want them to see the error of their ways and return to the old faith!"

Will and I looked at each other and I lifted my brows. He compressed his lips, a worried expression crossing his face.

"Sir, how can you possibly bring about such a thing?" Stephen asked.

"I have asked him that very question," Will said.

Thomas smiled ruefully. "I cannot say now. But you will know, you will all know, in good time."

"Maybe 'tis time for you to leave Hoghton Tower, go on to another home that is not under suspicion. You would be safer," Stephen said.

Thomas raked a hand through his hair. "God bless you, but I cannot leave. Although I know I would be welcome in many places, I have need of the library here." He put his hat on and bowed. "Now we must leave you to your rest. Thank you both again for what you did. I shall pray for you."

When their footsteps had faded away, I looked at Stephen and said, "Nice try."

He smiled, but his face looked haggard. "If only Thomas would leave here. That would be the simplest way of preventing his influence over Shakespeare."

"Did you notice how Will looks at him? You can tell he's worried about Thomas's agenda. It's almost as if he feels it's his duty to protect him."

"Which means the threat to Shakespeare is double edged. Even if he decides against taking his vows, he may feel some moral obligation to safeguard Cook's life."

I sank onto the settle. "As if we didn't have enough to worry about." An idea struck me. "Stephen, have you ever thought maybe Thomas is writing something? Why else would he need the library?"

He looked at me, considering what I'd said. "You may be right. Something to persuade the queen."

"He's determined to stay until he's completed his work, whatever it is."

Stephen's eyelids were drooping. We'd been talking for far too long, and he must be exhausted.

I rose. "Before I go, please drink some of Jennet's concoction. She asked me to insist."

"Aye, 'twould probably do me good."

I helped him sit up. He clung to me while I put the cup to his mouth, and drank all of it in one gulp. "God's breath, that was vile!"

I laughed. "I'm sure it will have you feeling better in no time." I set the cup down and turned to leave, but felt Stephen's touch on my arm.

"Stay with me until I fall asleep. It should take only a minute or two."

I sank back onto the settle. "May I ask you one question?"

"Go ahead. I know I could not stop you."

I was pretty sure that wasn't a compliment. I sneaked a look around to make sure we were alone and lowered my voice to a whisper. "The visions . . . Couldn't you have foreseen what was going to happen with the sheriff and prevented it?"

"It does not work that way. I cannot summon them at will."

"Have you ever tried?"

"Olivia, since I have no wish to see the future, I have not tried." He shifted and moaned, and I could see I was upsetting him with my questions. "Go." He gestured weakly toward the door. "If you persist in tormenting me, I shall do without your company."

"I'm sorry." I reached down and touched his cheek where the worst of the bruising was. "Does this hurt?"

"Not there. Here." He slid my hand slowly under the coverlet, placing it over his ribs. So close to his heart, I could feel its life-affirming, steady beat. "That's where Simon kicked you," I said, not moving my hand.

"Mmm." He was drifting off. Reluctantly, I slipped my hand away and dropped back onto the settle, where I remained until Stephen's breathing became measured and even. And until my heartbeat slowed to its normal rate.

Chapter Seventeen

A FEW DAYS AFTER THE BEATING, Stephen had healed enough to sit by the fire and read or, if he could find a willing partner, play cards. I looked in on him before heading off to meet Will. Our get-together had been postponed until today, Tuesday, because of the sheriff's raid. I knew he was expecting me because he mentioned it last night after dinner.

Stephen held an open book in his lap, but his gaze was focused somewhere off in the distance. "Olivia," he said, when my presence finally registered.

"I can't stay. I just wanted to check on you."

"Ah. You tempt me with your company only to disappoint me. Who has claim upon you?"

I gave him my best woman-of-mystery look. "This morning is my meeting with Will. I mustn't keep him waiting."

"Hmph. Off you go, then."

"See you at lunch."

His eyes held a bewildered look, and I knew he was dying to find out what I had up my sleeve. I waved and hurried away.

"Fare thee well," he muttered under his breath. I smiled to myself.

On my way to the classroom, I heard footsteps behind me. Curious, I turned and glimpsed Samuel, the man who'd carried my trunk upstairs on the first day. He was holding a folded and sealed paper in his hand.

"Is that for Master Shakespeare, Samuel?"

"Aye. Father Thom—that is, Master Cook asked me to deliver it to him."

"I'm on my way to meet with Will. May I take it for you?"

"I do not know. . . . I-I promised I'd put it directly into Master Will's hands."

I didn't want to get the man in trouble, so I smiled and said, "You must do so, then." He hurried off ahead of me after a quick bow. The letter had been sealed, I could see, so I wouldn't have been able to read it anyway. And the handwriting would have been a challenge for sure. Why would Thomas write Will a letter, since they saw each other every day and had plenty of opportunities to talk?

"Good morrow, Will," I said when I entered his classroom.

He leaped up from a table that he'd obviously claimed as his personal workspace. It was situated near the windows, and the sunlight streaming in dappled the papers and books spread out on its surface. The letter was not among them. *Damn!*

After kissing me on both cheeks, Will said, "Welcome, mistress. I have been looking forward to your visit."

"Samuel passed me on his way here. I offered to bring your letter, but he insisted upon doing so himself."

"Aye, well, I shall read it later. Come, sit down." He led me to one of the student tables. After I was seated, he hurried off and collected some of the books and papers I'd noticed before. When he sat down across from me, his eyes shone with excitement. I couldn't help smiling at him.

"I cannot tell you what a pleasure it is to be acquainted with someone who is interested in my writing! Although you may change your mind once you have heard some of it."

"I have a feeling it will please me exceedingly," I said.

He leaned forward. "Since my arrival at Hoghton Tower, I've been composing a play! Scattered scenes that have come to me little by little. Would you give me leave to read some of it?"

Now, this was interesting. "I love drama and the stage! Tell me a little about it before you begin."

"'Tis about a lady named Kate, who's known as a shrew. Her father betroths her to a man she hates, Peter. He's a braggart, full of himself, but once he learns her father is wealthy, he is determined to have her and tame her."

My God, he's describing the Shrew!

And after a few lines, I recognized the scene. To keep myself from falling off my stool, I gripped the table and held on for dear life. I, Miranda Graham, aka Olivia Langford, was listening to William Shakespeare read an early version of *The Taming of the Shrew*.

The scene was from Act II, when Petruchio tells Katherine

their marriage is a done deal. It begins with their first meeting, which doesn't go well. After Petruchio says they'll marry on Sunday, Katherine replies, "I'll see thee hanged on Sunday first."

I realized Will had stopped speaking. He was gathering up his papers and circling the table toward me. "I have the most enlightening idea, mistress! You read Kate's part, and I shall read Peter."

I nearly panicked. "Nay, Will, I could not do it justice."

"'Twould be most instructive for me to hear you read the words. I beg you oblige me, Olivia."

I accepted the pages from his outstretched hand. Of course, I knew the lines, and although they'd be somewhat different from those in this early version, I could always pretend I couldn't read his writing. Which, I remembered, was true.

"Very well. If it pleases you, I shall."

And so we spoke those famous lines together. Several times, Will plunged his quill into the ink jar and made changes based on what I said when it differed from his working copy and he liked the wording better.

"Aye, aye, 'beware' is much livelier than 'avoid.'"

"'Yet you are withered.' 'Tis more on the mark than 'shriveled up.'"

"Ah, 'oaths' fits the scheme, where 'curses' does not. You are quite skilled with words, Olivia."

I smiled. "I love this, Will. These characters have wit and liveliness."

"Truly?" His eyes sparked with excitement.

"Absolutely. Are you working on any other plays?"

"I have many ideas, but have written only small bits as yet." He smiled to himself, as if at some private joke. "Royalty make good fodder for drama, do they not?"

I ducked my head so he wouldn't see my grin. "Indeed! Are you planning to write about English kings?"

"Someday, when my time is more my own."

"Well, then," I said. "I believe you will."

We stared at each other for a moment, and something passed between us. A link fragile as the finest thread, yet strong enough to bear the weight of centuries. It didn't feel romantic, but it was deep and profound, nevertheless. Whatever happened, we would always have it.

I broke the spell. "'Tis getting on toward the midday meal."

"Aye. My thanks for your help, mistress. You cannot imagine how much this means to me."

"Someday I expect to see you onstage, speaking the lines you have composed."

"That is my hope too. There is something bigger than life about the stage, is there not?" He looked dreamy for a minute, and then, unexpectedly, a shadow crossed his face.

"What is troubling you, Will?"

"I feel I shall disappoint Father Thomas if I choose the stage over the church."

"Only you can judge what to make of your life."

"I must consider the religious life. I have promised Thomas to think on it."

"It is dangerous right now to think of becoming a priest. One must leave England to do so, isn't that true?"

"Aye. It would be difficult to find the necessary funds, although I daresay Master Hoghton would sponsor me." He rose and began gathering up his papers.

"Certainly you do not want to commit to a way of life only to please another."

"When that other is a man of such dedication and devotion, 'tis difficult to discount."

So the wink he'd given me at lunch the other day had only been teasing. He was taking Thomas's advice to heart. *Sigh*. Will was definitely at risk. If money turned out to be the only thing holding him back, I was sure Alexander would be more than willing to pay for his Jesuit education.

I walked toward the door. Will was shuffling papers, but even so, I thought I heard a sound in the passage. Footsteps scurrying. I yanked open the door, but the hallway stood empty and silent.

Will joined me and we headed for the banqueting hall. On the way, I counted all the doorways into which someone could easily have slipped. The eavesdropper had six rooms in which to conceal him—or her—self.

"I hate this!" I shouted, heaving my needlework across my chamber. It was late afternoon, and day was beginning its slide toward evening.

Jennet giggled. "Patience, Olivia. When I first learned to stitch, I near threw it onto the hearth many a time."

I walked over and picked up the embroidery frame, adjusting it so the linen was taut. "Look at this! It's—'tis a fright. I've ripped this out so many times, my aunt will guess the truth."

"Give it to me," Jennet said. I handed it over gladly.

I'd never like needlework—that was a given—but why shouldn't I enjoy an afternoon with a girl my age? Even if I didn't quite trust her. It was a welcome break from the gloom around the Tower. Despite everyone keeping to their usual routines, faces were strained because Alexander was still in jail. For something to do, I'd asked Jennet to help me with my embroidery, in case I was asked to produce it when Elizabeth returned. And as Stephen had suggested, it was a good way of drawing out the other girl.

Jennet was explaining something. "I'll form a new design in this corner, so the wear on the fabric will not be noticed. Pray, why did your mother not instruct you in needlework?"

The thought of my mother with any kind of needle in her hand made me want to hoot with laughter. "My parents believe educating oneself is more important, but Mother would not want my aunt to know that."

"Your secret is safe with me."

Ha! Was any secret safe with Jennet? I had serious doubts about that.

Oddly, the mention of my mother released a flood of homesickness. I missed my grandfather. And Macy. Not being able to text, call, or contact anyone was definitely weird, not to mention lonely. Stranger still was Stephen's explanation that time was standing still while I was . . . away. I couldn't get my head around the idea.

"Is something amiss, Olivia?"

"Nay . . . pardon me. I was thinking of something. Did your mother teach you, Jennet? You are very handy with the needle."

Sorrow shadowed her eyes briefly. "Aye, before she died. I was but four years old when we began. She was called to God after giving birth to my youngest sister, Honor, when I was ten years old."

"It must have been hard to lose your mother when you were so young."

She nodded briefly in acknowledgment.

"You have another sister?"

"Aye, Joan." While her face had softened when she spoke of Honor, mention of Joan seemed to have the opposite effect.

I pierced the fabric with my needle. Jennet had traced a simple design of a flower onto the cloth. I would start with the petals, practicing the satin stitch. "You must have borne great responsibility in the care of your sisters after your mother died," I said.

"Joan has caused me much trouble. She is stubborn by nature, and lazy and silly besides. I do not mind caring for Honor, though. She's a sweet and loving little thing."

"I have always wished for a sister."

"And I for a brother! Your brother is such a gentleman, and so well favored. I am glad he has made a good recovery."

I glanced up in surprise, since I'd thought Jennet had eyes only for Will Shakespeare. She had a bit of a sly smile on her face. If she were the writer of the note questioning my identity, perhaps she was testing me, to discover my true relationship to Stephen.

"Aye. You are not the first young lady to remark upon his charms." I forced a giggle, and Jennet laughed too. "Is it customary for the females in your family to marry at a young age?"

Her head jerked up. "Why do you ask me such a question?"

Obviously I'd hit a nerve, so I decided to dig deeper. "No reason, only I have heard that Puritan young ladies are expected to take a husband early."

She paused with her needle in midair, her eyes studying me. Then she plunged the needle into the fabric, drew it through, plunged again. Her hands were shaking. "My father has chosen a husband for me," Jennet said, revealing this tidbit with a certain degree of bitterness. She stuck the fabric again, as if her intended's face were trapped within the frame.

"You do not like him."

"He is a widower with three children, one of whom is but a few years younger than I. Father believes him to be a suitable match for me because he is one of the church elders." She snorted. "Elder describes him well. He must be at least two and forty. The last time I saw him, he had a large wen protruding from his cheek."

"A wen?" It must be a pimple or a blemish of some kind. *Good lord.* Why would Jennet's father want her to marry such a man? "Surely there are other suitable men more of an age with you?"

"Of course there are." Her gaze shifted for a moment, and I wondered if she was thinking of Will Shakespeare. "But he is not to be swayed. He says I must—" She stopped speaking and shrieked, dropping her needlework.

I thought maybe talking about her betrothed had pushed her over the edge. "A rat!" she shouted. We both leaped to our feet, and I glimpsed a hairy rodent scurrying along the wall. This was no little field mouse. It was big and evil looking. I grasped Jennet's arm and pulled her toward the bed. "Up here!" I yelled. She gave me a strange look, but climbed up on the bed with me. All I could think of was rats being flea infested, and fleas carrying the plague. Of course, nobody had figured that out yet.

"Help!" I cried, watching the disgusting creature tear around the room.

"Mistress, 'tis only a rat," Jennet said. "Vile but harmless."

"You're the one who screamed," I replied.

Will burst in. "What in God's name is the trouble in here?"

I pointed. "A rat!"

Out of the corner of my eye, I spied Stephen entering the room. "God's eyes! I thought you were being killed."

I pretended I hadn't heard him. "Get it out of here! Rats carry disease."

Stephen picked up a stool and chased after the rodent with it, until it scurried down the passage, off to do its dirty work in other parts of the house. *Wonderful.*

"I shall ask the steward to summon the mole catcher," Stephen said when he returned.

"How did it get in here?" I asked, jumping off the bed.

"Down the chimney, most likely," Will said. "Or perhaps through the servants' door." He eyed the back wall. "There may be a small hole somewhere. You would be amazed at the tiny openings they can squeeze through." His eyes sparkled. "No doubt it has spent many a night curled up in your bed while you lay sleeping. Right, Stephen?"

"Aye," Stephen said. "'Tis said they are so still, one does not sense their presence."

"Very amusing, eh Jennet?" I said.

"Indeed." Her mouth tightened and jealousy flared in her eyes. "'Tis near mealtime," she said. "We'd best prepare."

"I shall escort you to your chamber," Will said. Jennet took his arm and he smiled warmly at her. Well, that should fix things, I thought.

Stephen watched them leave. "They get on well," he said.

I shrugged. "I told you she has feelings for him. She looked like she wanted to bite someone's head off just now. I think she thought Will was flirting with me."

He pondered what I'd said for a moment. "In truth? I confess I did not notice."

Guys were so clueless.

"Olivia, if you are not occupied, will you ride with me tomorrow?"

That was the last thing I had expected him to say. I'd been bracing myself for a lecture regarding my lack of progress with the seduction.

"Pardon me?" I sneaked a look at him, but he was gazing off to the side. A weird habit of Stephen's.

Now he looked directly at me. "Ride with me, in the afternoon. I believe I am well enough healed now."

This was interesting. "Stephen, you know how poor my riding is."

"When I said 'with me,' I meant exactly that. On my horse, as we did riding back from Preston."

I should say no. I definitely should say no. But I heard myself say, "Okay." The truth was, I'd be thrilled to leave these four walls behind for an afternoon, especially in Stephen's company.

"Will tomorrow after the midday meal suit you?"

I hesitated. "Are you sure you're well enough?" Almost of its own volition, my hand reached out and I traced my fingers over the broken places on his face. The cut above his brow, and the purplish bruise surrounding his eye. Gingerly, I touched his damaged nose, then rubbed my thumb across the cut on his lip, now nearly healed. He didn't move a muscle, but his eyes glowed with a warmth I hadn't seen before. Then, in one swift motion, he grabbed my hand, stilling it. He clutched it to his chest for a moment before releasing it. I thought he might kiss me, but he said, "Until later," and strode from the room.

I stood there a long time, dazed, that giddy feeling pulling up through me.

After a while, I picked up my embroidery again, determined to master some of the stitches. I remembered my conversation with Jennet right before the rat had distracted us. She'd started to say something important. "He is not to be swayed. He says I must . . ." I would have loved to know the ending to that sentence.

Chapter Eighteen

THE NEXT DAY TURNED OUT to be windy but warm. A few fleecy clouds blew across the sky. Nothing to worry about. The wind whipped my hair in different directions, but I didn't mind. Although bruises still dotted Stephen's face, he claimed to feel only a little soreness in his ribs. He was no longer willing to let that stop him from his usual pursuits.

My high spirits plummeted when I saw him leading Peg as well as his own horse. "I thought you said I wouldn't have to ride on my own," I said as he helped me mount.

"When we are out of sight of the manor, we shall tie old Peg to a tree and you can climb up here with me."

According to Stephen, we were riding toward the southwest. He was in the lead, and faithful Peg seemed willing to follow Bolingbroke, Stephen's horse. Much to my relief, I didn't have to do anything but hold on. We were climbing, and when we reached the top of a rise, Stephen reined in. "This is Duxon Hill," he said.

Peg stopped too, and I tugged on the reins to turn her so that I was beside Stephen. He gestured back toward the manor, and when I actually paid attention to the view, my breath caught. "It's gorgeous!" I said.

Spread out below was western Lancashire. Because the day was clear, I could see villages nestled into the valleys and smoke curling from chimneys. Hedges enclosed pastureland, and church spires stretched to the sky here and there. "What's that larger town?" I asked.

"That's Preston. I did not think you would want to ride in that direction."

I shivered. Mere mention of the name stirred up painful and still fresh images of the burning. "Thank you. I'll be happy never to see that place again."

"Turn your gaze slightly toward those ridges," he said. I must have looked in the wrong direction, because he reached out and, grasping my chin very gently, turned my head the other way.

"If you look closely, you can glimpse the Ribble and its estuary going out to sea." I strained my eyes, but what I was seeing could have been a stone wall, or possibly a river. "Sort of."

"Concentrate."

I closed my eyes and imagined what it would look like. Maybe like a thin silver ribbon, barely visible at this distance. When I opened my eyes, that was exactly what I saw. "Yes!" I said. "It's right there, at the horizon."

"Aye. It would be, would it not?"

I quirked my mouth at him, realizing he was teasing me. But it was good-natured. We turned the horses and rode on, through rolling farmland with trees scattered about. After a while, Stephen said, "Let's stop here. We can tie Peg and then continue on." He helped me down and found a tree to wrap Peg's reins around.

"Won't she need water?"

"We will not be gone that long. She can graze here, where she's out of the sun."

He climbed back onto Bolingbroke. I set my foot atop his in the stirrup, and he wrapped his arm around my waist and pulled me up. When I was comfortable, we set off at a walk.

"What do you think of our little corner of Britain?"

"It's beautiful. I haven't been anywhere other than London. And Stratford, of course, for my parents' performances. You said they'd performed at Hoghton Tower, didn't you? They've never mentioned it to me." I was babbling, my happiness at being free of the confines of the house bubbling over. Ever since the sheriff's visit, an air of worry and fear had hovered like a gloomy presence, oppressive and suffocating, over everything we did. I leaned back against Stephen. His smell was familiar and comforting. Soap, sweat, an herb I couldn't identify, all blending into what had come to represent my own safety and well-being.

Olivia, you're slipping, I warned myself. *You're supposed to fight off any romantic feelings for Stephen.* "It's so fresh up here," I said, sitting up straight. Pale yellow blooms peeked out along the path. "What are the flowers?"

"Cowslips. We shall take a different route back, through the woods. Bluebells and wild garlic may be blooming after all the rain we've had, though 'tis rather early yet."

"What about heather?"

"Sorry. It flowers in late summer and through the fall. Gorse is just beginning to bloom, though. The bright yellow hedges." He pointed and I drank it in.

I let myself relax, trying not to dwell on the fact that Alexander was still imprisoned. I didn't want to think of Shakespeare, or Thomas Cook and the Jesuits, either. I closed my eyes and felt contented.

After an hour or so, we crested a hill. Outcroppings of rocks pushed up here and there, and Stephen steered us toward one. He dismounted and then helped me down. "I hope you brought food," I said, eyeing the rolled-up bundle at the back of the saddle. We scrambled over some small rocks and up to a shelflike area that spread out underneath the massive stone. "The ground is still damp, I fear." He unfastened his doublet and spread it out for me to sit on.

"That's very gallant of you."

"Anything for your comfort, mistress." After unrolling the bundle, he sat down next to me, and before long we were nibbling on bread and cheese and drinking ale from a flask. We were quiet, and comfortable with each other without talking. Whenever I had a moment alone with Will, I felt it was my duty to engage him somehow. Flirting or prying information out of him. Trying to encourage his writing and acting. Even though I really liked him, sometimes it was a burden. I exhaled a deep sigh, and Stephen heard.

"What's troubling you, Olivia?"

"I was thinking it is more enjoyable to be in your company than in Will Shakespeare's. Because of my . . . assignment."

"I think, for today, we should not talk of Will. Let today be only for our pleasure."

I smiled at him. "You're granting me a day off? Thank you for allowing me an entire afternoon during which I'm not required to think about my duty here."

He winced. "Am I so strict a taskmaster as that?"

"You are." I finished a bite of cheese. "Stephen," I said softly.

"Olivia?" His mouth curved teasingly.

"Tell me about Mary." The words formed without my permission. He looked stricken.

"Who told you about her?"

Should I apologize and change the subject? No. The door was open, and he didn't seem angry. A little surprised, but not angry. "Bess mentioned her. It was on Easter, actually."

His eyes were shadowed. "Of course. She assumed my sister would know. What exactly did she say?"

"How sorry everyone was when Alexander told them she died." *Should I tell him the rest? That Bess asked if he has courted anyone else since Mary's death?* But Stephen's voice hushed me.

"Mary and I were betrothed. Even though our parents had arranged our marriage, we fell in love and I very much wanted to wed her. She wanted it too. At least, I always believed she did, right up until the end."

"Would you tell me what happened?"

"Mary took her own life. She walked into the river one night and drowned." His head had been bent, and now he looked up at me. His eyes shone with tears, and I felt my own tearing up.

"Could it have been an accidental drowning?"

"Nay. She had weighed herself down with stones, so there was no doubting her intention."

"Did she leave a note? A message of any kind?"

He nodded. "It said only that she loved me, and her family. And she begged to be forgiven."

"Oh, Stephen, I'm so sorry."

"I have tried to understand why she did it. Since she died, I am tormented with dreams of attempting to save her. But I am always too late. She disappears beneath the cold, murky water before I am able to rescue her. And I am left with the same question: Why?" He'd been sitting on the rock, hands clasped together between his knees. Now he got to his feet, and I did too.

"Was her behavior different than usual leading up to her death? Was she sad and withdrawn?"

He frowned at me. "She *was* melancholy and kept to herself more than usual, no doubt of that. But she was always of that bent. I spoke to her parents about it, and a practitioner visited her. There was simply nothing to explain it. Was not and is not."

"But you blame yourself." I'd read about the symptoms of clinical depression for a school project, and Stephen's description of Mary sounded like it fit.

"Certainly I do. Would you not?"

I grasped his arms and said, "It seems like guilt is always part of grieving. But Stephen, if you lived in my century, you'd know that some people lapse into deep depression for no reason. We have drugs and special doctors who treat the condition. It sounds like that's what Mary suffered from. You mustn't blame yourself."

He blinked away tears. "Would that we had lived in your time, if Mary could have been saved." He walked away, turning his back to me, and I was sure he was struggling not to weep. After a minute, he pulled out a handkerchief and wiped his nose and eyes. He twisted around to look at me. "'What a piece of work is a man,'" he said with an ironic look.

"Quoting *Hamlet* now. That's not an encouraging sign." His mouth curved up, not quite a smile, but the beginning of one.

Rejoining me, he said, "I am indebted to you, Olivia. For listening and not judging me. This was to be our day of pleasure, and I have spoiled it. Mayhap we should be going back."

I wasn't ready yet. I especially didn't want our day to end with Mary's sad story. But I shrugged and said, "All right. If you think it's time." I bent down to collect the remnants of our lunch. "I haven't told you about my visit with Will the other day," I added.

Stephen snatched up his doublet and slipped it on. "I have been trying to guess what you were about."

"I'd asked him to share some of his writing with me—and you won't believe it, but he read me some of the *Shrew!*"

"Great God! Has he finished it?"

I shook my head. "He said he'd written scattered scenes. Then he had the idea for us to read the lines together. I nearly panicked until I realized I knew them from memory."

"What scene was it?"

"It was the first scene in act two, Katherine and Petruchio's first meeting."

"And was it the same?"

"Not quite. He made some changes based on what I was saying. I have the feeling he thinks I'm some kind of genius with words!"

"That scene is one of the best in the play. The verbal parrying is quite amusing."

"I love it too, even though Petruchio steals it."

"Katherine has some great retorts, though. And I'm fond of the 'Kiss me, Kate' bit. Could you and I practice that?" He stood there staring at me, his head tilted sideways.

I thought he was joking, but a spark gleamed in his eyes. Then his gaze dropped to my lips. His seemed infinitely kissable. I closed my eyes and leaned toward him. Cupping my chin in his hand, he kissed me, and my heart went spinning. After a few intense seconds, Stephen coaxed my lips apart. He slid his tongue inside my mouth, exploring, tasting. I put my hands against his chest and felt his warmth and his strength radiating into my body.

He drew back, gently but firmly.

"Wh-what . . . ?" I felt dazed.

Looking amused, he brushed his fingers lightly across my skin, stroking my cheek. "Come, we must start back or we shall be late for the evening meal."

Well. Thanks for the kiss, Olivia, but we wouldn't want to be late for dinner. Gritting my teeth, I handed him the bits of bread and cheese that were left, and he packed them up with the now empty flask.

Something occurred to me on the way back. I hesitated to ask, but my curiosity won out. "Stephen, could I ask you one more question about Mary?"

I could feel his body tense slightly. "Whatever you wish."

"With your visions, couldn't you have learned what was going to happen and intervened? Stopped it?"

Abruptly, he reined in Bolingbroke and practically flew off the saddle. Then he reached for me and hauled me down in front of him.

His eyes were solemn, hard, and his fingers felt like steel bands around my arms. "You asked me this before, do you not remember? I would not use the visions for personal gain. Ever. I have never tried to summon them, and most likely never will."

"Is that in the wizard code of behavior?" I asked, and immediately regretted it.

I felt the sharp reproach of his look, unwavering and intense, until I was forced to look away. "Sorry," I whispered, hoping I hadn't spoiled the closeness between us. He turned, and I reached out for him. "Stephen, I truly am sorry. Are we okay?"

His eyes softened, and he nodded briefly. After hesitating a moment he said, "I cannot speak for my ancestors who have held the power, but it would be wrong for *me* to use the magic for myself. Even apart from material gain. Like it or not, I have a higher duty. Beyond that, I must live my life the same as anybody else."

Something akin to shame, and heartache for him, pressed against my chest. "You're a good man, Stephen Langford," I said in a shaky voice. "I'm sorry for thinking you might use the power to benefit yourself. I see now you would never do that."

"God save me," he said, "come here." He reached for my hand and drew me close, then pulled me into an embrace. Exactly what I'd been longing for—his arms around me. This time, I kissed *him*, each of the wounded places I'd touched yesterday. I wanted him to feel how much I cared about him. He held me as if he were afraid I might try to run away, and in the end, his lips found mine again.

Breaking the kiss, he said, "You are . . . I am . . ." but never finished his thought. Instead, he rested his cheek against my forehead. We stood there like that for the longest time before we pulled apart and climbed back on Bolingbroke.

Neither of us said much on the way back. Resting against him, I was lost somewhere in the magic of the day. Between the swaying of the horse and the rise and fall of Stephen's chest as he breathed, I felt completely relaxed, and even dozed for a while. I jerked awake when we stopped, and he helped me down and then up onto Peg.

As we approached the spot where we had taken in the magnificent view earlier in the day, Stephen pointed out a lone horseman riding slowly up the drive. "'Tis my uncle returned home," he said. "Thank God."

Chapter Nineteen

THE RAIN RETURNED WITH A VENGEANCE, but it didn't affect the lightness of my mood. My day with Stephen had been so nearly perfect that the memory stayed with me and bolstered me, no matter how dreary the weather. I couldn't stop thinking about kissing him.

I asked him if he'd rehearse the *Shrew* with me. After all, when I arrived back in the present, I'd have to perform it again. "You know Petruchio's lines, don't you?"

He gave a wry smile and said, "Well enough." I hoped he was thinking about "Kiss me, Kate."

We managed to steal a few afternoons in the library to practice, and gradually, I began to feel more confident about my acting. One day, after we'd gone through the wedding scene, Stephen grabbed my hand and squeezed it. "You did well, Olivia! I thought your playing had the right degree of anger and irony mixed."

"Thank you," I said, a happy glow filling me. And right then, it occurred to me that for the first time, I'd said the lines the way my mother had taught me, finding the natural flow of the words, rhythm, and meter. "Character flows from language," Mom had insisted when she was coaching me for the part. Irritated, I'd rolled my eyes and insisted I knew what Katherine was all about, thank you very much, without her help.

"What are you thinking?" Stephen asked.

I gave him a sheepish smile. "That my mother was right about something. Very difficult to admit, since I've sworn to ignore any of her advice about my acting for all time." I rolled my eyes, and he laughed.

"That would be a costly mistake, I believe."

I plopped down on the settle. "Do you think Katherine and Petruchio truly love each other?"

"What do you think?" he said, throwing the question back at me.

"You sound like a shrink."

"A what?"

"Never mind. I'm convinced they do. They must! Did you know *The Taming of the Shrew* is still one of the most performed of Shakespeare's plays? How could audiences be so into it if, deep down, they didn't believe Katherine and Petruchio were in love?"

"Couldn't a modern audience simply think it funny?"

"Sure, some people would. But Petruchio's so mean to Katherine. He wants to marry her for her dowry. He's late for their wedding, and then he won't let her stay for the wedding feast. And he offers her food and clothing, and ends up taking it all away. Even Petruchio's servants think he's cruel."

"Nay, I do not agree. He is simply teaching her to obey him. A thing every God-fearing man wants in a proper wife."

"What? Are you serious?"

"'Tis in the Bible, Olivia, that a woman must obey her husband. And as you must have noticed by now, it is the established belief among people of *this* time."

"But that's disgusting!"

"To you, maybe. In this century, the audience would think, 'Well done, Petruchio! You have put Kate in her rightful place.'"

I knew he had a point, but nevertheless it galled me. Especially because he seemed to share that view. "So that's what you think too?"

He shrugged. "I am a man of my time."

"And I was really starting to like you. You're nothing but a sexist."

He laughed. "Is that like a clodpole or blockhead?"

"Not really."

"I do not know the word, but it sounds like a fault. Can you not overlook it in me?"

I grabbed the nearest cushion and lobbed it at him. "You better watch it, Langford."

He dodged out of the way just in time, chuckling. "I surrender, mistress. I will never require an obedient wife."

"You'll be lucky to get any wife." I laughed, but my mind was still on Katherine, and how to portray her. Long before Mr. Finley had chosen the *Shrew* for our spring play, we'd read and studied it. He'd lectured about the different interpretations of Katherine. Some scholars tried to put a modern spin on her character, while others insisted there was only one true interpretation—the straight reading, the one Stephen so enthusiastically endorsed.

I'd have to put my own stamp on the role. My performance

somehow had to be a blend of Elizabethan and modern sensibilities. I wanted to keep my expression soft, to show I was in love, even while Petruchio was trying to break my spirit. And the "advice to the wives" speech at the end. Ironic? Humorous? I wasn't sure yet, but I still had time to work it out.

"Your mind is elsewhere," Stephen said.

"I'm sorry. I was still thinking of the performance."

"Come, be seated for a moment." Stephen had lowered himself onto the settle before the fireplace and now motioned me over. I sat next to him, my skin tingling. I wasn't thinking of the performance anymore.

"How do you fare with your reading?" he asked.

My heart plunged. "Reading?" I echoed. *He wants to know about reading?* "I haven't had much time to work on it."

"Would you care to do so now?"

"Now?"

He twisted a corner of his mouth. "Are your ears plugged, mistress? Aye, now."

No kissing today, apparently. *Damn!*

"If you are called upon to read a letter to a servant, or my aunt should require you to read a Bible verse, you must not hesitate."

His mention of letters and servants triggered a memory. "I need to tell you something about Will first. I was so excited about reading the *Shrew* with him, I forgot all about it."

He raised a brow. "Go on."

"On my way to the classroom the other day, a servant passed me. He was carrying a letter to Will from Thomas Cook."

"And?"

"And nothing. I mentioned it to Will, hoping he might open it and tell me something about what was in it. But he didn't bite. He said he'd read it later. Why would Thomas write to him when they could as easily talk?"

"They cannot speak often in private. The letter may contain something important. If you should see it lying about . . ."

"I don't know when that would be." I frowned at him.

"On another visit to his classroom, mayhap?"

"Maybe. I'm supposed to meet with Will again, so I guess it might as well be there."

"We must move things along, Olivia."

"I know. I promised you I'd . . . take this to the ultimate outcome, and I will." *The "ultimate outcome." What does that even mean?* The last time we'd talked about this, I'd told Stephen I couldn't wait to make love with Will. My lack of enthusiasm must have registered, because his eyes softened and he grasped my hand. "Soon. We must—you must—do it soon."

I nodded, and he said, "Let us look at Ovid and see how you're progressing."

Wonderful.

On a rainy Monday afternoon I settled myself in the ladies' withdrawing room, practicing my newfound needlework skills. No one could fault me for lack of effort. It was April 10th, my twentieth day in the past. I'd been keeping track in my head. I knew Stephen was right about moving things along. At this point, I was growing desperate for an opportunity to work my wiles on Will. For the time being, I felt I'd done all I could to encourage his writing and acting, and I'd keep working that angle.

It still nagged at me that the sheriff had asked us about "young Shakespeare." We had never figured out why he wanted to know, though I suspected the sheriff and his goons weren't all that picky about who they arrested and tortured if they thought he might have information they could use against their perceived enemies.

I'd just returned to my room, trying to decide what to do next, when I heard someone walking quietly through the passageway. It was Jennet, wearing a cloak with the hood pulled up over her head. My chamber was dark, and I hadn't been in it for the last few hours. There was no way she could have known I was in there. Since it was pouring outside, I couldn't imagine why she'd be venturing out, but I made an impulsive decision to follow her. Even if it came to nothing, at least it was a chance to take some action.

I waited until she'd descended the stairs and the courtyard door had closed behind her before following. Even though I'd thrown my own cloak on and pulled up the hood, the steady downpour soaked me within a few minutes. Jennet headed toward the thick forest beyond the rose garden, and I stayed as close as I dared. If she turned around, she'd spot me immediately in the open area between the trees and the tilting green.

Jennet entered the woods and hesitated, apparently uncertain about which path to follow. Please don't turn around, I begged silently. Evidently she made up her mind, because she continued. When I arrived at the spot where she'd paused, I looked around and spied a bit of red cloth tied to a low-hanging branch. Someone had marked a trail! That would make this easier. Walking beneath the trees protected me from the rain, at least. I turned briefly and looked toward the house, at the bulk of the great keep rising into the sky. Should I turn back?

I decided to keep going. I waited for Jennet to get farther ahead of me, since I knew I could depend on the red markers to guide me. The sound of the rain was muted under the trees, and a musky smell of dampness and rotting leaves drifted up from the ground. I zigzagged around trees, fallen logs, and dripping ferns, watching for the red pointers. When something deeper in the woods caught my eye—a rapid movement, a blur of color—I stopped. I thought I could make out two figures huddled together. I crept closer, the leaf-covered ground muffling my footsteps.

When I'd gotten as close as I could risk, I hid myself behind a clump of dead trees and watched. Jennet was talking to a man with a huge hook nose. No one I recognized. Her hood had fallen away, leaving her exposed to the rain. Dank hair clung to her companion's forehead. Dressed in a doublet and hose, he wore nothing else to protect himself from the wet weather. Unable to hear anything, I crept away before they discovered me. On the way back, I played a guessing game with myself as to the identity of the mystery man, and what exactly Jennet had to say to him.

Back inside, I waved to Stephen as I walked through the passage. Pulling my cloak off, I threw it on the bed just as Bess, bearing hot water, entered through the servants' door. She took one look at my scraggly appearance and said, "Why were you outside on such a day, mistress?" She walked over and began toweling my hair dry.

I didn't blame her for asking, since I'd wondered the same thing about Jennet. "I needed some fresh air after doing needlework for a few hours." That was the best I could come up with.

She chuckled. "You're not one for the needle, are you, mistress?"

While I washed, she laid out a fresh smock and bodice, and also chose a kirtle and petticoat for me to wear. After she fixed my hair, I hurried to Stephen's chamber, knocking lightly before barging in.

"Enter," he called. I walked in to find him donning a fine-looking doublet, slashed to show off its vermillion lining. Still working the fastenings, Stephen turned toward me. He looked up and stared. "You look quite beguiling," he said.

I felt a blush spreading up my neck to my face, but accepted the compliment with a thank-you.

He blinked, as if to refocus. "What did you wish to tell me?"

"Is there somewhere we can talk without the risk of being overheard?"

"Now? Before dinner?"

I nodded. "It's important."

He grabbed my hand and we walked back to my chamber, toward the servants' door. We stood on the landing, and I related my story of Jennet's mysterious meeting in the woods.

"A lover, mayhap?"

"In the rain? Besides, they were only talking." I wrapped my arms around my body, trying not to shiver.

Stephen sighed. "I cannot see what significance it could have. We have no reason to suspect her of anything, except perhaps fancying Will Shakespeare."

"And writing the mysterious note! Don't you think it's weird that she'd be out in the pouring rain meeting with a strange man, unless it was on some secret business?"

"Aye. But I fear it proves nothing, nor does it reveal what, if any, mischief she's up to. And we've no proof that it was she who sent you the message."

We stood there, at an impasse. "You're right, of course. It probably means nothing."

"For the present, I do not see that we can do anything." He squeezed my hand. "Come, we must go to the evening meal. They'll be waiting for us."

From my spot across the table from Alexander, I had my first good look at him since his return a few days before. He didn't seem well, but then I'd always thought he looked sickly, even from the first day I met him. After spending time in jail, it was no surprise that his face would appear even more pale and drawn. I wondered if he was ill, and if his imprisonment had made his condition worse. Elizabeth had not yet returned, so that probably didn't help his health. Apparently her sister-in-law was on the verge of death, and despite learning of Alexander's arrest, she'd been unable to leave.

"I have some rather unfortunate news to impart," he said during a lull in the talk. I could tell everyone was holding their breath, waiting for him to make some devastating announcement.

"The Earl of Derby and his son, Lord Strange, will not be visiting us as we'd hoped. Lord Strange sponsors a company of players, as you know."

A collective exhalation ensued, and some people resumed eating. "It did not seem the most propitious time for such a visit," he continued. "But Master Cook has an announcement which may ease your disappointment."

Now heads turned toward Thomas, who was seated near one end of the table.

"We are going to stage one of the Corpus Christi pageants, set for the same day Lord Strange's players were to have performed. As the pageant master, I shall be calling on all of you to help with designing sets, sewing costumes, and, of course, playing the various parts."

"Which pageant?" Fulke asked

"The flood," Thomas said. "Noah and the flood. 'Tis humorous and has many parts. Of course, I will play God—" He was interrupted by hoots of laughter. Thomas, I'd noticed, liked a good joke as much as the next man. He grinned broadly, his eyes good humored. When the table had quieted, he went on. "Fulke will play Noah, and Will Shakespeare has agreed to take on the role of Noah's wife." This prompted clapping and jeering, and Will stood up and bowed.

"When do we begin?" Fulke asked.

"Tomorrow morning we shall meet in the schoolroom. Will's scholars are going to help with the scenery, and several will be in the pageant. We do not have much time; April twenty-third is only two weeks away, so we shall need to work hard."

Fulke and his father, along with Will, continued to question Thomas about the play. Stephen whispered in my ear. "Shall I explain?"

I nodded, remembering Will's mention of the plays during our ride to Preston.

"When people were all of the old faith, these plays were performed by the guilds. Their purpose was to educate common folk about Bible stories. Each guild performed a different one."

"So there were others?"

"Aye. The fall of man, the birth of Christ, the death of Herod.

Many more. Noah's story is very comical, if acted well. I daresay it will be of interest to us to see Master Shakespeare as a player, will it not?"

"Absolutely."

Stephen turned to his uncle then, and they talked about spring planting and the effect all the rain was having on the crops. I stole a look at Jennet, and then surveyed the room. No sign of her friend. Not at our table, or at the one in the middle of the hall. If he wasn't from the estate, then who was he? Maybe Jennet had a secret lover, but that wasn't what it looked like. If I were having a tryst, I'd find somewhere warm and dry. I watched her as much as possible during the rest of the meal, but she acted like her usual self.

Chapter Twenty

ON MOST NIGHTS, people scattered after the evening meal. To-night, after the toothpicks had disappeared into their special cases, Alexander signaled us to wait. "The rain makes us dull," he said. "Men, let's retire to the guinea room for primero and some very fine sack I've been saving. What say you?"

There was general agreement among the men, who pushed back from the table laughing and rubbing their hands together. All but Will Shakespeare, who looked panicked. Stephen whispered something to him. He flushed, but after Stephen clapped him on the shoulder, he smiled and nodded. I assumed Will was short on money, and Stephen had offered a loan.

"I shall enjoy your sack, sir, but not the wagering," said Thomas. "Mistress Olivia, may I speak to you?"

I was standing around, just waiting for everyone to disperse. I intended to hang out in my room for the rest of the evening. "Of course."

"Would you be kind enough to serve as the prompter for our pageant? Since you may not take one of the roles, I believe this would suit you and allow you to participate."

"Uh, sure. That is, I'd be happy to." God, I was always stammering around him.

He smiled and inclined his head. "Excellent. I will explain your duties during our meeting tomorrow."

After bowing to me, Thomas followed the rest of the men to their card game. He always seemed vaguely uncomfortable with me—with women in general. Overly formal, more so than he was with the men.

I lit a candle to take upstairs. When I entered my room, Copernicus greeted me with excited little whimpers, and I absentmindedly patted his head. I'd better study my reading. I couldn't believe I'd just agreed to handle the prompt book for the pageant. That was probably a mistake. I lit more candles and curled up on my bed with a stack of books I'd borrowed from Alexander's library. Within a few minutes I was yawning and would probably have fallen asleep if Bess hadn't popped through the servants' door.

"I brought you some clary, mistress. I warmed it for you." She set a mug down on the table by my bed.

Clary? "Thank you, Bess. You're so thoughtful." I raised the cup to my lips, and the pungent odor nearly knocked me backward. Maybe "clary" was another name for spiced ale. I sipped cautiously. "Mmm. Good." Actually, it wasn't bad. It tasted like wine rather than ale. I took another sip and choked a little. If only they didn't make these drinks so peppery.

"Do you need anything else, Mistress Olivia?"

I shook my head. "Not now, thank you."

I was concentrating on my book when I heard her exclaim. "I stepped on this paper. I did not see it."

Bess was holding out a familiar-looking piece of parchment, neatly folded. I waited until she left, then quickly opened it. The same scrawl as before jumped out at me.

You are not Stephen's sister.

I gasped. Someone knew the truth. But how? More to the point, who? The words seemed like a threat, even though, as in the first one, the note said nothing about what the writer might do with this little morsel. Tucking it into the waistband of my skirt, I pulled my bodice over it. When Stephen returned to his chamber, I'd dash over and show it to him.

I studied my books with the magnifying glass and was pleased to realize I'd made some headway. I could actually read whole pages now. But I was too wound up to concentrate for very long. I set the books and glass on the floor and decided to go in search of the men. I made my way to the guinea room. Once there, I hesitated and considered whether or not a young lady would be welcome. I decided on "not." The corridor was deserted, and the door was ajar. Throwing caution to the wind, I put my back to the wall and listened.

I recognized Stephen's voice. "'Tis a wonder the queen has time for anything save the secret missives from Walsingham's spies."

"And the spies are after our priests." That was Alexander. "They should seek actual criminals to harass."

"I still believe the excommunication was unnecessary," Stephen went on. "It didn't serve any useful purpose other than to turn the queen and Privy Council even further against Catholics."

"'Tis true, things have grown worse for us ever since," Alexander said.

"It is not for us to question the pope's decisions." Now Thomas Cook was speaking. "But that particular one has forced English Catholics into hiding. Arrests and fines. Torturing and killing of priests. I ask myself whether this is too high a price to pay. It has not changed Elizabeth's course."

"All this religious strife." That was Will's voice. "Does it not serve to turn people from God?"

"There is no doubt men are confused," Thomas said. "That is why we Jesuits have come back. To help England regain the true faith of the church fathers and the saints." Even from the doorway I could hear the fire in his voice.

"I—I fear for your safety, Thomas," Will said. "For your life."

"Before we left Rome, we spoke much of torture and death. One brother said he'd always wanted to be a few inches taller." There was some uncomfortable laughter at his reference to the rack. "For myself, I hope to be able to walk to the scaffold on my own, with my dignity intact and my privy parts covered."

Thomas would have been humiliated if he knew I'd heard that last bit about his . . . parts. Nevertheless, I brazenly continued eavesdropping.

"Pray do not say such things!" Will pleaded.

"I find humor comforting, Master Will. But do not worry; I have much work to do before I face such eventualities."

I wondered how he could be so cavalier about his own execution. *He doesn't fear death*, I realized. *That's the only explanation. But what about the torture certain to come before?* I shuddered.

The conversation wound down, and after a brief silence Alexander said, "Gentlemen, I'm for my bed." I heard footsteps and realized I was about to be discovered. I burst through the door before that could happen and dropped a curtsy. "Pray pardon me," I said, flushing. "Is Stephen here? I need to speak to him."

Five puzzled sets of eyes stared at me. The sixth, belonging to Stephen, shot daggers my way. He didn't waste any time striding over to stand beside me.

With an iron grip on my arm, he said, "Gentlemen, I bid you goodnight. I shall escort Olivia to her chamber."

"God keep you, Niece," Alexander said.

"Fare you well, Uncle," I said, stumbling slightly as Stephen jerked me away. His fingers bit into my flesh, and he hurried me along so fast I was practically gliding. "You're hurting me. And slow down!"

He relaxed his grip on my arm and slowed his pace. "Would you care to explain what you were doing?" he hissed.

"Seeking information. What's wrong with that?"

"You cannot loiter in passageways and eavesdrop!"

"Why not?"

"Because you're sure to be caught, as you very nearly were. As it was, everyone thought you impertinent at best and unhinged at worst. Promise me you will not do anything so foolish again."

"All right! I promise. Where are we going?"

"To the library, where we might have some privacy."

In a few minutes, I was lounging on the settle while Stephen coaxed a pitiful flame to life in the fireplace.

"How much of our conversation did you hear?"

"Enough to make me afraid."

"Thomas seems to be fearless." Seating himself next to me,

Stephen shook his head, baffled. "I believe he is overly confident about his present safety. After the sheriff's raid, I do not see how he can be so unconcerned."

"Will Shakespeare seems worried about him. I wonder what he would do, how far he would go, to protect Thomas."

Stephen looked at me, his expression inscrutable. But I had the feeling he was making a valiant effort to keep quiet about my . . . duty. Shrugging, he said, "There is little you or I can do about it tonight."

"You mentioned something about Walsingham's spies. I don't know who Walsingham is, but the whole spy thing intrigues me."

"Olivia, this is not something meant to amuse you."

I bristled. "Is that what you think?"

In an instant, his expression changed from annoyed to apologetic. He reached over and took my hands. "Forgive me, of course I do not. I grow tired of the whole business, that is all I meant. Pray continue."

"Well . . . haven't you wondered how the sheriff knew there was a priest here?"

"People wish to say their confessions and hear Mass. Word passes from one family to the next. 'Tis only natural."

"But the sheriff knew there was a *Jesuit* priest on the premises. Doesn't that make a difference? Aren't the Jesuits the ones they're really after?"

"Aye, you are right. 'Tis the Jesuits they fear." Stephen rose and paced around the room.

"So . . . I have a theory. Do you want to hear it?" I hurried over to him.

"Do I have a choice?" I narrowed my eyes and he laughed.

"I think there's a spy right here at Hoghton Tower!"

"You have an exceptional imagination, mistress," he said, eyeing me skeptically.

"The first day I was here, when we were outside dancing, someone was watching us. I saw the curtain pulled aside, and it fell back into place when we turned to come in."

"That could simply have been a curious servant."

"And something else. During my meeting with Will, I could have sworn I heard footsteps in the hallway right before we left the room. Nobody was there, but there were lots of hiding places."

"Why did you wait so long to tell me these things!"

"I didn't think they were that important, but now, too much has happened for us to ignore anything." Stephen looked annoyed, but more willing to listen.

"Getting back to my theory. . . . How did the sheriff choose this home to raid? He must have an informant!"

"And who is on your list of most likely suspects?"

I leaned in conspiratorially. "Jennet, of course. The man she met with in the forest could be part of a network of spies," I whispered.

"How exactly would that work?"

From the smug look on his face, I knew he was needling me, but I answered anyway. "Whoever she reports to passes on her information to someone else, who passes it to yet another person, and so on. Who knows where it ends up?"

"Who else is among your suspects?"

"One of the servants, maybe. I don't know. I just think it's too much of a coincidence that the sheriff knows there's a Jesuit living here."

"I've been acquainted with the servants since my childhood, and 'tis highly unlikely there would be a spy among them. They are fiercely loyal to my uncle. Jennet, I'll admit, bears watching. I hardly think she has anything to do with Walsingham, but she could be spreading rumors. Something likely to attract the attention of anyone who means to harm Catholics."

I reached under my bodice and extracted the note from my waistband. "There's this, too." I handed it to him. "I don't know what it has to do with anything. With Jennet, or Shakespeare and Thomas, or spies."

After raising his eyebrows at me, he looked it over. "Is the writing the same as the other one?"

"I think so. Since we burned the first one, I couldn't compare them, but I'm almost positive."

"I do not understand the purpose. Is it meant to scare you— us? Who could know we are not brother and sister? And what do they intend to do with the information?"

"I keep coming back to Jennet. She was away for Easter weekend and could easily have found someone to help her with the note. Plus, if she was the one watching us when we were dancing, maybe she thought a brother and sister wouldn't be quite so, well, enthusiastic."

Stephen smiled. "Indeed. And none of the others who can read and write seem likely." He walked over and stirred the fire to life with the poker, and then threw the note into the flames.

"I agree. By now, Jennet would be able to write a short note. Even though she's been friendlier to me lately, I think she's still jealous when it comes to Will. At least a little."

"Why? Thus far you've hardly given her a reason to be, have you?"

Immediately, tears filled my eyes. I put some distance between us so Stephen wouldn't notice and told myself to get a grip. "I can't think of a motive for Will."

"Nor can I."

"But Thomas might have a reason to threaten me. Maybe he's figured out I'm trying to get Will away from him. And the church."

"How would he know that? Even Shakespeare does not know, because nothing has happened!"

I was shaky, on the verge of tears. But I couldn't let that comment pass without a response. Voice trembling, I said, "More has happened between Will and me than you know about."

Stephen closed the distance between us in a second, but stopped short of any physical contact.

"You don't care what happens to me, as long as I do exactly what you want!"

He seized my arm. "Do you think I am enjoying this? Do you think I like using you this way?" When I didn't answer, he said, in a softer voice, "I do not. There is nothing to be done but get it over with." He lifted my chin and looked into my eyes. "I hate to see you thus, Olivia."

Our faces were only inches apart now. Somehow, my hands ended up on his chest, and he moved his to frame my face. Despite our argument, I wanted him to kiss me. *I really wanted him to kiss me.* He leaned in, and when our lips met, I opened my mouth a little to the softness of his.

He broke the kiss long enough to say, "You steal my breath, Olivia." Then he kissed me again, as if he never wanted to stop. Something stirred in my heart, and I moved my hands up and slid them around his neck.

And then he drew back, just like he had the other day.

"What's wrong?" I asked, hurt, not understanding.

"I forget myself," he said, starting to turn for the door. "This is not . . . Kissing you is not a good idea. It will only hurt us both."

"No! It's okay. Kiss me as much as you want." But he was already gone. Thank God. How mortifying was that, practically begging him to make out with me?

My fingers strayed to my mouth, where I could still feel the touch of Stephen's lips. How could the person who was practically throwing me at Shakespeare kiss me like that? And why was he so set on pushing me away?

Chapter Twenty-One

CURLED INTO A LUMP OF MISERY, I lay awake most of the night wondering about the mixed signals I was getting from Stephen. Did he care for me or not? Our feelings for each other aside, he was right about one thing. The seduction plan was going nowhere. Nor was I having any better luck with the antiseduction. Based on what I'd overheard last night, it was obvious that Will was devoted to Thomas. He'd probably be perfectly happy to remain under Thomas's influence, do his bidding, and follow him anywhere. For the time being, it seemed like seduction was the only way forward, if I could only find an opportunity for it.

Dawn was breaking as I hurried to the schoolroom, hoping to get there before anyone else. I wanted to search for the mysterious letter from Thomas. Given the situation, I thought it might be important to know exactly what it said.

I had no idea when the school day began, or what time Will and his young scholars arrived. The birds were twittering and swathes of peach and pink radiated through the sky as I made my way along the passages. Surely no one, even in this century, got to school so early.

The classroom door stood open, and I stepped over the threshold and closed it. Where to start? Will's personal worktable would be the most obvious place. The room was dim, and I chided myself for not bringing a candle. Since I didn't want to use up valuable time looking for one, I'd have to make the best of it.

I sorted through stacks of papers, all student work. Spotting a small wooden coffer resting on a shelf behind the table, I lifted it down and carried it over to one of the windows. There were several letters inside! I worked quickly, unfolding and glancing at each one. Some of them were from Shakespeare's father. Two were from Alexander arranging Will's employment as schoolmaster, and a few others were from various people I'd never heard of.

I unfolded the last one and had to clap my hand over my mouth to keep from crying out. It was to Anne Hathaway, incomplete and never sent, obviously.

> *My dear Mistress Hathaway,*
> *You have bewitched me with your beauty.*
> *When I should be tending to my duties, I think*
> *of you instead. The fullness of your breasts, the*
> *lovely slope of your neck, your delicate ankles*
> *peeking out from beneath your skirts. I long to*
> *see you again. Pray wait for me*

He'd crossed out the part about waiting for him. Not knowing what his future held, was he afraid of giving her too much encouragement? If I could take one thing home with me . . . this would probably be it. What a stroke of luck to have even seen it!

I replaced the letters and returned the coffer to the shelf. Glancing around the room, I could find nowhere else to look. There was a narrow alcove with wooden pegs, where the students put their coats, but it contained no shelves or drawers. Tables and stools for the students, now standing lonely and deserted, were the only other pieces of furniture. Will must have taken the letter to his chamber. I'd have to search it one day while he was teaching.

It was time for me to get out. I pressed my ear to the door for a second, to make sure nobody was in the passage. Then I slipped out and back to my room, where I had time to undress and climb into bed before Bess could discover I'd been up and about at such a ridiculous hour.

After lunch, I drew Stephen aside. "I need to talk to you."

"About what?" he asked, giving me a brief look before turning his gaze to the side.

"Privately," I whispered. "It's about Will. I searched—" Alexander was approaching us, so I closed my mouth around the rest of the words.

"Lad, when you and Olivia are done, I need a moment."

"We are done now, Uncle," Stephen said, walking away. "I shall see you this evening, Olivia."

I nodded. *If only I had that branch, I'd smack him with it again.*

Later, I was lying on my bed fantasizing about kissing Stephen when he appeared in the passageway. I bolted up, embarrassed to be caught daydreaming. He strode over to me.

"Olivia, guests are expected tonight. This is what my uncle wanted to tell me."

"So?"

"There is to be music and dancing after the evening meal. This could be a prime opportunity for you, for the seduction." *So aloof.* He couldn't look me in the eye when he said it.

"Great. I'm looking forward to it, and to going home." I kept my eyes on the coverlet, pulling at some loose threads.

"About last night," he said. "I should not have kissed you the first time, and certainly not a second. It was wrong of me, and I entreat you to forgive me."

My head jerked up. *There was so much more than a kiss between us.* He was keeping me at a distance because of what he was asking me to do with Will. That was the only thing that made sense. How could he let his feelings for me show when he wanted me to seduce another man?

"No apologies necessary," I said coldly.

"But—"

"Please, let's not discuss it."

"As you wish." There was a distinct lack of emotion in his voice. "You started to tell me something."

"Remember the letter Will received from Thomas? I said I'd try to find it."

He nodded, and even plunked himself down on the edge of the bed.

"After what they were discussing last night, I thought I should look for it. I was up at dawn and made a thorough search of the classroom, even found some letters. But none were from Thomas. Do you want me to search his room?"

"I could do it, but you would be more likely to recognize it."

"I'll find a time when I'm certain he's busy somewhere else. You could be my lookout, though."

He nodded and headed back to the door, turning briefly. "Wear the crimson gown tonight, and make sure Bess arranges your hair."

"Leave me alone," I said, flopping backward on the bed.

After Stephen left, I lay there a long time going over the pros and cons of making love with Shakespeare. In the plus column was the fact that nothing else seemed to be keeping him from caving in to Thomas. While Will hadn't made any major moves on me, other than a few kisses, I knew he liked me, especially since I was interested in his writing and acting. I was pretty sure he'd be a willing partner. In fact, there'd been a few times when I'd thought he was seducing *me*. Stephen, acting all cold and formal, had hurt me. After everything we'd shared, I was hoping he'd say there was no way he would *let* me do it. Maybe my going through with it would drive him wild with jealousy. *Right*.

On the negative side, I simply didn't know if I had the audacity to carry it off. I realized this was the complete opposite of how I'd felt before, and certainly the opposite of the impression I'd been going out of my way to give Stephen. At first I'd been awed by Will. Just being in his company had been a thrill. It still was. Losing my virginity to him, someone I so admired and revered, would be so cool. And there was that ridiculous idea of one-upping my mother—as if she'd ever know.

But all this was before Stephen. Before I'd fallen for him. I desperately wished he would be the one I'd be making love with tonight.

And then I was struck by an idea so perfect, so obvious, and so right, I wondered why I hadn't thought of it sooner. I needed help planning the seduction. Not only planning, but practicing. Who better than my host, my guide, and, coincidentally, the man I truly desired . . . Master Stephen Langford? *Brilliant, Olivia!*

I flew off my bed and went in search of my prey.

He wasn't in his chamber, the library, the billiard room, or any of the drawing rooms. I was about to give up when I heard his voice drifting in from outdoors. Peering out the windows, I glimpsed him striding through the courtyard, dressed in riding clothes. My knees turned to jelly.

Back in my room, I swept the hairbrush through my hair a few times; then I straightened my skirts, smoothed my bodice, and fervently wished I had some blush and mascara. Meanwhile, I heard Stephen moving around next door, and after a decent interval, I moseyed on over.

"Knock, knock," I said, peeking in. He'd stripped down to his shirt and was drying his hands and face with a towel. I could tell by his look he was surprised to see me.

"Olivia. Do you need something?"

I sauntered over to him and gave him my version of a smoldering look. "Yes. I need your advice regarding tonight. The . . . events . . . of tonight."

He must have guessed I was up to something, because he narrowed his eyes at me and tilted his head to one side. "Indeed?"

"Indeed. Can you spare me some time?"

He sighed. "Very well." He stood there staring at me, waiting.

"Not here," I hissed. "We could be overheard, or someone could walk in."

"The library, then?"

"Oh, no." I shook my head slowly. "We need more privacy than that."

Now he really looked suspicious. Turning his back on me, he went to his wardrobe and found a doublet. When he'd finished fastening it, he said, "Come. You'd best get your cloak. And bring Cop, if he's there."

Once outside, we set off for the forest, picking our way around trees, fallen logs, and ferns. I was glad to have Copernicus loping along beside us, since there was nothing between Stephen and me but silence. Before long, a few rough buildings came into view in a clearing.

"Where are we?"

"These are sheepfolds and shepherds' huts." After rapping on the door of one of the thatch-roofed huts, Stephen pushed it open. He commanded Copernicus to stay, and we entered. "Cop will alert us if anyone approaches."

"Aren't we trespassing?" The hut was snug and clean, the floor covered with fresh-smelling rushes. The only furnishings were a small wooden table and a bench. There was no fireplace, but I'd noticed some fire rings outside. We sat next to each other on the bench.

"The shepherds are hospitable folk. If they should find us, they would probably think it an honor. Now, would you care to tell me what we're doing here?"

I sucked in a deep breath. "I think we should practice the seduction."

"What you should say?"

"No. What I should *do*."

"Ah. *Do*. Well, then." He barked a laugh. "What game are you playing, Olivia?"

"This is *not* a game, Stephen. I told you I've never seduced anybody."

He dropped his forehead into his palms and nodded. "I remember."

"I think you should teach me."

He kept his head in his hands. Was he going to refuse?

Finally he looked up. "What is your plan as to how things will proceed tonight?"

I gave an exasperated shrug. "Talk. Dance. Flirt. Suggest we go somewhere we can be alone. Then—"

Eyes laughing, he said, "I am familiar with the rest."

"Wonderful, because your job now is to show me."

Looking at me mischievously, he slapped his hands on his thighs. "Very well. Let's get started. How many men have you kissed, Olivia? Besides Will and myself, and that youth in the play?"

"Dozens!" My face burned at the lie.

"Truly? You just said you were not practiced in seduction."

"But I've *kissed* lots of guys. I'm not a total dork!"

"Mayhap I should have put it differently. Do you still maintain you've never made love with any of the *dozens* you've kissed?"

"You know I haven't."

"You are right, then. It would mayhap be wise for me to instruct you." He scooted closer to me, so our thighs were touching. I inched away, and my cheeks burned hotter.

"Is something wrong? I thought you wished to practice with me. We must begin with kissing. 'Tis the sweetest part of wooing."

My heart beat wildly. "No, everything's fine," I said, without moving any closer.

"Come, Olivia. I have kissed you before, and I do not believe you found my kisses offensive."

His brown eyes were unreadable. Even though I knew he was calling my bluff, I wasn't about to back down now. I slowly reached up and stroked his cheek, and he smiled.

"I love your overlapping tooth," I said, and immediately felt back in control of things.

"I knew someday I would be glad of it." He set his hands on my shoulders and leaned in to kiss me.

At the touch of his lips, my heart gave a gentle leap. I threw my arms around his neck, and his hands brushing down my arms made me lightheaded. He grasped me around the waist and pressed me close, both of us trembling.

It was barely a whisper, but I heard him say, "Ah, Olivia." Drawing back, Stephen looked at me with glazed eyes. "If he does not kiss you, you may have to—"

"Make the first move. I know," I said, placing my mouth back against the warmth of his.

At last we broke the embrace. "What should I do after we kiss?" I asked. "Should I touch him—?"

"No! He will know what to do next. Good God, Olivia, give the man a chance."

"But I'm seducing *him*. Maybe he'll try to resist me."

"Ha! I assure you, he will not."

"Humor me. As I was saying, maybe I should put my hand here?" I rested my hand on his thigh and slid it slowly upward. Stephen slapped it away. I couldn't believe I was being so bold.

"Enough, Olivia! I'm warning you—"

I loved seeing him flustered. "About what?" I asked, batting my eyes. "Should I undo his doublet? And slide my hands up under his shirt, like this? Along his bare skin? Would he like that?"

I hadn't reckoned on how electrifying the touch of Stephen's skin would be. I was seriously thinking about climbing onto his lap when he rocketed off the bench, cursing. "God's breath! This must stop, Olivia."

"But—"

Just then, the door burst open. A man I'd never seen before entered, obviously shocked at seeing us there. "Sir?" He looked from Stephen to me blankly.

Stephen adjusted his clothing as he spoke. "James, I beg your pardon. My sister and I needed a private place to talk. We were just leaving."

I rose, and after a quick curtsy to poor James, I followed Stephen outside. Dozens of black-faced sheep, bleating loudly, were milling around, bumping against each other. I couldn't believe I hadn't heard them. Stephen snapped his fingers at Copernicus, who seemed inclined to hang around with the sheep.

"So much for your great watchdog," I commented as I hurried to keep up with him.

"He barked. I heard him."

"Why didn't you warn me?"

"I barely noticed, so caught up was I in your little scheme!"

"Slow down! My 'little scheme'? What's that supposed to mean?"

"You know what I am speaking of. Your clumsy attempt to seduce me, when it is Shakespeare you must entrap!"

I opened my mouth, but found myself stuttering. I couldn't

deny the truth of what he'd said, and a stab of pain, deep and visceral, cut into me. He had not only inserted the knife, but also twisted it. He didn't welcome my attentions, and he thought they were *clumsy*, for God's sake! Even worse, he wanted to humiliate me for foisting myself on him.

"It would be best if I went ahead of you. You can walk at a more leisurely pace. I shall see you at dinner," he said coldly.

"Fine," I bit off. Tears gushed from my eyes and flowed down my cheeks, and I was grateful he'd left me to walk alone. At that moment, I wished fiercely that I were home in Boston, in my predictable, safe little cocoon. It might not be perfect, but it was better than rejection.

I would take great pains to prepare for the evening, so I'd look gorgeous. I would look so beautiful and desirable that King Henry, were he still alive, would want me for his seventh wife. Shakespeare, Stephen, Fulke, every man present would desire me. I'd flirt with the others and reject Stephen, and he could cry into his pillow every night, from now until forever. I doubted that guys did that, but however it happened, I hoped he'd suffer.

Chapter Twenty-Two

I DRESSED WITH CARE in the red gown and wore my finest silk smock underneath . . . and nothing else, no kirtle or petticoat. I even asked Bess to put a rose from the garden in my hair. A pale pink, to contrast with the red of the gown. By the time I was ready for the evening meal, I still hadn't made up my mind about tonight's outcome. I intended to flirt with Will and see how it went. For starters, I'd sit beside him at dinner and try to "woo" him. Prominently featured in my plan was driving Stephen wild with jealousy.

I headed downstairs early and was one of the first to arrive. Lingering by the table on the dais, I noticed once again what a magnificent room the banqueting hall was. The days were growing longer, and the last bit of daylight was seeping in through the windows. The flames from hundreds of tapers bathed wood and stone and tapestries in a warm radiance. Above the hall, the railings surrounding the gallery were festooned with spring greens and flowers. Someone had gone to a lot of trouble to impress the visitors.

Right after Will arrived I sidled over to him and said something really seductive, like "Good even, sir. May I sit next to you?" Of course, he smiled and said he'd be honored. He was too polite to say anything else. Jennet was eyeing us from across the table, but Stephen sat down and distracted her.

Bess had told me Elizabeth arrived home earlier today, but I hadn't seen her yet. In a moment, Alexander entered the room with his wife on his arm, and I thought he looked healthier already. The visitors accompanied them, and we all rose while the two men were introduced. They were dressed in leather doublets and trunk hose. One looked middle-aged, the other, younger. "Allow me to present my guests," Alexander said, "Master Timothy Hale and Master Robert Lowry. They are stopping here on their way west, where they have business."

After the hand washing, I grabbed my tankard of ale and drank about half of it. "I am looking forward to the dancing tonight," I said to Will.

He looked at me, a naughty gleam in his eye. "Truly? May I have the first dance, then?"

"You may." I finished the ale, and a servant immediately refilled my mug. *If I drink too much, I'll make a fool of myself on the dance floor—and elsewhere.* I decided to reconsider my strategy.

Jennet was leaning toward Stephen, her gorgeous hair cascading over one side of her face in a perfect fall. They were laughing about something. Well. Who knew she could be funny? Stephen didn't even glance my way.

I couldn't think of anything to say to Master William

Shakespeare, funny or otherwise. *Seen any movies lately? Are you into graphic novels? What's on your iPod? You should start a blog! That would really get your name out there. Do you tweet?*

I broke off a piece of manchet and chewed on it. One of the visitors, Timothy Hale, had struck up a conversation with Thomas Cook. The younger one, Master Lowry, singled out Will. "Master . . . Shakespeare, was it?" When Will nodded, he went on. "What is your business here?"

"I am the schoolmaster."

"You seem quite young for such an occupation."

"Perhaps." Will shrugged him off and turned to me. "I should like to read more of my writing to you, Mistress Olivia."

"I'd like that too, Will."

I glanced at Lowry, who was sitting across the table diagonally from me. He turned his head to speak to someone on his other side, and for the first time, I saw him in profile. Something about him . . . I knew him from somewhere; I'd seen him before, I was sure.

Abruptly, Lowry turned back to continue his conversation with Shakespeare. "Pray, lad, how did you come by this job?"

It was then that I noticed Alexander watching us. He held a wine glass in his hands, rolling it back and forth between his palms. He seemed wary of something.

Will must have noticed too, because he flashed a glance toward Alexander before addressing Robert Lowry. "My own schoolmaster recommended me for the post."

"Tell me, sir, are you licensed?"

Will flushed. This was becoming awkward and uncomfortable, almost like an interrogation. Stephen and Jennet had stopped talking and were listening to the conversation.

"Pardon me, Master Lowry," I broke in. "What brings you to Lancashire?" I gulped noisily at my ale, hoping he would think I was an impertinent, and maybe intoxicated, young lady.

He shoveled a bite of beef into his mouth and chewed before answering. "We are on Privy Council business," he said curtly.

"In truth, you must be very important visitors then. Tell me, why did you choose to stay at Hoghton Tower? Are there not grander places for privy councilors?" I asked, deliberately misunderstanding. These two rough-looking men might work for the Privy Council, but I doubted they were members.

"Come, Olivia," Alexander said. "Allow our guest to eat in peace. He has had a long journey here. Let us not trouble him with our questions."

All of a sudden I knew where I'd seen him before. A rain-soaked day in the woods. A man in a clearing, dressed almost the same as he was now, with a distinctive profile. Robert Lowry was the same man Jennet had been talking to in the woods the other day. An icy trickle of fear crawled down my back.

"So shall he not trouble us with his," I said, looking at Lowry straight on.

Stephen cleared his throat. I shifted my eyes his way and tried to figure out if he was warning me or laughing at me. Before I could decide, he said, "Pay no heed to my sister, sir. I know my uncle and aunt are always pleased to welcome guests."

If Lowry were a spy or a government informer, goading him wouldn't help us. "Pardon me, sir, for my rudeness," I said, my face flushing.

He tilted his head very slightly to acknowledge my apology, and things returned to normal. Will and I looked at each other, and in his expression I saw a mixture of amusement and respect. I held his eyes for as long as I could, trying to bewitch him. It was hard to do that, to hold someone's gaze that way. I looked back at my plate and stabbed a piece of fowl, smiling to myself. I felt bold and seductive.

Will and Fulke went off to organize the music. I looked around the room at the clusters of people who had split off after the meal. Lowry and Hale were conversing with Alexander and Elizabeth, too far away for me to see their expressions. Thomas and Stephen were huddled together talking. Jennet was nowhere to be seen. Desperate to tell Stephen about her and Robert Lowry, I was tempted to interrupt his conversation with Thomas. But then I'd run the risk of losing any chance of up-close-and-personal time with Will.

I tried to make sense of Jennet's relationship with Lowry. She'd met secretly with someone who, in all probability, was a Privy Council spy. How long had she been sneaking off to meet with him? What did it mean? My best guess was that she was reporting to him, and had been all along. Now I understood how the sheriff had known, before the raid, that a Jesuit was hiding here. How she'd figured it out was unclear, but I'd found out plenty from listening and watching, and she could have done the same.

Whatever was going on, I had to tell Stephen right away so we could decide what to do. The music was starting up, chords from the lute and recorder floating among the guests. As I looked around, I recognized some of the neighbors drifting in for the dancing. In a moment Fulke's voice called out, "Ladies and gentlemen, choose partners for a galliard!"

"Mistress?" Will said, suddenly appearing at my side.

We lined up with the other dancers. After the honor, we began a series of little steps and hops, circling around each other and grasping hands now and then. It was an energetic dance, and I had to focus my attention on performing the steps correctly, so there was really no chance for talking. I smiled up at Will whenever the movements allowed. I was beginning to like Elizabethan music, which no longer sounded so odd to my modern ears. It was playful, lively, and eminently suited to dancing.

I looked at Will and said, "'If music be the food of love, play on.'"

His eyes lit up. "You say the cleverest things, Olivia. I may borrow that line someday."

"I hope you will." Duke Orsino's words from *Twelfth Night* had always stuck with me because Mr. Finley said they were a perfect example of iambic pentameter. When Shakespeare wrote that line, would he believe he'd stolen it from me?

"I thank you for coming to my rescue with our arrogant visitors," Will said while we both caught our breath.

"Who are they, do you know?"

"Privy Council business," Will said, his lip curling. "Privy Council spies, I fear."

With Will's confirmation of my own suspicion, my stomach tightened. And I had acted like a spoiled brat. A lot like Katherine, I thought, wincing. That was probably what Stephen was thinking.

"Would they have come here for a particular reason?"

"In truth, I do not know. I believe they travel about, stopping at different manors and seeking information about religious and political matters. They could have been sent to finish what the sheriff started."

"To find Thomas and arrest him?"

Will nodded slowly, looking around us. "Soft," he cautioned.

"Yet Thomas ate with us as usual. He's not hiding."

He shrugged. "'Tis a strange situation. Mayhap 'twas thought he was best concealed in the open."

"I don't—do not see them," I said. "Do you think they've left?"

"Nay. I would not be surprised if even now they were questioning Master Hoghton. Tomorrow they will travel on and bother some other blameless citizens." The music started up again and Will offered his arm. "Come, let's forget about them."

And if this night was to go according to plan, I must force myself to forget, at least for now. The dance was a pavane, the music slower paced and better suited to flirting. There were lots of opportunities for circling around and staring longingly into your partner's eyes. When we took each other's hands and stepped close together, our bodies actually touched. I knew Stephen was watching from the edge of the dance floor; I could feel his eyes on me. No way would I give him the satisfaction of returning his gaze.

When the dance ended, Will leaned in close. "Let's walk outside. A breath of air would feel good." We clasped hands and threaded our way through the room. Feeling abandoned and a little desperate, I looked back to find Stephen, but he'd dissolved into the crowd. *Get with the program, Olivia. This is what you're here for. Just do it.*

We reached the inner courtyard, and I realized we were not alone. Other couples were already there, embracing, kissing, murmuring. There could be no doubt as to why Will had brought me here. He led me to an unclaimed stone bench and pulled me down beside him. Without any preliminaries, he put his arms around me and drew me close. His eyes met mine for a moment, as if asking permission. I didn't flinch. Slowly, he lowered his head and kissed me.

I threw my arms around his neck and returned the kiss. He smelled a little of sweat, but he'd sweetened his breath with mint. After a minute, he ran his hand over my cheek, down my neck, and over my bodice. Every so often he paused, as if waiting for me to stop him.

Oh, my God. I'm making out with William Shakespeare! I nearly laughed out loud. But instead I turned my attention to where Will's hand was at this moment. Running down my leg to my ankle, making its way underneath the soft folds of my gown. "Olivia," he said in a choked voice, "we must go somewhere else."

"Let's go through the main entrance. Most people are still in the banqueting hall."

He grabbed my hand and we raced off. I bunched up my gown with the other hand and tried to keep up with him. We flew up the steps, pausing briefly to make sure Stephen wasn't in his room. When we reached Jennet's chamber, the passageway door was closed. Not a good sign, since she'd vanished after dinner. Will and I looked at each other, and he motioned for me to wait in my own room while he investigated. After a moment, he reappeared and signaled to me. I hurried over and we passed through Jennet's room and into Will's together.

Immediately, he closed the passageway doors and locked them. Then he came over to me and kissed me gently. He nuzzled my neck for a minute. "I'll light some candles. Stay right there."

When that was done, he approached me again. "You look so lovely in the candlelight, Olivia."

Embarrassed, I ducked my head. "Thank you." Why was he making this so hard? Part of me wished he'd act like a jerk, so I wouldn't feel anything at all for him. Instead, he was being romantic and sweet.

"Come." He led me to the bed and we sat. And then he scooped up a handful of my hair and wound it around his fingers. "Your hair . . . 'tis like the finest spun silk. It shines like mahogany."

"Um . . ."

"Your skin. All satin and velvet. So fair and"—he leaned over and kissed a dozen different places on my face—"it tastes like the sweetest nectar."

I closed my eyes. *Maybe I did love Will a little.* When I opened them, I found him gazing adoringly at me. I leaned toward him and he took the hint, swooping in for a kiss. His arms went around me, drawing me close.

"I love the slope of your neck, the swell of your breasts." Hmm. That had a vaguely familiar ring.

He lowered his head and dropped kisses on my . . . swell. I could easily get used to a man worshipping me. And then the oddest sensation swept over me. Was Will truly so enraptured by my beauty, my soft skin, and my shiny hair? Or did he just want to have sex with me? I guess it didn't really matter which of us seduced the other.

I realized he was whispering to me. "Your gown."

"M-my gown? Oh, the fastenings are in back," I said, my voice quavering.

Will unfastened it about twice as fast as Bess was able to. In no time at all I was standing there wearing nothing but my thin smock, and I began to shiver. My stomach was roiling, queasy. After tugging off his doublet and the shirt underneath, Will grasped me around the waist from behind. Slowly, his hands slid upward.

My mind flashed to Stephen, and how he'd watched me while I danced with Will. And earlier, kissing him, holding him. Was this what he wanted for me? What I wanted for myself? I twisted around and kissed Will passionately, buying time. In a minute, it would be too late to change course. I withdrew slightly from the embrace.

I thought I was going to be sick.

Chapter Twenty-Three

WILL MANEUVERED ME BACKWARD to the bed, yanking at the coverlet with his free hand. "Lie down," he whispered. Heart hammering, I did as he asked. He lay down next to me, and before I knew what was happening, he'd grabbed the hem of my smock and was tugging it over my head.

God's breath! I'm completely naked! I squeezed my eyes shut. *I'm an actor. It's only a role I'm playing. It's not really me, Miranda. Or even Olivia.* I clenched my jaw and steeled myself.

But it *was* me. It was my body, something precious to give. I wasn't sure about giving it to Will, especially since I was in love with Stephen. Will reached for me, his voice interrupting my muddled thoughts.

"Oh, Anne, sweet, I love you so much."

Huh? I pressed my palms against his chest and pushed him away. Had he just called me Anne, as in Anne Hathaway? I studied his face, and could tell by his horrified look that he knew exactly what he'd done.

"Pardon me, Olivia. I do not know why—"

He'd just given me the perfect out. A chance for a graceful exit. "Pray, who is Anne?" I tried to sound hurt.

"A lady from Stratford. I—I . . ."

I interrupted. "Forgive me, Will, but I do not wish to make love with you."

He cursed under his breath. "I called you Anne. How can you ever forgive me?"

"She must be someone you care for very much."

"Aye, but I care for you, too. Are you certain about this? *Carpe diem*, Olivia! Life is short."

I recognized that phrase from a novel I'd read, and knew it meant "seize the day." From Ovid, probably. *Nice try, Will.* "I think both of us were mistaken in thinking this was what we wanted."

"But—"

"Nay, Will. This is not right."

He rolled over and out of the bed. "As you say, mistress."

We both hurriedly dressed and, gentleman that he was, Will offered to refasten my gown. I told him not to bother, since I was going directly to bed. When the silence grew uncomfortable, I headed toward the doors. After he unlocked them, Will touched my shoulder. "Olivia—"

"You do not need to say anything more, Will." He nodded, a guilty expression crossing his face.

I made sure the coast was clear before scurrying back to my room. It was late, and the strain of this never-ending day had caught up with me. After preparing for bed, I let the crimson gown pool on the floor, stepped out of it, and wearily climbed under the covers. Tomorrow I'd face Stephen, and together we would figure out what came next.

I awoke to Stephen's touch. So deeply had I fallen into sleep that it seemed a long time before I sensed and finally reacted to his hand clasping mine and his voice gently calling to me.

"Olivia, wake up."

I smiled at the sound of his voice. *Was I dreaming?*

"Olivia—"

I opened my eyes. "Let me go back to sleep. Please." What was he doing here, anyway?

Smoothly, Stephen lifted me up, coverlet and all, and carried me to his chamber. A fire blazed and crackled in the grate, and he put me down on the settle, directly in front of it.

I yawned, pawed at my tangled hair, and blinked my eyes a few times.

"Here, drink this."

Scooting over to make room for him, I accepted a cup from his hand and sipped. "Wine. That should really wake me up."

"Do as I ask. Believe me, you'll feel better."

And after a while, I did. He gave me the time I needed to regain my senses, and gradually it dawned on me that he wanted to know what had happened with Will. Of course he did. Might as well come clean.

"I couldn't do it, Stephen. I tried, but at the last minute, I couldn't go through with it. I'm sorry . . . to disappoint you." I watched his face, sure he'd be furious with me, and waited for his expression to harden.

Instead, on a sigh he said, "I am very glad you did not." His voice was husky and his eyes gleamed in the firelight.

"You are?" I couldn't keep my surprise and shock from showing. "I've been agonizing over it for so long, and now you say you're glad it didn't happen!"

Stephen winced. "I beg your forgiveness. I should never have asked you to do it. I thought only of myself—what would be least troublesome for me. It was unfair to you."

Somewhat grudgingly I said, "It wasn't all your fault. I was intrigued by the idea at first. Losing my virginity to the great Will Shakespeare seemed appealing. Now it just seems wrong." *Because I'm in love with you.* "And I don't think it will change his mind about becoming a Jesuit."

"Mayhap you are right about that." He had an odd half smile on his face.

"What are you smiling about?"

"You did not tell me you were 'agonizing.' Most recently, you said you were 'looking forward to it.'"

Only to make you jealous. "Uh, well, I never thought it would work, so I agonized about it. That's all I meant."

"Do you wish to tell me what occurred?"

"No!"

He shushed me. "You will wake the others."

No way could I tell him about my almost-sex with Will. I felt myself flush, knowing his eyes were riveted on me. "Maybe another time," I said. *Like never.* "What should we do?"

"We must think of a new tactic, something involving us both."

"I had my own plan, you know."

When he looked blank, I said, "Talking to him about acting, asking about his writing, seeking his advice about reading."

"I did not realize that you hoped to lure him from the priesthood in that way."

"It hasn't made much of an impression, except I think it made me more attractive to him. But he seems as devoted to Thomas as ever." I paused a minute to sip at my wine. An idea struck me and I seized Stephen's hand. "What if we tell him about his destiny, and even how we know?"

"He would not believe us."

"You're the one who told me Elizabethans believe in the super-natural to explain weird happenings. Maybe it wouldn't seem so far-fetched." I expelled a quick breath. "It's the truth, after all."

"Will views us as friends and companions—not sorcerers or seers."

"You'd have to tell him—"

"I am not revealing my powers to Will Shakespeare, Olivia! I will not yield on that."

I nodded. *Another part of the wizard code of ethics. Never reveal that you are one.*

We sat in silence for a few minutes. Eventually I remembered my "aha" moment at dinner, and that I needed to tell Stephen about it. "How was Jennet during the meal? You two seemed to be laughing a lot."

He shrugged. "I was teasing her a bit, and poking fun at the visitors."

"Did anything about her behavior strike you as odd, or different?"

"Not at all. Why?"

"Her tryst with the man in the woods."

"What about it?" His voice was sharp.

"At the time I noticed he had a huge, hooked nose. He wasn't wearing a cap, and I could see him clearly. The man was Robert Lowry."

Stephen leaped to his feet. "Jesu! You are certain?"

"As soon as I caught a glimpse of his profile tonight at dinner, I knew he was the same person."

"I must confess something to you as well. I thought about keeping it from you, but in light of this new information—"

"Just tell me!"

"The moment I met Lowry, I recognized him as the other man in my vision."

"Oh, God. So he's important, somehow, in all of this." I tried to piece it together. "Robert Lowry and the sheriff are plotting against . . . whom? Thomas Cook?"

"Who else?"

I mused out loud. "Jennet's got to be reporting to Lowry, who we now know from your vision is working with the sheriff. They already knew there was a Jesuit here, so what else could she be telling them?"

"One thing to consider," Stephen said. "Thomas studies in the library. If he carelessly left some of his papers lying about, she may have looked at them, may even have seen this document he's writing."

"But you're forgetting she can't read—at least, not that well."

"What if that's all been a ruse? Mayhap she reads and writes as well as you or I. We have only her word on it. And given what he's writing about . . ."

A tiny ping of doubt struck me. "I don't think so," I said, shaking my head. "It would mean she's been lying the whole time she's been at Hoghton Tower." I stood and paced, glancing at Stephen. "Her creepy father may be involved in this somehow. I wouldn't put it past him to use Jennet to push his own agenda, whatever that is."

"Perhaps. We must keep an eye on her. If we notice anything else out of the ordinary, we will go to my uncle and let him decide what to do."

"I guess that's a plan." Feeling an overpowering weariness take hold of me, I yawned and stretched. "I'll need to talk with Will tomorrow, to make things right between us."

"Perhaps you should allow him to approach you. As a gentleman, he would want it that way."

I nodded. "I'll wait for him to come to me. But right now I need some sleep. I'm too tired to think about this anymore. Something will come to us."

Stephen stepped close to me, right into my personal space. Fine by me. "I admired the way you stood up to Lowry. It took courage to speak to him as you did, although it may not have been the wisest course."

"I did it for Will's sake. Lowry was practically interrogating him. And I *did* apologize."

"'Tis no matter. He has other fish to fry."

I nodded. "I hope they're not swimming around here at Hoghton Tower."

Stephen smiled, and I felt my eyes practically begging him to hold me, kiss me. "Good night, then, Olivia. Sleep well."

"Good night, Stephen."

"I am glad—relieved—that matters did not proceed as we once wished." Placing a hand on either side of my face, he leaned in and kissed . . . my forehead.

Chapter Twenty-Four

PREPARATIONS FOR THE CORPUS CHRISTI PAGEANT were now in full swing. Most mornings, the actors and musicians rehearsed in the gallery above the banqueting hall, with Thomas directing the whole enterprise. The day after the botched seduction, I sneaked away to the ladies' withdrawing room with a book. If I was to help with the pageant, I had to keep practicing my reading.

I left the door open so I'd be able to hear Will's voice, and when I did, I intended to make sure he saw me. I wanted to provide every opportunity for him to apologize. I hoped Stephen was right about Will taking the blame for what had happened—or not happened—between us.

Stephen. I wished I knew what he was thinking and feeling about me. Loving each other was hopeless, a dead end. I couldn't stay here forever, and he couldn't come back with me to the present. Of course we'd never discussed either possibility, because the feelings between us had never been acknowledged, exactly. And I was forever getting mixed messages from him.

"Good morrow, Olivia."

It was Will, standing in the doorway. I threw my book aside and leaped to my feet. He reached for my hands, but kept me at arm's length.

"Pray forgive me for last night," he said. "I behaved abominably." His flushed face showed that he was truly ashamed. "I need a friend, not a lover. Can you be a friend to me, after I have taken such advantage of you?"

"I would be honored to be your friend, Will Shakespeare." It was a no-brainer.

"Thank God. I feared you could not forgive me." He dropped my hands and began to pace around the room. "My conduct would be such a disappointment to Thomas. He expects more from me, and he is right; I should attend more to the love of God and the care of men's souls—my own included."

"Master Cook is immersed in his faith," I said, stating the obvious.

"Thomas is willing to give his life for his beliefs. He expects it, anticipates it, and spends much time contemplating how he will fare when racked and put to death. He even jokes about it."

I felt the blood drain from my face at the prospect. "Why does Thomas not continue his travels? Surely others wish to meet him, you said so yourself. People seem willing to risk their lives to hear him preach. Dead, he is of no use to anyone!"

"He is weary," Will said, coming to a halt in front of me. "He has been hiding since his return to England near a year past. None of us would like his kind of life, having no home, always on watch for spies and government agents."

"Why does he remain so long at Hoghton Tower? It's dangerous!"

"Because of his work. He has been writing an important document, which will rebut the Protestant religious arguments. In it, he exhorts the queen herself to return to the true faith."

"Surely there are fine libraries in other Catholic homes that would be just as useful to him."

"Believe me, I have urged him to leave now, not to wait until after the pageant. If he chooses to turn a blind eye to the dangers, there is nothing more I can do."

"You . . . will not go with him?"

"I will see him safely to the next hiding place. I've told Master Hoghton I wish to do so."

"Please, Will, do not take this upon yourself," I said, forcing him to look at me. "My uncle will send someone else, a servant or a laborer. Someone who would not be suspect." On their journey, wouldn't it be tempting for Thomas to press Will to join the Society of Jesus? And for Will to easily succumb?

"Thomas is willing to sacrifice his life. Should I not do the same for his sake?"

No, I wanted to shout. *No, you most definitely should not.* "When will he leave?"

"I believe almost immediately after the performance. His work is completed, and he must deliver it into the printer's hands. In secret, of course."

"Will, I know it is not my business, but I am your true friend." My cheeks burned. If he was remembering last night, he must be thinking about what an understatement that was. I plunged on. "As your friend—will you tell me the truth? Do you intend to join the Jesuits?"

His gray eyes darkened, and I thought I'd made him angry. "Aye. How did you know?"

I groaned inside. "You saw what happened to that poor man in Preston! That could be you, or Thomas."

"Thomas believes we can proceed safely to another location and eventually cross the channel to France. From there I will travel to the Low Countries, to the university for priests."

I placed my hand on his chest. "Is this what you really want? In your own heart, are you ready to give up a wife and family? You have more than one young lady smitten with you, and that's just here at Hoghton Tower. And then there is Anne. . . ."

He blushed and turned away from me. "That is a weakness which must be overcome. Thomas did so."

"Is love a weakness, then, Will? Do not forget, Thomas did so because becoming a priest was his heart's desire. He has zeal, a passion for God. Do you have that same passion?"

He pulled a hand through his hair, which caused it to stick out in all the wrong places. "I do not know!"

"And what about becoming a player? You told me yourself that is what you wished to do. And your writing—"

"Did you know Thomas himself has written plays? The Jesuits are known for their oratory and their acting. 'Tis part of the way they teach and learn."

"There are other kinds of learning. One learns from being out in the world, from engaging with others, from experience. Learning doesn't come just at universities. And you have a whole library right here at your disposal." My voice shook, its pitch rising.

Will sighed and dropped down onto a cushioned chair. "What am I to do? Thomas is a man of God, a truly good man. I want to be like him!"

"Maybe you can emulate him in some other . . ."

Someone was approaching. It was the man in question.

"Master Will, mistress, pray pardon me for disturbing you." Thomas swiveled and looked directly at Will. "We are ready for you now, sir. And Mistress Olivia, we shall have need of you for the remainder of our rehearsals."

"Ah, certainly. I shall be there," I said, trying to keep the panic I was feeling from my voice.

I was glad for the interruption, because I didn't know what to say next. Sad eyed, Will rose and bowed to me, and I felt sorry that he was so torn. He left the room, and I sank down onto the settle by the fire. We were—I was—failing. Friend or lover, I couldn't possibly hope to overcome the priest's influence. Will seemed more convinced than ever that he should follow in Thomas's footsteps. It was time to make a little foray into Master Will Shakespeare's chamber. The mysterious letter held the key to Thomas's sway over him, I was sure of it.

I ticked off the whereabouts of everyone who might possibly catch me snooping. Jennet was in the stillroom with Elizabeth for the morning, and Will of course was at rehearsal. No one else, except

Stephen and me, had a chamber in this passageway. The servants should have straightened the rooms by now, so I didn't think one of them would catch me. Stephen was supposed to be my lookout, but I had no idea where he might be.

I found him in his room, seated by the fireplace, Cop curled up at his feet. "What are you doing in here? I thought you'd be hunting or doing something else outdoors."

"Come, be seated. Nay, I do not feel up to anything; I am brooding."

I didn't ask what about. "I want to search Shakespeare's room. He's at rehearsal, and no one else is around. A perfect opportunity."

"Are you certain?"

"As certain as I can be. Come on, I need your help."

I grabbed his hand and pulled him toward the passage. "Wait!" he said. "We need to form a plan."

"I *have* a plan. I'll look for the letter while you keep watch. With all the doors open, you can see in either direction. If someone's coming, your job is to distract them."

"Linger in the passage? That will seem suspicious indeed."

"Why are you acting so weird? Nobody has a reason to suspect you of anything. If someone shows up, talk in a loud voice, so I'll know you're warning me."

He looked skeptical, but nodded. "As you say." He seemed awfully distracted, but I didn't have time to worry about that.

I slipped into Will's room, glancing back to make sure Stephen was in place. Once inside, I slowly twirled around, trying to decide on the best place to start. Will was not exactly a slob, but he wasn't Mr. Neat, either. Books and papers were piled on a writing table.

He'd tossed his sleeping smock onto the settle. His bed had been made, probably by a servant.

With its jumble of papers, the writing table seemed the most likely place to start. Pushing an ink jar and dirty quills aside, I sorted through the stack of foolscap quickly. Most of the documents were closely written in what I recognized as Will's hand and looked like the beginnings of poems—sonnets, perhaps—with several crossed-out words and smudges.

I abandoned the writing table in favor of the wardrobe, sorting through some clothing. Not that he had much. A few doublets, a couple pairs of hose that looked like they could use a good washing, one linen shirt. Apparently he had only one pair of boots—the ones he was wearing. I exhaled my frustration. Nothing there.

I lifted the mattress off his bed. It was light, like my own, made with some kind of ticking. After I removed it, I could plainly see the ropes, sagging from one end of the bedstead to the other. But no letter. I even ripped off the bed linen, quickly replacing it when it yielded nothing. *Damn!*

Stephen stuck his head in. "Are you almost done?" he hissed. "'Tis near mealtime."

"Oh my God, you scared me!"

"Well, are you?"

"Yes! Get out of here." He disappeared.

Now I began to feel desperate. I swiveled back to the writing table and eyed it again, thinking about where I might stash a letter. Perhaps he'd slipped it into one of the books. As I leafed through the second book in the stack, a folded parchment fell out, and I recognized it instantly because of the sealing wax. I grabbed it, returned the volume to its place in the stack, and dashed down the passage to Stephen's room. I closed the doors at my end while Stephen took care of those at the far end.

Hiding the letter in the folds of my skirt, I kept my expression flat.

"God's breath!" Stephen said. "I guess we should give up. Mayhap it would not have helped anyway."

"Ta-da!" I whipped the letter out and held it up.

He looked shocked at first, but then grinned and said, "You are quite the little thief, mistress."

I unfolded the paper and— "Oh, no. It's in Latin."

"Ah. Clever of him. Only a well-educated person would be able to read it, were it discovered."

"And that would include you, no doubt," I said, passing it to him with a smirk.

I followed Stephen to the settle, where he unfolded the letter and began reading out loud, pausing now and then to sort out the phrasing.

> Good Master Will,
>
> May God's mercy and grace be upon you, my friend.
>
> Please accept this missive as my attempt to guide you in your understanding of my mission here in England. It is easier for me to lay down my thoughts in writing than to explain it in the short periods of time afforded us to speak privately.

*Out of all Europe, the English have retreated
farthest from God. Although I have had to live
abroad many years, England is my home, and
restoring her to the Catholic faith would bring
untold honor and glory to the church.*

> *I come here on no political business, as some
believe, but only to hear confessions, say Mass,
and preach. In all earthly laws, my obedience is
to the queen as my sovereign. But there is only
one sovereign of the church, and that is our Lord
Jesus Christ.*

"He doth protest too much, methinks," Stephen said wryly, before going on.

*In my youth, I had the honor of meeting
Queen Elizabeth. I much admired her for her
great learning, understanding, and godliness. I
have since taken a different path from our noble
monarch. Would that I could persuade her to
cast aside the ways of the reformers and restore
her to the one true faith.*

"He met the queen," Stephen murmured. "Why would Thomas Cook be acquainted with Elizabeth? If that is true, he must be so remarkable a man that she requested an introduction to him."

"So? Thomas *is* remarkable. You've said so before."

"Exactly. Mayhap too remarkable for an obscure Jesuit."

I tried to follow his thread, but couldn't see where his thoughts were leading. "Read the rest."

> As long as there are folk who wish to
> adhere to the old faith, my work here continues.
> As long as there is one more soul to save, I must
> keep on. I seek no honor or glory for myself, only
> for God. May God's grace be with you always,
> Will.
>
> Your humble servant in the Lord,
> Thomas Cook

"Pretty impressive, Stephen."

He waved off my praise. "Schoolboy Latin. 'Tis a very straightforward letter, and for our purposes, disappointing. It tells us nothing we do not already know." He threw the letter in the air, and it slowly drifted to the floor.

"I better put it back while I have a chance."

"Aye," Stephen said absentmindedly. He propped his elbows on his knees, hands cupping his face.

Scooping it off the floor, I glanced at the letter one last time, turning it this way and that, as if I might be able to ferret out some secret it held. My fingers rubbed against the seal. I looked at it closely, and then I stopped in my tracks.

"Stephen, this seal doesn't have Thomas's initials. It says *E.C.*"

Stephen bolted to his feet. "Let me see that!"

I handed it over, watching his face turn pale. "Can it be?" he said. "Edmund Campion?"

"What are you talking about?" Although the name sounded vaguely familiar, I couldn't remember in what context. "Please, Stephen, explain!"

"Edmund Campion, the Jesuit priest. The most wanted man in all of England. Walsingham, the spymaster, would do anything to get his hands on him. Do you not see? Thomas Cook *is* Edmund Campion."

Chapter Twenty-Five

"THE LEADER OF THE JESUITS? The charismatic one?" I asked. "It finally makes sense why Will is so in thrall to him."

"Go, quickly, and put the letter back. Then we shall talk."

I dashed back down the hall into Will's room. Just as I reached the writing table, I heard Stephen's voice.

"Will! How is the play practice progressing?"

I jammed the letter back into the book.

"Very well, I believe," Will answered, probably wondering why Stephen was shouting.

"Ah, I am glad to hear it. Will you perform indoors, in the hall? I was wondering if out-of-doors would be more realistic, such as was done in the old times."

I dashed into my room.

Stephen and I had no further opportunity to talk until late in the day. During lunch I realized I hadn't even told him about Will's almost certain decision to join the Jesuits. But I put that out of my mind for now, because I was sitting next to Jennet. This could be a chance to learn something.

"Are you helping with the pageant, mistress?" Jennet asked me while I nibbled on bread and sipped my ale.

"Thomas has asked me to be the prompter. Females, as you know, cannot be players." I rolled my eyes and she laughed. "And you?"

"Nay, I cannot take part. My father would remove me from here if he got wind of it. Indeed, I will probably have to leave on the day of the performance. When is it to be?"

"I believe a week from Sunday next."

"I shall ask Cousin Alexander to arrange for me to go home the day before."

I drank some ale and pasted an innocent look on my face. "Pray, what is the harm in watching such a play?"

Jennet's expression sobered. Her eyes slid away from mine and she said, "'Tis a practice established by the old faith, regarded as frivolous and heretical by Puritans." Her cheeks flushed. "Also, my father considers men dressing like women an abomination against God's laws."

"Do you regard it thus?"

"I have nothing against it. It seems like harmless fun." She shrugged. "Master Will says 'tis funny."

"They are performing the story of Noah and the Flood."

"And Will plays Noah's wife. That would be a sight to see."

"Where I come from, 'tis sometimes said of parents that 'what they do not know cannot hurt them.'" I gave her a sly smile.

"I will think on it. Mayhap my father need not know."

"Speaking of your father," I said, "what news of your betrothal?"

"None. And that is another good reason not to go home." We laughed, but I shuddered to think what it would be like to be forced into a marriage with a widower years older, unappealing in every way, and then be expected to sleep with him, raise his children, and nurse him in his old age. Ugh. I couldn't help feeling sympathetic toward her.

At the other end of the table, Thomas, Will, and Fulke were entertaining the others with stories about the pageant. "Master Will makes a fine nagging wife for Noah," Thomas said.

"And you a most excellent God Almighty," Will jibed. "Though we all know you fancy yourself thus already." Thomas took it good-naturedly. Alexander looked as if he thought Will had gone too far, but must have realized it was all in fun since he ended up laughing too.

Stephen sent me a look, darting his eyes away after a second, and I knew he was wondering the same thing I was. Did Will know Thomas's true identity? With the initials on the sealing wax—a totally careless act on Thomas's part to have sealed the letter that way—how could he not? And all the discussions they'd had, probably in private as well as among company. Alexander most likely had known from the start. A devout Catholic, he would have been honored that such a man would want to reside at his home while writing his manifesto, or whatever it was.

"Olivia?" Jennet poked me in the ribs. "Master Cook is addressing you."

So deep in thought I hadn't even realized anyone was speaking to me, I jerked my head up. "Pray, what did you say?"

"Can you come to our rehearsal this afternoon? Your job is quite an important one, as you will save us all from the shame of forgotten lines and missed cues," Thomas said.

"Oh, aye. I shall be there." I smiled, as though I had nothing on my mind but an amusing production of the Noah's ark pageant.

Stephen and I finally caught up with each other after the evening meal. "Get your cloak and meet me in the rose garden."

I rolled my eyes at his bossy tone. "Yes, sir. Will do." As he hurried up the staircase ahead of me, I took a long look at him. He was always impeccably dressed. Tonight he wore a black doublet with an aubergine-colored lining over a fine linen shirt. Dark velvet Venetians—best described as billowy shorts—stockings, and boots completed the look. He could have been on the cover of a Renaissance edition of GQ. *Stop it, Olivia.*

I grabbed my cloak and tugged on the gloves Will had given me. It had rained earlier, and both landscape and buildings were shrouded in mist. The moist grass dampened my slippers and wet the hems of my skirts. While I waited for Stephen in the garden, I tried to identify the birdsongs. My grandmother always said robins sang the day to sleep, but I didn't know if that was true in the here-and-now. The then-and-now. Whatever.

A form appeared out of the mist, and I gasped.

"Did I frighten you?" Stephen asked.

"It's just that I couldn't see you coming."

"Let's find a bench and sit down." He reached for my hand and led me around blooming crabapple trees and down a path until we reached the bench.

"I noticed you conversing with Jennet during the meal. Did you learn anything?"

I wrapped my cloak closer around myself. "Only that she intends to leave the day before the Corpus Christi pageant. Her father wouldn't approve. I tried to talk her into staying."

"Any luck?"

"Hard to tell. She says she doesn't want to go home. Her father wants her to marry a much older man who sounds pretty disgusting."

"You raised the question earlier, and I cannot but wonder if her father is involved in this. It makes sense that he would be the one aiding the Privy Council."

"I keep thinking about that too. If that's true, he may have enlisted her help."

Stephen nodded. "It is beyond belief that Edmund Campion has been in our midst all this time and I've been completely unaware. There were signs. I should have guessed."

"It explains why Will is so confused. I think he truly *is* torn, Stephen. When I talked to him today, he seemed so dejected." I shivered, feeling the mist drifting closer, wrapping us in its dampness. "Is there any doubt in your mind that Shakespeare knows Thomas is really Edmund Campion?"

"None. 'Tis the reason for his indecision. With such a powerful influence as Campion, Will must feel a great pressure to do his bidding."

And then I grabbed Stephen's arm so hard he flinched.

"What is it?"

"I just figured something out!"

"Soft, sweeting," he whispered. "Someone could be about."

Oh, God. I moved closer, close enough to smell his soap, and wished desperately we were out here for a much different reason than the true one. "Jennet knows. She knows Cook is Campion!"

"We have no proof of that."

"We've been wondering what she told Lowry. That's got to be it."

" 'Tis a big leap. She may have identified Thomas as the Jesuit, but how could she know he's Campion?"

"You said last night she could have been tricking us all along, that she may be as good a reader and writer as you or I. If she got her hands on the document he's been working on, maybe something in it gave away his identity."

"We cannot be sure, Olivia."

It seemed perfectly obvious to me, but maybe watching all those reruns of *Law and Order* with my grandparents had skewed my perspective. "Will did have one encouraging bit of news. He said Thomas—Campion—is leaving right after the play. But that also means we only have about a week and a half to make sure Will doesn't leave with him. What should we do?"

"Let us agree on one thing first. We should continue to call Campion Thomas. If we start talking and thinking of him as Campion, the name will doubtless slip out when we don't want it to. Agreed?"

"Of course."

"In answer to your question, we may have to resort to extreme measures to prevent Shakespeare's leaving with Thomas."

"Define 'extreme measures,'" I said, slanting my eyes at him.

"Lock him in one of the rooms on the lower level."

"But that's ridiculous," I said, loud enough that Stephen had to shush me. Again. I lowered my voice to a whisper. "He'd never come along willingly!"

Frowning, he said, "We wouldn't keep him locked up for long. Just enough time so that it would be impossible for Will to catch up with Thomas. Then we'd release him. 'Tis not as if he would be our prisoner."

"Good luck convincing *him* of that!"

"It may be our only hope."

I lowered my voice. "I think we should talk to your uncle. If we explain the situation to him, maybe he won't allow Will to escort Thomas, and then we wouldn't have to deal with it."

"Tell him Thomas wants Will for the brotherhood? I'm not sure it would matter to him. Indeed, he'd probably be pleased."

"But surely Shakespeare's family should have some say. If you had a young man working for you, one as young as Will, wouldn't you feel obligated to ask his parents before sending him off to become a priest?"

Stephen exhaled a frustrated breath and his shoulders drooped. "You are right. I will ask to speak with him."

"I want to be there too."

"Absolutely not. Females are not involved in decisions of this nature."

"Please, Stephen. I'm part of this. And I can be persuasive."

He grinned. "That you can. Very well. Let's go in, then. Perhaps I can find him now and arrange a time." When we reached the outer courtyard, Stephen said, "Go first; I will follow shortly."

I nodded. He brought my hand to his lips, brushing them gently across my fingers. Neither of us spoke. I walked toward the door, turning back once. But I couldn't see him. He was already lost in the mist.

Chapter Twenty-Six

STEPHEN WASTED NO TIME in arranging our meeting with Alexander. As I stepped hesitantly over the threshold of the billiard room, I recalled that it also served as an office. After Stephen shut the door, his uncle gestured for us to sit down on the oak chairs in front of the desk.

"I suppose, since you have closed the door, this must be a serious matter," he said, raising his brows.

"Aye, Uncle, it is indeed."

"You had better tell me what is amiss."

Stephen and I looked at each other. We'd agreed that he would speak first, and I'd chime in if necessary. *Absolutely* necessary, Stephen had said. I was grateful for the decision, since I felt slightly nauseous. I wished I hadn't eaten quite so much quail at dinner, and I should have skipped the pear tart with cream altogether.

"Uncle, we're concerned for Will Shakespeare. It seems obvious Thomas Cook is attempting to persuade him to join the Society of Jesus." Stephen paused, apparently unsure about what to say next. "Olivia and I do not believe . . ." He tried again. "We do not think Master Will is suited to the priesthood."

I jumped in, ignoring Stephen's warning. "Will told me he wanted to write poetry and someday become a player. Now, he seems prepared to abandon all his plans for a life that may not be right for him."

"Even if this is true, why does it concern you?" Alexander's expression was solemn and somewhat annoyed. He peered at us, his fingers steepled.

"Because we've come to care about Shakespeare," Stephen said. "Thomas has a passion for God. He is a most holy and learned man, but Will is more passionate about earthly things. He is not a zealot, like Thomas."

"Mayhap he will turn his passion toward God."

"Uncle, you sound as if you already know this to be true," I said.

"Indeed. I have discussed it with Thomas. I have even given my consent to the plan, not that Thomas needed it."

Oh, no, I thought. *Oh, no.* "But what about Will's family? Have they consented?" I asked.

"My dear Olivia, I am not convinced you should be privy to this discussion at all. But since you are my niece, I shall allow it. You may rest assured that I have written to the lad's father." Lips pursed, he sent Stephen an irritated glance, as if he thought my brother should keep a tighter rein on me.

Stephen persevered. "Olivia and I have both become friends to Will. We are only concerned that he do what is best for his own life."

"That cannot be for either of you to judge."

Stephen lowered his voice and leaned forward. "Nor for someone else, especially not Father Edmund Campion, who has much to gain in the matter." A smothering silence fell. Stephen's uncle gripped the edge of his desk until his fingertips grew white. He cleared his throat and finally spoke.

"How long have you known?"

"Not long. The point is, with such a one as Campion pressuring him, how can Will make a proper decision? If he decides against the priesthood, he knows he will be disappointing one of the most venerated men in all of Europe. That is a strong motivation to choose against his own interests."

Alexander sighed. His face looked haggard, and I thought then that he probably spent many sleepless nights knowing he was sheltering an outlaw, a man wanted by the Privy Council, and so was endangering his entire household.

"Thomas Cook leaves on Sunday, directly after the pageant. Will has agreed, in fact asked, to escort him to the next home. It is up to young Shakespeare to make his own choice. I . . . I understand that you mean well, but I will not prevent him from going. That is all I shall say on the matter."

"But—"

"Olivia, our uncle has made his decision, and we must abide by it. Let us say no more." Stephen took my arm and I rose and curtsied, glaring at him. Why were we giving up so easily?

As we turned to leave, Alexander spoke once more.

"Do others know?"

Stephen shook his head. "I do not believe so."

Jennet. Tell him Jennet might know.

"You will be discreet, I trust. I do not need to tell you what would happen if word got out."

We nodded and wished him good night.

"God keep you both," he said.

Outside in the passage, we paused. "Let's go somewhere we can speak privately," Stephen said, heading toward the library. Instead of the settle, Stephen led me to the window seat. "We know now that my uncle will not help. It is up to us."

"Yes."

"I believe we have done all we can for the present. Your making a friend of Will allowed you to plead with him to do what he loves. Other than Thomas, you have the most influence on him."

"I do?"

"Of course you do! If not for you, he and Thomas would have sneaked away in the night before now. He would not be doubting himself."

"But the play, and Thomas's writing."

"The play could easily go on without them. And I think Thomas finished his document weeks ago. Nay, I think 'tis because Will is yet undecided that they remain here."

"Even though it's so risky for Thomas to stay?"

"For him, recruiting a man of Shakespeare's intelligence and sensitivity to the priesthood is foremost. He's willing to take the chance."

"I've tried to get Will alone in the last few days, but he's always rehearsing for the pageant. If I could have one more chance to try to convince him . . ." I tapered off, knowing that in this case, nothing was a sure thing.

"We must be vigilant, in case they're prepared to leave before Sunday. Then we must intervene."

"By locking him up?"

"Can you think of a better idea?"

"No," I admitted. "Shouldn't we have told your uncle about Jennet?"

"Ah. I thought about that, but I hate to cast suspicion on someone if it turns out they've done nothing wrong. After what we said about Thomas and Will, I have the feeling he'd think we were a couple of gossiping goodwives."

"But she met with Lowry!"

"Can you be absolutely certain about that? It was raining, the light must have been poor—"

"I'm sure. I had a clear view of them both. It was Lowry."

"It has been many days since their visit, and nothing has happened. I do not think we need worry about Mistress Jennet."

I sighed. "I don't get it. Just the other night, you said you thought she might be conspiring with her father to pass information to Lowry. What changed your mind?"

"I do not discount that as a possibility. 'Tis only that I am more concerned about Thomas Cook leaving and taking Shakespeare with him. We must concentrate on preventing that from happening."

"Your call." I wasn't at all sure he'd made the right one, though. I was still mulling everything over when I heard his voice.

"Olivia," he said, in that funny way he had. He'd stood up and planted himself in front of me. He looked serious, his dark eyes without even a glimmer of humor.

"What?"

"Do you think about going . . . back?"

"Of course. I hope you have a plan for getting me there."

Studying me, he said, "You need not worry. The magic has not failed me in the past."

Since I didn't really want to talk about going back, I said, "Speaking of which, I've been wondering about some of your other...adventures. This isn't the first time you've had to, uh, step in, is it?"

"This is only my third adventure, as you put it."

"Would you tell me about the other ones?"

He put his hands loosely on his hips and stared me down. "Truly, Olivia, you wish to hear of this now? You are diverting me from my purpose, which was to talk about you."

"Pick one—your first one. Give me the short version."

He shook his head. "You're incorrigible, wench."

"Hey, Langford. You're treading on thin ice." His lips quivered, and I giggled. And then we were both laughing. After a minute I said, "You're not off the hook, you know."

He sighed. "You've heard of Sir Francis Drake, who sailed 'round the world?"

"Of course! Sixth-grade social studies."

"I spent time aboard one of his ships." He shuddered and gave me a mock-horrified look. "Bad experience. I was horribly seasick. I pray my work will never involve a sailing vessel again."

I snorted. "But what did you do? Your mission?"

"Would that you were not so persistent, mistress. A planned mutiny would have placed Sir Francis's life at risk. I made sure it did not take place, because I knew Britain needed Drake in the future. And that is all I will say."

"But—"

"No more! We were talking of you, not me. I was thinking about your life when you return, and how you are feeling about everything."

"Why do you care?"

The vulnerable look flashed in his eyes. "Do you think I have no feelings for you, Olivia?"

"I don't know," I said truthfully. "Do you?" I looked into his eyes, wishing he'd say how much he adored me.

He dropped his gaze and didn't answer. "Are you still determined to give up acting? You've been playing what will surely be one of the greatest roles of your life. I look upon you sometimes and am convinced you stand with one foot in the present and one in the past. I am all in awe of you."

Something fell away inside of me, maybe the final barriers to trusting him completely. "That's the nicest thing you've ever said to me. Thank you, Stephen."

"I only say the truth." His voice was low, but forceful. "You have fooled everyone into believing you are my sister, an Elizabethan young lady. Only a great actor could have succeeded."

And I loved every minute of it! The thought slammed into me and, suddenly light-headed, I had to grab the edge of the window seat. Stephen seized my arms and pulled me to my feet. "I don't want to give up acting," I said, laughing a little. "It's how I want to spend my life."

His hands gripped me hard. I looked in his eyes, recognizing the pain and longing there, and my face crumpled. "But I don't want to go back! I can't stand the thought of leaving you." Stephen crushed me against his chest, holding me so tightly I could barely breathe. Then he pushed me away far enough to look at me. Devour me. I felt the warm caress of his breath on my face before he kissed me, so deeply I feared he thought it was our last kiss. My legs turned to mush, and I would have fallen if not for his arms encircling me.

"This cannot be," he said, breaking the kiss and resting his forehead against mine. "You will return to the . . . to your present, and my life will go on without you." He stepped resolutely away from me. "Please, Olivia, leave me now."

I threw myself against him. "No. Don't make me!"

Gently, he pushed me away. "Pray do as I ask."

His face looked full of sorrow. I backed away, blinking back tears. Right before I left the room, I looked at him once more. He was staring out the window, his back to me. I stepped into the corridor and closed the door. Slowly and hesitantly, I began walking away, doing as he asked. Leaving him. I didn't get very far before turning back. Every part of me wanted to go to him. *But no, Olivia. He doesn't want it.*

In the morning, Stephen was gone. Vanished, without a word to me or to anyone else, apparently. And he'd taken Copernicus with him. When he didn't return after a couple of days, I began to feel frantic. How would I get home? Fear, emptiness, and an ache deep inside rendered me nearly incapable of functioning. And anger. I was furious with him for abandoning me when I needed him most.

Chapter Twenty-Seven

I'D FORGOTTEN THAT IN SHAKESPEARE'S TIME, usually only one copy of a play, called the "book," existed. In a real playing company, it would have been my job to copy out each person's lines. Thank God, Thomas hadn't asked me to do that. Each actor had taken a turn at writing out his part on foolscap—if he *could* write—or simply used the time to memorize the lines. That was why the prompter was important. I was the one in charge of that single, precious copy, of letting people borrow it, making sure it was kept safe, and, in many cases, helping the younger players learn their lines. My reading had improved enough that I could handle it without worrying. After Stephen's disappearance, I devoted myself to the job.

When people asked me where he was, I said our father had needed him. Maybe it was the truth. Possibly Alexander knew where he'd gone. Stephen could hardly have disappeared without telling his uncle, but I decided not to ask him. Wouldn't he wonder why Stephen hadn't told me himself?

Forget about Stephen, I told myself. *Be glad he's gone.* This strategy worked most of the time. Being involved in acting was healing in its way. The rehearsals had progressed to the point of full-scale productions. Thomas was an exacting pageant master, an Elizabethan Spielberg. If he wasn't satisfied, the players repeated their lines until he was.

I decided to try one more time with Will, and after pageant rehearsal one morning, I approached him. The rehearsal was over, and he was instructing a group of his youngest students, who were playing some of the animals on the ark. "What sort of sound does a lion make?" Will asked. "He's a fearsome beast!" Will was squatting, at eye level with a small boy.

"Like this! *Rrrrrrr—RR!*"

Will fell backward, as if the lion had frightened him to death, and the boy giggled. "Aye, very good, Luke," he said, rising. "Practice that for a moment while I speak to Mistress Olivia."

He grasped my elbow and we moved away from the children. "I've been wanting to tell you what a fine job you're doing as Noah's wife," I said. "How does it feel to play a female?"

"I do not like having to pitch my voice higher. It runs the risk of sounding silly rather than funny. On the London stage, younger boys whose voices haven't yet changed would play the female roles."

"Have you seen a play in London, then?"

"Nay, I have never been there, but touring companies stop at Stratford on occasion."

"You haven't given up on the idea of becoming an actor, have you?"

He eyed me suspiciously. "Can you sit down for a moment?" he asked, leading me to the table in the center of the hall. "You have a great interest in my future, Mistress Olivia. I am curious as to . . . precisely why this would be the case."

I was struck dumb. After all, I was the one who was supposed to be asking questions, not Will Shakespeare. Did he think I was a spy or something? I stared at him for a few seconds, my brain whirring so loudly I thought he might hear it.

Worse yet, I felt a flush suffusing my skin all the way from my neck up to the top of my head. "I, well, that is, in my family, we believe it is important to follow your dreams." *Oh, God, that sounded way too modern.* I tried to recover. "You see, my father did not wish to be a farmer. He has always regretted not speaking his mind on the subject."

"I see. So he did not wish to work the land that had been in his family for generations?"

"Nay. He wished to study . . . uh, law. Aye, he wished to be a lawyer." I was really warming to my subject now, digging myself into a deeper and deeper hole. "Legal matters have always fascinated him."

"Truly? I am surprised he would have had any knowledge of the law." Since Will's eyes met mine with curiosity and amusement, I was pretty sure he was deliberately putting me on the spot.

"Aye, well, he did. He does not like to talk of it, but our mother has told us." I looked down and ran a thumbnail along a deep groove in the table.

"And your brother. What does he wish to do with his life?"

I huffed out a breath, as if it were obvious. "Stephen? He loves the land. He wants nothing more than to supervise the farming and the tenants. To marry and raise children and live in our family home." I thought all of that was true, since he'd told me so himself when we talked about the visions. The idea of him married to . . . whoever . . . put an annoying knot of jealousy in my gut.

"What do *you* wish for, Olivia?"

"Me?" I forced a phony laugh. "I'm simply a poor female, marking time until my father arranges a marriage for me to a respectable man."

"Oh, I'm certain he will have no difficulty doing so." He shook his head slowly while he spoke.

I swallowed uncomfortably, my throat feeling like it was about to close up around all the lies I was spouting. Why the interrogation? Will seemed to be having a good time with it. Since I didn't think I could stand one more minute of it, I shot to my feet. "I must go. I promised to help my aunt with, um . . . something."

Will burst out laughing. "Pray forgive me, Olivia. I have teased you unmercifully."

"Aye, you have done. I do not understand the reason."

He must have sensed he'd hurt me, because he sobered. "Since the Privy Council's men were here, I have become suspicious of everyone. I am finding it difficult to judge who is trustworthy. I wished to know if you were someone I could rely on, since I have entrusted you with my secrets."

"And what have you concluded?"

"One thing I know for certain, Olivia, is that you have my best interests in your heart. Indeed, I do not understand why, but I believe it is so."

I placed my hands on the table and leaned forward, so I could look Will in the eye. "In that you are correct," I said. I bobbed a quick curtsy. "Good day, Master Will."

I got out of there as fast as I could without breaking into a run. Will had turned the spotlight on me, and I couldn't very well turn it back on him. I hadn't been able to question, cajole, or influence him any further.

~~

Later, at the noon meal, Jennet told me she'd made up her mind to stay for the pageant.

"That is good news indeed! I think you'll enjoy it. Why did you change your mind?"

"Your advice that what he does not know cannot hurt him. And I have no desire to see the man my father wishes me to wed."

She didn't joke about him today. Her eyes looked hard, and I wondered if perhaps the marriage was imminent. Her intended must be really horrid for her to have such a strong aversion to him, I thought.

She bit off a piece of bread, chewed, and swallowed. "It would have been nice to see my sisters, but I can visit them another time."

I nodded, washing down a bite of partridge with ale. If Jennet stayed here, it would be much more difficult for her to communicate with her father, the lugubrious Master Hall. Yet her sudden change of heart seemed strange. She'd seemed so certain before.

I noticed that Alexander was not present. He hadn't been at the evening meal last night, either. Curious, I turned to Fulke and asked him if he knew where my uncle was.

"He's gone to the horse market in Preston. Every landowner picks up new horseflesh this time of year." He seemed puzzled. "Does not your father do the same?"

I gulped. "Aye, he does. I've lost track of time since I've been away from home for so long." I nibbled at a strawberry tart and then realized Jennet was speaking to me.

"Mistress Olivia, how do you progress with your needlework?"

"Not well, I fear. I need another lesson. Are you busy this afternoon?"

"I am. Cousin Elizabeth and I will be in the stillroom brewing decoctions and tinctures. On the morrow, mayhap?"

"I will appreciate your help."

Since Stephen's mysterious departure, I'd given up on everything except Will. So I made a decision. I'd take advantage of this perfect opportunity to search Jennet's room. Maybe I could learn something about her relationship with Robert Lowry, Privy Council spy.

After lunch, I excused myself before anyone could ask yet again about Stephen. Hurrying past his chamber, I couldn't help picturing all the "Stephen" things I knew were there. The stack of books near the bed. The miniature portraits of his parents on his nightstand. Foolscap, an ink jar, and quills scattered over the small writing table. *Oh, for God's sake, Olivia. You're not supposed to be thinking about him.*

I waited for an hour or so, to be on the safe side. I'd told Bess I was tired and wanted to rest. Will was helping to supervise set building this afternoon. When everyone had gone off to their respective tasks and the house had grown quiet, I approached the double doors separating my room from Jennet's.

I called her name and rapped softly a few times before sneaking in, then closed both doors behind me. Jennet's chamber, smaller than Stephen's and mine, had the austere aura one might expect for a Puritan girl.

A twin-size bed with a plain coverlet stood against the back wall, the washstand next to it. A painted cloth depicting a martyrdom in gruesome detail—a Protestant one, no doubt—hung on one wall, and beneath it, a table displayed a book called *Foxe's Book of Martyrs*. I fanned the pages, but no papers fell out. Next I searched her wardrobe, quickly riffling through her clothing, all the same unrelenting black and white garments she wore every day. I reached to the back of each shelf and felt around with my fingers, but found nothing.

I examined her bed as thoroughly as I had Will's, removing both the mattress and the sheet, but came up empty. Where else to look? There was no desk, nothing on the table but the one book. If Jennet had any secrets, they weren't to be found here. I was turning to leave when something caught my eye.

Beside her wardrobe, a small painting of Jesus hung on the wall. Why would a Puritan girl want this in her room? "Papist" was the word that came to mind. I walked over and examined it more closely, but nothing about it jumped out at me. I lifted it off its nail and flipped it over. A piece of foolscap was stuck between the back of the painting and the edge of the frame.

I paused to listen for any sound of footsteps or voices, but heard nothing. With trembling hands, I unfolded the paper. Bold script crawled across the page. I scanned it rapidly, and it looked as if I'd be able to get the gist.

> *Daughter,*
>   *On Thursday next, 20th of April, after yr*
> *midday meal, proceed to the alehouse at Riley*
> *Green. There you will meet with RL and sheriff*

to arrange date for arrest of Campion and WS.
Do not fail to oblige me in this. You know what
will transpire if you do not do yr duty.

Stunned, I read the words over and over, to make sure I had it right. They knew! They knew Thomas Cook was really Campion. Jennet had figured it out and told Lowry. It must have been after the privy councilors had dined here. If they'd known then, they would have arrested him that night. There was no signature, but Jennet's father was obviously the writer. Tomorrow was Thursday, April 20. My hands shook as I replaced the note, rehung the painting, and beat a hasty retreat back to my own room.

I paced, my heart thudding. My first impulse was to go straight to Alexander, but then I remembered he was gone. Given his feelings about "females," I wasn't sure he'd believe me, anyway, even if I provided irrefutable evidence.

I should warn Will, I knew. *I should definitely warn Will.* But if I did, he'd be obligated to tell Thomas. Then the two of them would ride off into the sunset, never to be heard from again. I couldn't risk it. I'd have to follow Jennet to the alehouse and listen in on her conversation with the two men. I didn't know where Riley Green was, but it couldn't be that far if Jennet had to show up there right after lunch.

One major obstacle stood in my way. Jennet knew me outright, and both Lowry and the sheriff would recognize me. I felt fury building, aimed directly at Stephen. If he hadn't left, I wouldn't be forced to deal with this on my own. We could've figured something out together. I kicked the small stool near the fireplace, and it slid approximately five feet. Not worth it for the amount of pain it caused.

"Ouch! God, that hurt!" I hopped around on one foot, cursing, and only then did I notice that Bess had entered the room through the servants' door and was standing stock still, watching me.

"Mistress, is something amiss? Have you injured yourself?"

I stared at her for a moment, considering whether or not I could enlist her help. She undoubtedly would be familiar with Riley Green and the location of the alehouse. But could I ask her without arousing suspicion? "Nay, Bess, I am fine. I stubbed my toe. And I'm angry with Stephen." At least that much was true.

She smiled sympathetically. "If you do not need me, I'll help in the stillroom."

I nodded my permission. As she turned to leave, I blurted out, "Bess, where is Riley Green?"

"The village?"

"I guess." My face went red. "Aye, the village. There's an alehouse there."

"Why, 'tis just at the bottom of the road up to the manor."

"Toward Preston?"

"Nay, the other way." She shot me a suspicious look. "But you will not go there by yourself, mistress?"

"Someone mentioned it, and I wondered why I'd not seen it. That's all."

"The alewife and her husband are friends. Even so, young ladies do not . . . should not—"

"I would not dream of entering an alehouse unaccompanied."

Judging by Bess's look and warning, I'd have to disguise myself as a young man. Olivia Langford could not enter an alehouse unaccompanied, but *Oliver* Langford most definitely could. That meant borrowing clothing. Will and I were of similar size, but he had few clothes. I'd have to borrow from Stephen. Doublet, hose, shoes, hat. I had my Uggs, had hidden them away where even Bess hadn't found them, so I'd wear those and hope nobody would notice their unique look. I thought about raiding the costume trunk for the Corpus Christi play for a fake beard, but that would have been totally over the top.

I gathered the pieces of my disguise. Good thing Stephen was so vain about his appearance. He had plenty of everything, including several hats to choose from. My boots were exactly where Stephen had told me to hide them, at the bottom of an unused cupboard in the passageway. I stashed everything else in there with them, just in case Bess stuck her nose into my wardrobe. All was ready.

Edgy and inattentive the following morning, I repeatedly lost my place during pageant rehearsal. Thomas sent me away, saying, "You are unwell, mistress. We shall go on without you." I breathed a sigh of relief.

During lunch I said to Jennet, "Shall you help me with my embroidery this afternoon?"

Her face colored faintly, though not noticeably unless you were expecting it. "Pardon, Olivia, I have promised Cousin Elizabeth I would gather herbs today."

I faked disappointment with a frown and sigh. "Very well. Another day, then."

I'd told Bess to help Elizabeth in the stillroom again this afternoon. Since she'd been away for so long, they were behind in brewing up their little potions, or whatever it was that went on in that place.

As soon as Bess left, I began my transformation into a young man. The hose were the biggest challenge. I pulled them all the way up to the tops of my thighs and tied garters around them. No matter how tightly I tied, though, the hose still bagged around my knees and ankles. My boots would cover the worst wrinkles, so I wasn't too worried. I'd chosen the thickest doublet I could find in Stephen's wardrobe and left my bodice on underneath to add some bulk. While I pinned my hair up, I stationed myself by the passageway windows. When I saw Jennet walking through the courtyard carrying a basket, I bolted toward the staircase, plopping the hat on as I went and praying I wouldn't run into anyone.

Suddenly conscious of the true import of my little scheme, I paused and took a ragged breath. I'd either find out the day and time of the raid—or I'd fail. Worst of all, I might get caught. If I were sent to prison, could Stephen send me back to Boston? Would he even be allowed to visit me? I had no answer, and since I didn't even know where he was right now, what was the point of speculating? After making a final adjustment to my baggy hose, I headed for the trees.

Low, feathery clouds rode the sky earlier, but a steady wind had risen and blown them out. It was still windy, but not unpleasant with the sunshine. My plan was to walk through the forest, where the risk of being seen would be less. After what seemed like forever, I spotted the main road. Keeping to the woods, at last I glimpsed the alehouse by the side of the road. Farther on, I could see a few cottages and thatch-roofed huts.

Now that I'd found the place, my courage was wavering. And then Jennet emerged from around a curve in the road. I ducked behind a large fern, peeking around the fronds. She walked up to the front of the place and, presumably, right through the door. I needed to make my move.

I stood, brushed myself off, and walked toward the building. When I rounded the corner to the front, I nearly freaked out. There were horses, dogs, and lots of men standing around. *Damn!* I hadn't expected a crowd. I tried to put a swagger into my step. Difficult when a bunch of rotten little mongrels were jumping at me and nipping at my ankles. Some of the men snickered, and one of them called to the dogs. I scurried inside, pulling my hat low over my forehead.

I knew I would have only a moment to size up the situation. If I lingered too long in the doorway, I'd draw attention to myself. After a minute, I saw Jennet and her buddies over in one corner. I walked to a table near them, but not close enough to be obvious.

The alewife approached me. I lowered my voice an octave, hoping to sound like a teenage boy. "Ahem. A tankard, if you please."

She nodded and turned. I should order some food. Less suspicious that way, and eating would keep me occupied. "And, uh, I'm hungry. What's on the menu?" I smiled up at her, and she shrugged.

"The usual. Mutton pottage and bread, sir."

"Excellent. I'll have some of that." *Oh, geez. I sounded like I was dining at some fancy restaurant in contemporary London.* I felt my cheeks flushing.

It looked like Jennet and company hadn't gotten down to business yet. The sheriff and Lowry were scooping pottage into their mouths and mopping up gravy with hunks of bread. There were few other people in the place, and the alewife soon plopped a tankard of ale in front of me. Jennet, I noticed, was neither eating nor drinking. After a minute, the three of them began talking quietly. I'd be lucky to hear anything.

The sheriff's strident voice suddenly surprised me. "Mistress Hall, it is not your place to question what we do!"

I jerked to attention and pricked up my ears.

"I am simply saying if you get the one you really want, why do you need the other? He can be of no use to you," Jennet said.

"You will do as you are told!" The sheriff again, roaring his disapproval at Jennet.

I scooted my stool slightly sideways so I'd have a partial view of them. Jennet had stood, and Lowry's hand shot out and grasped her arm. But when he spoke, it was to the sheriff.

"Restrain yourself, sir! We are in a public place."

My food arrived, and I busied myself breaking off a piece of bread and dunking it into the stew. Lowry was speaking to Jennet now. She'd sat down again.

"We need young Shakespeare to give evidence against the Jesuit at his trial."

I couldn't hear her answer, just bits and pieces of it. Basically, it sounded like she was saying they'd never get Will to cooperate.

I shoved some food into my mouth and washed it down with the ale. The whole mass landed with a sickening thud in my stomach. *They wanted to use Will to testify against Campion!* That was why the sheriff had been interested in Will all along.

"We have ways of persuading, mistress. Your friend will not wish to endanger his family. Or himself, for that matter." Lowry again.

I waited, but none of them spoke. *Tell them when they're supposed to come for Shakespeare and Campion! That's what I really need to know.*

What happened next was so unexpected, so amazing, that I hardly had time to react. The door burst open, and Copernicus came bounding through. He sniffed around for a minute, and then made a beeline for me. Flinging himself at my chest, he licked my face joyfully, nearly knocking me off my stool. Stephen sauntered in and looked around for his dog.

Stunned, I did nothing for several seconds, just let Copernicus lick and whimper. Then my brain finally kicked into gear. By now, everyone's eyes, including those of Jennet, Lowry, and the sheriff, were riveted on me. I jumped to my feet and pushed the huge dog away. "Down, boy!" I commanded in my young man's voice. I threw some coins on the table and rushed out, shoving past Stephen. Heading for the woods at a run, I realized too late that Copernicus was chasing me.

Chapter Twenty-Eight

IN NO TIME, I heard Stephen calling Copernicus. I glanced quickly behind me. He was gaining on me, but I kept on running. I couldn't risk being seen by Jennet and her pals.

"Stop!" Stephen yelled.

I was losing steam fast. When I sensed him right at my heels, I stopped abruptly and spun around. I had a wicked stitch in my side. Bending over, my hands grasping my thighs, I tried to catch my breath.

"Sir! That is my dog. I only wish to—"

I rose and pulled the hat off. Stephen stopped speaking in mid-sentence.

"Olivia! I might have known. Explain yourself."

I gave him the evil eye. "Keep walking with me. That sneaky wench Jennet and her friends Lowry and the sheriff are in the tavern. I can't let them see me."

"By God, they've already seen you!"

"They didn't recognize me."

"Because of that clever disguise you're wearing? Men's clothes and a hat." He took a closer look. "My doublet, no less. And that must be my shirt and hose, too. Aye, you look like a real man, Olivia."

I felt like slapping him. "I fooled *you*, didn't I? You disappear for days and then have the nerve to question what I'm doing. And what gives you the right to be so . . . so condescending?"

He stopped, hands on hips, and watched me. "Forgive me. That was uncalled for. You did indeed fool me." He smiled his captivating Stephen smile, but I was in no mood to be charmed.

"I must return for my horse. If I did not, it would look suspicious, although I expect they'll have fled by the time I get back."

"Fine," I said.

"We shall talk later." He whistled to Copernicus and off they went.

I made my way back through the thick trees, feeling half sick. I'd missed out on the crucial piece of information—the timing of the raid and the arrest of Shakespeare and Campion. All because Stephen, after disappearing for a week, had chosen this exact moment to show up. And then he'd had the nerve to give me a hard time!

I decided to enter through the servants' door to avoid running into Elizabeth or Alexander. Or worst of all, Jennet. As it turned out, I passed a few servants who seemed hardly to notice me. If they wondered who I was or what I was up to, they didn't ask. It took me a while, but I finally located the stairs leading to my chamber. I closed the passageway doors at both ends and changed back into my own clothes. Seated on my bed, I was pulling pins out of my hair when Stephen tapped on the door and asked if he could come in.

He didn't waste any time with small talk. Nor did he bother explaining where he'd been for the last several days. "Would you care to enlighten me as to what you were doing?"

I tugged the last few pins from my hair and began brushing it out. "Something came up while you were away." I quit brushing and met his eyes. "A new threat to Shakespeare far more dangerous than anything from the Jesuits. Lowry and the sheriff intend to arrest him along with Campion. They want Will to testify at Campion's trial, and they're going to force him into it by threatening his family."

"God's breath! You were right to suspect Jennet. She must have discovered Thomas's true identity and informed them."

I described the note I'd found from Jennet's father and how that had prompted me to take action. "Because you and Cop came bursting in, I couldn't stay to find out the one thing we desperately need to know—where and when the arrest will take place." I glared at him.

"Great God, is there no end to it? Will one threat after another crop up?"

"Something occurred to me—why Will Shakespeare? Why not Alexander? Or you, for that matter."

"I can only speculate, but Master Will is young and thus more likely to be intimidated by them—and they may know about his father signing the spiritual testament. Who has ever heard of the Shakespeare family? Alexander, on the other hand, has some powerful friends, and as for me, I am under his protection while living here."

I heard footsteps. "Shh! Someone's coming. Open the doors. I'm going to sit on the settle with my needlework. Let Jennet think that's what I've been doing all afternoon."

In a minute, both Shakespeare and Jennet came walking through the passageway. "Stephen, well met!" Will said. "Where have you been, friend?"

"My father required my help for a few days."

Jennet wandered over to check out my embroidery. Good thing I'd spent some time working on it since she'd last seen it.

"You are slow and deliberate, mistress," she said, laughing. "But you progress."

Ha, ha. At least I'd never betray my friends. "Aye, but you need not worry. I shall never be the needlewoman you are. How was your herb gathering? 'Twas a lovely afternoon for it."

"I gathered by the stream. Bladderwort and willow. Some fresh watercress for the kitchen."

"So we shall have some in a salad tonight."

"Perhaps. I must change for the evening meal," she said, exiting toward her chamber.

Will followed shortly, and Stephen said, "I must wash off the dust from the road before the meal. Until later, Olivia."

"Would you care to walk with me?"

I was on my way upstairs after dinner when Stephen overtook me on the staircase. "Come," he said, taking my arm.

I got my cloak and we tramped through the courtyards toward the tilting green, Copernicus loping after us. Neither of us spoke.

The longer the silence lasted, the hotter the anger and resentment inside me burned. After we passed under the great keep, it burst out.

"How could you have abandoned me like that?"

"You are angry with me."

"How perceptive of you, Stephen. Not angry. Furious!" I wrapped my arms around myself and clenched them tightly.

He stopped walking and set his hands on my shoulders. "I did not abandon you, Olivia. Pray let me explain."

"You must have known I'd worry . . . wonder where you'd gone, and why."

He let go of me abruptly. "I needed time and solitude to think," he said. His eyes held a desperate, almost pleading gaze. When I didn't respond, he went on. "I visited my home for a few days."

"Couldn't you have told me before you left?"

"Indeed, I should have done. I never thought you would be forced to deal with such as this while I was gone." I had to admit, he sounded as if he meant it. "Accept my apologies, I beg you."

I nodded, but refused to grant him a smile.

We resumed walking and reached the tilting green. I sank down on the bench, but Stephen remained standing. Something had changed between us. He was formal and distant, and the look I'd seen in his eyes, I realized, was simply a plea for understanding. Nothing more. Whatever feelings he had for me, he'd managed to overcome them during the days he was away. That must have been what he needed to think about. I felt an ache in my throat, and I prayed to some higher authority not to let me cry.

"My sister has recovered and wishes to join me here at Hoghton Tower."

"What? That can't happen!"

"I managed to put her off by saying there were a number of guests in residence and she must wait until some of them leave."

"What's to stop your sister from coming here when this whole thing is over? Then you'll be found out."

"When I return home, I shall say I'm ill or injured. She will not come without me."

"Why not?"

He looked annoyed. "How long have you been here? You should be more accustomed to our ways. Young ladies of this time do not travel unaccompanied. As my mother is unwell and my father is too busy at this time of year, there would be no one else save me."

Something broke free inside, unfurling right up through my chest. A profound loneliness and hurt. The person I depended on for my well-being, who beyond all reason I'd fallen in love with, was treating me like some minor annoyance that had to be dealt with and put in her place. And I'd thought—hoped—he returned my feelings. More than anything, I didn't want him to know how he'd hurt me. "It doesn't really concern me, anyway," I said, trying to keep the pain I was feeling out of my voice. "I'll be gone by then."

Without looking at me he said, "'Tis grown chilly out here. Let's return to the house."

"Fine," I bit out. We ended up in Stephen's chamber, where a fire burned and crackled in the grate.

"Pray be seated." He was over by his washstand doing who knew what. I didn't look. When he came to sit beside me, he carried two cups. "'Tis the wine we drank before."

I reached for the cup and drank. The burn hit my stomach and spread, down my legs to my toes and all through my body. Perhaps it was the glow and hiss of the fire, or it might have been the wine. I wasn't sure, but after a while I began to feel stronger. "I've been agonizing over whether to warn Will. What do you think?"

"Doing so would mean he and Thomas would leave immediately, and together. In that instance, the most likely outcome is that Shakespeare would join the Jesuits."

"I agree. I also debated telling Alexander, but he's not here. He's off at some horse show."

Stephen's eyes studied my face. "It seems I owe you another apology, Olivia."

"For what?"

"Not taking your concerns about Jennet seriously. You were right about her all along."

"Women's intuition." I smiled at him, longing to see one in return. He looked so serious. "What do you think we should do?"

"The pageant is Sunday, three days hence. Let's assume that Thomas still plans to leave immediately afterward. We must try, one final time, to persuade Will not to accompany him."

"And if that doesn't work, we lock him up?"

He scowled. "That would be the last resort, something we'd do if he left us no other choice. And I mean to be ready."

"By doing what?" I rolled my eyes, which Stephen ignored.

"I shall find some sturdy rope to restrain him, if necessary. I'll fill a flagon with ale and pack a basket of food and hide them in one of the lower chambers. If we're forced to lock Will up, he'll have all the usual comforts." He grimaced. "Some, anyway. We must find blankets and warm clothing—candles, too. It is cold and dank down there." Stephen squatted in front of the fire, as if even the thought of the lower rooms turned him cold, as it did me.

"I'll leave all of that to you. Saturday will be our final pageant practice, and I won't have time to help."

He nodded. "Our plan is thus: After the pageant, we stay close to Shakespeare. If he says he's leaving with Thomas, we shall try to convince him not to. If he insists, we shall forcibly escort him to the . . . lower chamber."

I couldn't picture myself taking part, but I didn't object. Stephen could handle Will, if it came to that. "What about Lowry and the sheriff?"

"Before Thomas leaves we must warn him, and confide in Alexander as well. He'll want to send a guard with Thomas, and devise a plan for the safety of Will and his family."

"Where would Will go? Back to Stratford?"

"Nay, the sheriff would look for him there. It would be safer to conceal him at another home, at least until we know what happens to Thomas—Campion."

I glanced up at Stephen and asked another question that had been plaguing me since the beginning. I'd been too afraid of the answer to ask. "What happens if we lose Shakespeare? If he goes off with Thomas and becomes a Jesuit. Or, worse yet, he's arrested and executed?"

"Then I am afraid his work is lost forever."

"But that can't be! I know it exists, has existed, through the centuries all the way into the future."

"Why are you such a skeptic? If there were no risk, I wouldn't have brought you back. We would not be doing all this. We're ensuring that Shakespeare will go on to write and perform his plays." He returned to my side, grasping my hand between his own. He looked somber, his face shadowed, eyes cheerless.

"You're scaring me."

He gave me a rueful smile. "The truth is thus: If we do not save Master Will Shakespeare, you will return to a different world."

I jerked my hand away and shot to my feet. "You said when we arrived here—no, you promised—that I'd return to my school, and I'd go on with my life as usual. You gave me your word." I couldn't hide the tremor in my voice.

"Not precisely. I agreed to help you travel back to your century. I never said what you would be traveling back to." He hesitated before continuing. "Do you recall I said certain limitations and restrictions existed? I cannot control the final outcome, much as I would like to, for your sake as well as Shakespeare's."

I walked to the windows, arms folded across my chest, feeling betrayed. It was deep twilight, that dreamlike time between the end of day and beginning of night. And that was where I found myself, somewhere in between . . . something.

Stephen's voice was low, regretful. "Then, I had no doubt we would succeed. Now, I am not so sure."

"I might have to go back to a world completely unknown to me?"

"Not completely. Much of it would be familiar. 'Tis hard to judge exactly what a difference Shakespeare's work has made in the world. Your mother and father, obviously, would not be engaged in their present work."

I spun around. "Oh, yes, obviously. I wouldn't be at the same school, I wouldn't have the same life at all. And where do you think my parents met? During auditions for *Othello*. Maybe I would never have been born!"

Stephen rose and grabbed my arms. "This is why we must not fail. Do you understand? *We must not fail.*"

I tried to imagine a world without Shakespeare, without the sonnets and the plays. Some of the beauty of life, the grace, would be missing. Some essential piece that defines what it is to be human.

"The world would seem . . . less radiant without his work. That's not really the right word, but—"

"I understand."

"Love would change without Romeo and Juliet. And that's just the tip of the iceberg. Power, rage, jealousy—what would they mean without Richard, Lear, Othello?"

"And much charm and lightness would vanish without the comedies."

"*The Taming of the Shrew.*"

"Aye."

"It's unspeakable."

"'Tis unthinkable."

"We can't let it happen."

"Good. Then we are in agreement. We shall use whatever means we must to prevent Will from following Thomas, and to protect him from Lowry and the sheriff."

"Absolutely." But a lump of worry and uncertainty lodged in my stomach. Could we save Shakespeare? And afterward, could I save myself?

Chapter Twenty-Nine

SATURDAY AFTERNOON, we held a final practice for the pageant, a dress rehearsal. We were to have music at the beginning and end of the performance, so instruments were brought out and set up in the minstrels' gallery. Two of the musicians, Fulke and Will, were also in the play. Stephen had agreed to be the third.

I stood with my prompt book offstage, behind a rood screen, an intricately carved wooden piece that had once been in a church, according to Stephen. He was hovering around, putting me on edge. "Don't you have someplace else to be?" I asked as he stared at the book over my shoulder. After my testy comment, he backed off.

"Will brings this play alive, does he not?" Stephen asked after we'd watched for a while.

I smiled in agreement. Whenever Shakespeare appeared as Noah's wife, he seemed to energize everyone else. Comical but not farcical, Will let the words convey the humor without overplaying his part. Fulke did a commendable job as Noah, who mostly re-acted, first to God and then to his wife. Mrs. Noah is annoyed with him because he didn't tell her about God's command to build the ark. She insists she's going home to be with her family and friends, even after Noah explains that the flood to end all floods is about to happen.

It was funny because of that timeless way men and women bicker with each other. I loved the wife's stubbornness, and the fact that her major quarrel with Noah was that he didn't tell her what he'd been up to. I thought a modern audience would laugh too. With this performance, I'd caught another glimpse of Shake-speare's genius. Will obviously reveled in his role. The play's suc-cess depended on him.

Stephen finally wandered off, but the rehearsal continued.

"Enough," Thomas said after three hours. "I believe we are ready."

After dinner, Stephen walked me upstairs. "How did things prog-ress after I took my leave?"

"Thomas seemed off balance. He forgot some of his lines, which he's never done before. And he hardly even noticed every-one else's mistakes."

"What about Shakespeare?"

"We didn't exchange a word."

"'Tis no matter. At this point, what will be, will be." We were standing in the passage outside Stephen's room. He pulled me in-side, far enough so that anyone else passing wouldn't overhear us.

"You sound very calm about the whole thing," I said.

"Only because I believe we've done all we can."

"Did you, er, make your preparations today?"

His eyes flickered toward mine. "Aye. All is ready."

I felt that knot in my stomach again. Just thinking about tomorrow and what could happen seemed to bring it on.

He raised my hand to his lips. "Good night, Olivia. Sleep well."

No way, I thought.

I awoke with the dawn chorus, well before the sun was up. I lay quietly and tried to clear my mind, to listen to the sweet peacefulness of the almost morning. Servants in the passage called to each other as they began their daily routines, and a few voices softly hummed or whistled. Stretching, I swept my eyes around the room, taking in the furniture, the tapestries, and the fireplace. I wanted to remember everything, to be able to picture it when I was back in Boston. I had the feeling I'd be going home soon.

I must have dozed, because I was still in bed when Bess breezed in with a tray bearing a ewer of warm water and breakfast. "Good morrow, mistress," she said, curtsying.

"Good morrow." I scooted up and watched her pour the water into the basin on the washstand. "Do you think I could have extra water this morning, Bess? If it's not too much trouble, I'd like a thorough washing."

"Oh, aye, mistress. When would you like it?"

"After breakfast?"

"I'll see to it."

When she left, I rinsed my face and ran my fingers through my tangled hair. Then I walked over to the table by the settle, where Bess had placed my usual bowl of pottage and tankard of ale. There was also a small basket of strawberries, sweet and juicy, an unexpected treat. Unfortunately, I couldn't eat much. After a few desultory bites, there was a tap at my door. Perhaps someone bringing the water.

But it was Stephen, dressed and looking fresh and handsome. "Kind of early for a visit, isn't it?" I asked, feeling shy about being in my sleeping smock.

He grinned. "Forgive me for intruding. I wanted to see how you were faring."

I shrugged. "Okay, I guess."

"Did you sleep?"

"Some. I woke up early."

"As did I. Are you going to eat these?" he asked, pointing to the berries.

"Go for it. I don't feel much like eating."

He polished off the berries and then tackled the pottage.

"Stephen?"

He raised a brow. "Olivia?"

"When am I leaving?" I hadn't had the courage to ask before, but now I couldn't stand not knowing. It wasn't just Shakespeare's fate hanging in the balance.

Stephen dropped the spoon into the bowl, leaned back, and gazed at me. "I would guess sometime in the next few days, if all goes according to plan."

"Just like that. It's over. Farewell, Miranda, nice knowing you."

"You know it is not that simple. Nor would I be so careless about it."

"No? You were careless about bringing me here. 'I have need of you, wench.' Those were your exact words."

Looking embarrassed, he leaned forward and held out his hand. "Let us not quarrel, today of all days."

I squeezed his hand, but I couldn't look at him. Somehow it hurt to look directly at him. "And if things don't go according to plan?"

"Well, then, we shall have to see."

"What do you mean?"

"Only that if Will eludes us somehow, maybe you and I will need to take action. If you are agreeable, that is. If not, you may . . . return home."

The water arrived. Several women carried steaming pails, and Bess followed them with a couple of extra basins.

"Enjoy your bathing, Sister. I shall see you at the midday meal," Stephen said before he left.

Standing by the long table in the banqueting hall, I clasped my hands together and tried desperately to act normal. Elizabeth had appeared unexpectedly beside me and was asking about my health.

"Are you unwell, Olivia? You look flushed, my dear."

"I am well, Aunt. Do not worry about me." I leaned closer to her. "'Tis my courses," I whispered.

"Ah." She patted me on the shoulder. "The womanly burden. See that you take care not to tire yourself." She touched my cheek with the back of her hand. "You do look feverish. Are you certain—?"

"Excitement about the performance, that is all."

She walked back to her place and I heaved a grateful sigh. I could feel my cheeks burning. That always happened to me when I was nervous or excited about something.

"What was that about?" Stephen asked as we found our seats.

"She thinks I look feverish."

He smiled. "Your cheeks are glowing, 'tis true. Your hair is passing lovely that way, Olivia." His eyes moved from my face to my hair. "The braid looks like a coronet."

"Thank you. Bess arranged it." I quickly changed the subject. "Where is everyone?" I asked, noticing all the vacant places at the table.

"They're making final preparations for the pageant, I expect."

Sure enough, when I glanced toward the opposite end of the room, I spotted Fulke lugging pieces of an ark that had been roughly constructed for our set. In addition to the ark, we had a painted cloth of azure to represent the floodwaters, a rainbow sewn from scraps of brightly hued fabric, and a cut-out dove that would, at the end, hang from the ark by a string. Apparently, this was similar to what had been done in the days when the pageants were performed by the guilds.

I sipped my ale and took a few bites of the various dishes placed before me. Stephen spent most of the meal talking to his uncle about enclosures, lambing, and the horses he'd just purchased. I tuned them out, unable to think of anything but Will Shakespeare and Thomas. When the meal was finished and the tooth picking about to begin, I slipped away and dashed upstairs for the prompt book. After glancing at myself in the glass and smoothing my skirts, I turned to leave.

Without warning, Jennet and her father burst through the servants' door and into my chamber, scaring the life out of me. What were they doing here, and why hadn't they entered the house in the usual way? Master Hall shot me a menacing look, and I knew I was in trouble.

Chapter Thirty

"Jennet, Master Hall," I said, curtsying and trying to pretend nothing unusual was occurring. A much younger man whom I'd never seen before accompanied them. He was tall and built like the Hulk.

They came to an abrupt halt. Ignoring me, Jennet and her father gave each other a knowing look, and a tiny prickle of fear stirred inside. I started to back away, then whirled and made a dash toward the staircase. But the young stranger, despite his size, was quick on his feet. He grabbed my arm and jerked me to a stop.

"Sir, let go of me!" Before I got the words out, he had started to drag me back down the passage toward Jennet's room. She quickly closed the two sets of doors after us.

"What should we do, Father?" Jennet said, not even looking at me.

"I demand that you tell me what's going on!"

"Be silent, woman," Master Hall commanded. With one broad hand, he shoved me down on the bed. I fell backward and hit my head against the wall.

"Father!" Jennet protested. "Do not hurt her."

"They'll be ready to begin the pageant," I said desperately, rubbing my head. "Someone will come looking for me."

"Silence!" Master Hall said, glowering.

I clamped my mouth shut. I could learn more by listening. Sneaking out when they weren't so preoccupied with watching me was a better idea.

"We shall have to use her," he said. "She will become part of our plan."

I wanted to ask what plan but resisted the urge.

Jennet had moved to the windows and was peering out. "Have they arrived?" her father asked.

Oh, my God! This must be the raid. She's watching for the sheriff.

Jennet shook her head and whirled around to speak. "I do not see what use she will be to us, Father. We should find somewhere to lock her up." I was surprised to hear Jennet challenge her father. Good for her, even if she did want to lock me up.

"I think not. Mistress Langford will accompany us when we make our grand entrance into the hall. Mayhap we shall give her a line to say. Even more valuable . . . it can be she who points out which one is Campion."

Jennet gave him a sour look.

"I know you were to make the identification, Daughter, but *her* doing so will be a great humiliation for the family."

By now, I knew the performance must have gone ahead without me. I wondered why Stephen or someone else hadn't bothered to look for me. Jennet resumed her watch at the windows, and after a minute she said tersely, "They are come."

"I must meet them." Master Hall turned toward the young man, who had positioned himself near the doors. "Luke, do not allow Mistress Langford to leave. I'll return as soon as I've conferred with the sheriff." He clomped off down the passage.

There would be no chance of escaping to warn anyone, not with the Hulk guarding the doors.

Jennet and I glared at each other. "When did you figure out about Campion?" I asked.

"I found some documents, and other . . . items . . . in his chamber and described them to my father and Lowry. They figured it out."

"I saw you one day in the woods talking to Lowry. Stephen didn't believe you knew anything. He trusted you."

"And you did not?"

"Not really. I wanted to tell my uncle about your meeting, but Stephen said we couldn't be sure the man *was* Lowry. He did not wish to cast suspicion on an innocent person."

"Your good brother—if he is your brother—is too trusting."

"I followed you to the alehouse too."

"You did? How did you know—?"

"I searched your room. You are not the only one capable of deceit."

Her mouth hardened. "You shock me, Olivia. Indeed, I did not think you had it in you."

"It was you who sent me the notes. Why?"

"I watched you and Stephen, and the way you behaved in each

other's presence somehow did not seem right. Not like a brother and sister. More like a couple." She stopped and looked aside for a minute. "And I hated your wooing of Will Shakespeare."

I didn't dare admit anything about Stephen's and my relationship. What if she blabbed as a parting shot? "Who wrote the first note? I figured you'd be able to write the—"

"You are so very trusting and gullible, Olivia. 'Tis no wonder I never figured you for a sneak." She laughed and tossed her hair. "I tricked everyone. I've been reading since the age of six, you see. Most Puritans learn to read at a young age, not that we read anything other than the Bible and the *Book of Martyrs*."

"You had me completely fooled," I admitted. "I even felt sorry for you."

She lifted her chin defiantly.

"Why did you do it, Jennet? Betray the people who have cared for you and looked after you these past months? And why throw Will Shakespeare to the wolves? I thought you were in love with him."

She grunted. "He's nothing to me now. You do not understand, do you? I thought you might, since I had confided in you. Think, Olivia. Can you not put it together?"

A lightbulb flashed on. "Your marriage! Your father threatened to marry you to that disgusting man if you did not do his dirty work for him. That's what he threatened you with in the note— what would happen if you did not do your duty."

"Aye. Now you have it. I have had much practice, you see, at being my father's spy." She walked toward the bed and stopped in front of me. "Ever since I was a child, I've reported to him, telling him of misdeeds on our small holding. He especially wishes to be informed of fornication, the worst of all sins."

"How could you possibly know about the misdeeds of others? Especially . . . fornication?"

"You would be surprised how easy it is to spy once you have grown skilled. Since I looked after the sick and injured, it was simple to discover when someone was faking illness. And 'tis nothing to spy on the servants. They are prone to gossip and laziness anyway."

"But the . . . other. How could you have found out about that?"

"It is a simple matter to follow a couple. I would wait a few days to see where their little romances would lead them. Behind the dovecote is one of the favored locations for it. I could easily peek around the corner to see what they were up to without their knowing it."

"But that's despicable!"

She shrugged. "At first it seemed like a game, but there came a time when I no longer liked doing it. All who lived and worked with us came to despise me." She lowered her head, and when she raised it, her eyes shone with tears. "One day I realized that no matter what I did, I would never please my father. He believes women are of no worth—except for procreation."

"Why did you keep on, then?"

"Some of us have little choice, Olivia. I am caught in my father's net. Until I marry and have my own home, I must do as he says."

"What about this?" I gestured, meaning Hoghton Tower. "How did you end up here?"

"My father's connection to the Privy Council, Robert Lowry, asked him to place me here. I am related to the Hoghtons on my mother's side. And before you judge me, mark this: I refused to do it. I told my father it was over. I would no longer be his spy."

"And then he threatened you with marriage to—"

"The simpering Master Dugdale. A more repulsive man would be hard to find. So I agreed. After I met Will Shakespeare, I hoped we might . . . he might love me, or at least bed me and mayhap we would have to marry. But alas, you came along and ruined all hope of that."

As ironies went, this ranked high. I wasn't the only one at Hoghton Tower who'd planned to seduce Shakespeare. And even more ironic, my seducing Will had pushed Jennet toward betraying him.

"One other thing I've been wondering about," I said. "What hold does the Privy Council have over your father?"

"They promised to ignore certain deviations from the true Protestant Church. Father does not use the Book of Common Prayer in his services, for one thing, which is against the law. How clever of you to realize that Father must do their bidding, as I must do his."

It was a tangled web of alliances, secrets, and blackmail, I thought. "What will you do now? Will your father still force you to wed Master Dugdale?"

Before she could answer, Jennet's father stepped into the room. "All is ready. We must proceed to the hall."

I rose. He grabbed my arm, and this time I managed to jerk it away. There was really no escape route for me. He must have understood that, because he let me go.

Master Hall prodded me in the back, directing me down the stairs and out into the courtyard, where several of the sheriff's men were waiting. The sheriff himself hovered inside a little-used entrance. He glared at me and shoved me forward, forcing me to enter the hall proper. The play had begun. Noah and his wife and sons were all on stage.

Friends, neighbors, and villagers had been invited to Hoghton Tower for the performance, and most of them were spread out on the floor, some sitting, others standing. At first, no one noticed us. We moved stealthily up one side of the great room until Fulke, in midsentence, suddenly stopped reciting his lines. I blinked and stared. Someone else was playing the part of Noah's wife; if I was not mistaken, it was one of Will's older students.

The audience grew restive and began whispering, asking each other what was happening. After a few agonizing moments, as my heart thudded against my rib cage, heads turned toward us. My uncle started to speak, but the sheriff cut him off.

"The house and property are surrounded. It would be foolish for anyone to attempt to escape." A hush fell over the room. "Mistress Langford," he said. "Which one is Edmund Campion?"

There was a collective gasp, but no one spoke.

Frantically, I looked around for Stephen, but I couldn't find him. He wasn't in the minstrels' gallery, nor was he at the other end of the room with his aunt and uncle. The sheriff's strong hand yanked me against his side. "Mistress? I am waiting."

A player dressed in a white robe and wearing a wig and false beard stepped out from behind the rood screen. I recognized the costume immediately as the one for the God character. But something wasn't right. Whoever was wearing the costume, it wasn't Thomas.

Jennet cried out. "There he is! That's Campion!" And then chaos erupted. The sheriff abruptly let go of me and rushed the stage, followed by several of his men. Thomas, or whoever it was, didn't move. Audience members tried to flee, but the deputies pushed them roughly back to their places.

Only the actors seemed calm, too calm for what was happening. Simon, the thug who'd beat up Stephen, grabbed the arms of the person in the costume and jerked them behind his back while the sheriff ripped off the wig and then the beard.

It was Stephen.

"This is not the Jesuit, 'tis Langford!" the sheriff shouted. He fired a look toward my uncle. "Sir, you are harboring a criminal. A man who has committed treason. It would behoove you to tell me where he is."

"The man you seek is not here, Sheriff. You have been misled."

"Liar!" The sheriff turned to some of his men and gestured toward the audience. "Get these people out of here. If anyone acts suspicious, bring him to me." The crowd began filing out, unnaturally quiet.

"Family, players, musicians, everyone, come!" the sheriff commanded. All of us gathered around him, waiting. Jennet and her father hovered near the wall, apart from the rest. Stephen had removed the robe he'd been wearing, and when he was close enough, I mouthed the words, "Where's Will?"

"Safe," he whispered. He reached out and touched my shoulder. "Are you okay?"

"Jennet's father shoved me around a little, but he didn't hurt me."

The sheriff signaled to them to join the rest of us. Master Hall strode over, looking smug and insufferable. Jennet, however, hung her head, refusing to meet anyone's eyes.

"Tell them how you learned of Campion's presence here," the sheriff said. Jennet said nothing, apparently believing the question was meant for her father. "Mistress Hall!" the sheriff roared, and she finally reacted.

"It was obvious Thomas Cook was a priest, but I didn't suspect him to be Campion. Not at first. Then one Sunday I searched his chamber."

She paused, as though recalling the order of events.

"Tell them the rest, Daughter."

For the first time, defiance flashed in her eyes. "I knew he was saying Mass. Indeed, it was hardly a secret. I found papers in his room with Edmund Campion's name on them, and some other things. A signet ring, for sealing letters, was one of them. I got word to my father, and he told the sheriff and Master Lowry."

Done in by the ring and his own carelessness. I felt sure that this time he'd be caught. Alexander would have to tell them where Thomas was hiding to save himself. To save all of us.

"We know he is here. You need only reveal his hiding place," the sheriff said to my uncle. Just then, one of the deputies rushed in and asked to speak to the sheriff. They huddled off to one side and spoke in low voices.

"Cousin Jennet," Alexander said, reaching out his hand to the girl. "I forgive you. I know your father forced you into this. I do not know what he threatened you with, but he used you ill for his own gain. I am sorry for you."

She flinched.

"May you all burn in hell," Master Hall said, pushing his daughter aside and advancing toward my uncle. Jennet flushed. "Father, stop!"

The sheriff interrupted. "That's enough, Hall. We've learned from one of the grooms that a man fitting the Jesuit's description fled some time ago on horseback. He has eluded us, but we shall find him quickly. He looked pointedly at Alexander. "What is his destination?"

"I do not know who left here on horseback, Sheriff, and I certainly was not privy to his destination. This is a busy estate. We have men coming and going at all hours of the day, even on Sunday. It could have been anyone. A peddler, cooper, smith, rat catcher—"

"There is a rat involved with this, but 'tis not the catcher. We are wasting precious time." He barked orders to his men, appointing leaders and issuing instructions. They would divide up and head in different directions to hunt their prey more efficiently. "We will meet in Preston, one day hence," he said, "at the church. If you should find the man, send word. And do not let him escape!"

The sheriff turned to Jennet and said, "Which one is Master Shakespeare?"

"I—I do not see him. He was supposed to play Noah's wife in the pageant, but he is not here."

The sheriff let out a growl. "Did he go with Campion?"

Of course, nobody answered. I had the feeling I knew where Will was. Hiding in the room Stephen had prepared for him.

I stole a glance at Alexander. His lips were pressed into a straight line, his face colorless. Someone had brought a chair for Elizabeth, who looked like she was in shock. Stephen was hovering nearby, keeping a close eye on them. In a minute, the deputies began to file out, ready to give chase.

The sheriff turned to go. "I shall deal with you after we catch our prey, sir," he said to Alexander. "Do not be so foolish as to believe there will be no retribution for this." His expression terrified me, and his voice seemed full of barely checked rage. Only the urgency of catching Edmund Campion saved Alexander.

Chapter Thirty-One

AFTER THE SHERIFF LEFT, Stephen rushed downstairs to release Will. Alexander refused to answer any questions, and didn't even acknowledge Thomas's true identity. "Let us pray for Thomas's safety," he said, and that was it. We were dismissed, and everybody sought refuge in their chambers.

Within a few hours, I thought I might go crazy, so I took Copernicus outside for a walk. I was hoping Stephen might be in his room by the time I came in, but he wasn't. He hadn't been there all day. I thought he was probably with his aunt and uncle, offering whatever solace he could summon.

In the late afternoon, Bess brought me a snack. I was just finishing when Stephen appeared. Not until I actually saw him did I understand that deep down, I was terrified he'd disappeared again. I shot to my feet and hurled myself at him.

He held me tightly. "Here, here, what's this?" he asked in probably the gentlest voice I'd ever heard from him.

"Nothing, I'm fine. . . . I was worried because I hadn't seen you all day."

He rested his cheek on my forehead for a moment before releasing me. "My uncle needed me. Let's find Shakespeare and talk."

Stephen rounded up Will and suggested we move to the library, where we would have more privacy. On the way, he asked one of the servants to bring us spiced ale.

The three of us huddled before the fire. "So you have decided against becoming a Jesuit?" I asked Will.

He sipped at his drink before answering. "Over the last several days, I came to the realization the Jesuit life was not for me. I shall not follow Campion. He would not want me to endanger myself."

"Do you know where he's gone?" I asked.

"Aye. I was to have been his escort. But if I tried to find him, I'd only tangle with the sheriff and his men. Where would that get me but in a cell?"

"How did Thomas—Campion—know what was going to happen?" I asked.

"I believe my uncle has his own spies," Stephen said wryly. "Just before we were to begin the pageant, he told me I would be playing the role of God."

I laughed, the first time all day. "Did you know the lines?"

"Not exactly." His eyes danced with amusement.

"Didn't everyone wonder what had happened to Thomas? And what about me? Nobody came to look for me."

Will answered. "Master Hoghton informed everyone there was to be a raid, so confusion prevailed. I am sorry to tell you, Olivia, we hardly noticed you were missing, for all else that was happening."

I had to admit that, given the situation, I probably wouldn't have noticed either. "And Stephen hustled you off to the cellars?"

"That he did." Will smiled sardonically. "Your brother seemed to believe I wouldn't go willingly. He grabbed my arm and pushed me along until I persuaded him I wouldn't run after Campion." Will looked at Stephen, rubbing his arm and wincing. "You gave me a good bruising, my friend."

"We did not want you to do something foolish."

"So I gathered."

"Will, did you know . . . you must have known . . . that Thomas was really Edmund Campion," I said.

"Not when I first arrived here. But he was such a learned man and so passionate about religion, I soon made him out to be above other priests. When he began talking to me about becoming a Jesuit, I suspected he was something other than what he said."

"When did you know for certain?"

"Do you remember that day in the schoolroom, when I received a letter? He'd sealed it with the initials 'EC.' Can you imagine anything more foolish? Typical of him, though, to be careless of his own safety."

Stephen and I locked eyes. "What?" Will said. "Did you know too?"

"We guessed. Like you, I thought his intelligence and religious zeal went beyond that of other priests I'd met," Stephen said. He didn't mention that we'd read the letter.

"I wonder what will happen to him. 'Tis a cat-and-mouse game, all subterfuge. Who can outwit whom," Will said.

"I fear the worst. Maybe not tomorrow, or the next day, but

Campion cannot escape Walsingham's brand of justice indefinitely," Stephen said.

"Jennet's participation in the scheme shocked me," Will said. "I thought her a harmless and sweet girl, tractable and eager to please. I wonder why her father involved her."

"A few days ago, when we were talking, you said you'd felt suspicious of everyone since Lowry and his friend were here. I thought you meant Jennet," I said.

"Nay, I had no one in particular in mind. If anyone, I guessed a servant, or a laborer. Someone who needed money, and thus might be easily bribed. Did you suspect her?"

I nodded, and gave Will a brief explanation of why I'd never trusted her. "A part of me still feels sympathy for her, though. I cannot help wondering if her father will force her to marry the man she finds so repulsive. She did what they asked of her, even though things didn't turn out the way they wanted."

"For her sake, I hope not. Perhaps she still has a chance for a happy marriage," Stephen said.

"What will you do now, Will?" I asked.

"I think I can answer that." It was Alexander. "I've been looking for the three of you." Stephen and Will shot to their feet.

"Be seated, Uncle," Stephen said.

Alexander claimed Stephen's place on the settle. "Will, on the morrow I am sending you to my friend Sir Thomas Hesketh, a relation of my wife. He resides at Rufford Hall. He's an amiable man, and I believe you will be happy there." He smiled at Will. "Sir Thomas keeps a company of players."

"Indeed!" Will said, his eyes dancing. "I shall be sorry to leave here, but I believe the stage is my true vocation."

"Do not forget about your writing!" I said.

Will grinned. "The two blend well."

"I think it would be in your best interests to change your surname," Alexander said. "Later, when all this business is finished, you can change it back."

" 'Tis a good plan," Stephen said, looking at Will. "If the sheriff is inclined to search for you, it would make things more difficult for him."

"Where is this Rufford Hall, sir?" Will asked.

" 'Tis twelve miles southwest of here, roughly," Alexander said. "Nephew, you're familiar with it, are you not?"

"Aye. My sister and I shall be happy to escort Will. 'Tis on our path home." Stephen shifted his glance toward me. "Our parents have need of us. It is time to take our leave of Hoghton Tower, is it not, Olivia?"

I nodded. "Aye. 'Tis past time."

"I shall lament the loss of your company," Alexander said, looking sad.

We finished our ale and said good night.

In the morning, I hugged Bess and thanked her for everything she'd done for me. Elizabeth and Alexander awaited us in the courtyard. They kissed me goodbye on both cheeks.

"We shall hope to see you again soon, dear Olivia," Elizabeth said.

"It is my hope too, Aunt." I couldn't imagine how Stephen would explain everything to his family. It was one of the few reasons I was happy to be leaving.

"God keep you, Niece," Alexander said as he helped me onto my mount. "It has been a joy having you with us."

I felt like the lowest of life-forms. Possibly lower.

For once, I was glad to be on the sidesaddle. It allowed me to look around and behind me more easily, to soak up my last view of Hoghton Tower. The forest, the tilting green and rose garden. I wouldn't be coming back, I knew. Not in this century, anyway.

At first, our route took us by pastures where sheep and cows grazed, looking like figures in a landscape painting. Sometimes the road cut through farmlands, with enclosed areas for crops. In other places, the forest grew thick enough that the road seemed barely able to forge a path through the trees. Under the canopy of leaves, wild garlic and bluebells were beginning to bloom.

Where we could, we urged the horses into a trot. But the road was deeply rutted from the recent rain, and we didn't want to risk an injury to one of the animals or to ourselves. So most of the time our pace was fairly slow, and we rode three abreast whenever we could.

"I'm worried about our uncle," I said. "Will the sheriff make good on his threats?"

Stephen and Will glanced at each other. "I believe it depends on what happens with Campion," Stephen said. "If he is captured and brought to trial, Alexander will be forgotten. If he is not caught, the sheriff may return to exact his revenge."

"I am still aghast that they intended to arrest *me*," Will said, shaking his head. "I cannot imagine what I should have done if they'd forced me to testify against Father Campion."

"'Tis still possible, Will! Be cautious. Stay close to Rufford Hall until this matter is settled and do not speak of it to anyone," Stephen warned.

Dropping back to ride alone, I gradually forced myself to think about what would come next. After we said our goodbyes to Will, I'd be returning to the present. If only I didn't have to leave Stephen, I'd be happy to go home. The truth was, I ached to talk to my grandfather and Macy, and even to my parents. I missed acting, TV, movies, my iPod, my laptop, and, most of all, modern plumbing. But I'd give it all up in a heartbeat if I thought Stephen wanted me to stay. I was almost positive I would. Wouldn't I?

But I'd looked at it from all angles and had to admit that Stephen had never given me any indication he wanted me to stay. To ease the unrelenting ache in my heart, I told myself that he did care for me. Maybe even loved me a little.

About midmorning we reached a crossroads, and Stephen reined in Bolingbroke. Will and I followed suit.

"Will, can you ride on to Rufford Hall without us? Our home lies in the other direction."

We all dismounted to bid each other goodbye, and I looked at Shakespeare, feeling a surge of emotion. "I wanted to say, Will, it has been an honor to know you." I hesitated a minute, choking up. "I believe you chose well. Let Edmund Campion attend to men's souls. You have the power to capture their hearts and minds."

Holding my hands, he kissed me on both cheeks. "You have been a valued friend to me, Mistress Olivia, always believing in me. I shall never forget you." His gray eyes seemed genuinely sad.

"Trust me, Will. I couldn't forget *you* if I tried."

He slanted his eyes at me, but kept his thoughts to himself. "Thank you for . . . for helping me find the way to my true destiny. I hope we shall meet again someday."

I blinked. *Not me. Stephen, maybe.* "Now, go and make a name for yourself," I said, giving his hands one more squeeze.

Stephen and Will hugged, clapping each other on the back. "You'll have to ford Martin Mere," Stephen said.

"Thank you," Will said. "I'll manage." He remounted, and Stephen and I watched him ride away.

Chapter Thirty-Two

"We did it," I said, glancing at Stephen. I should have felt triumphant and insanely happy, but I didn't. Not now. Stephen's reaction was subdued too. We turned the horses and rode in the opposite direction.

"Where are we going?"

"To a deserted abbey. It was pillaged during the Dissolution, but the ruins still stand."

"That was King Henry's doing, right? That man was a real tyrant, wasn't he?"

Stephen grimaced. "On your TV, I noted that England is still ruled by monarchs, even in your time."

"But they don't have any real power. Their role is more . . ." I struggled for the right word. ". . . symbolic, I guess you'd say. They do a lot of charity work and christen ships and hold state dinners, that kind of thing."

"I see." He chuckled. "Far less dangerous that way."

Up ahead, I glimpsed the abbey ruins rising from a grassy area surrounded by woods on three sides. Nearby, rolling farmland stretched out as far as the eye could see. I recognized gorse and rhododendron bushes growing wild among the fallen stones, which were all higgledy-piggledy. A tower remained intact, standing watch over the countryside.

"It's beautiful," I said.

We dismounted and Stephen took my hand, leading me through the ruins, pointing out the cloisters, the cruciform shape of the old church, the monks' cells. Sunlight dappled the stonework here and there. Birdsong and the whir of insects distracted me, but even so, I felt a heaviness weighing me down. We walked out into the sunlight.

"I have brought your things, Olivia, just as I promised. I want you to change into your modern clothing." He pulled a bundle from behind Bolingbroke's saddle. My backpack.

"No, I can't. Don't—"

"I beg you, sweetheart. Do as I ask, and then we'll talk."

I sighed, knowing it was futile to protest. I found a giant stone to stand behind and removed my traveling clothes. I pulled on my jeans, T-shirt, and hoodie, feeling myself sliding back toward the present, to Miranda's life. After tugging on my boots, I fastened my watch, noticing it was about six in the morning in Boston.

When I reappeared, Stephen said, "Let's sit a moment." He pointed to a huge, flat piece of stone.

Neither of us said anything at first. I leaned back, placing my weight on my hands, letting the sun shine on my face. My foot swung, seemingly on its own, my boot heel hitting the stone over and over.

"I cannot think how I shall get on without you, but 'tis time for you to go," Stephen said at last. I turned to look at him, fighting back the tears I knew I could keep at bay for only so long.

"But first, I have a gift for you," he said.

"You do?"

"Do not look so surprised. Did you think I would let you go without giving you a token to remember me by?"

As if I could ever forget him. He handed me a small object wrapped in a white linen handkerchief. I opened it carefully, and a pendant fell out into my palm. A small oval, it was set with a sapphire surrounded by tiny pearls. I gasped. It was stunning.

"It belonged to my mother. She gave it to me when Mary and I were betrothed. I—I had planned to give it to her as a wedding gift."

My heart surged. "Oh, Stephen. Are you sure? What if—"

"It means the world to me for *you* to have it, Olivia."

I smiled up at him, caught his eyes with my own. "Then I accept. Thank you."

"Would you like to put it on?"

I nodded, not trusting myself to speak.

"I brought a length of ribbon." Stephen threaded the ribbon through the circle on the pendant's top edge. "Let me tie it around your neck." He held it out and I lifted my hair as he knotted it. I started to turn back, but he stopped me, kissing the back of my neck. The touch of his lips sent a thrill through me.

"I've wanted to kiss you there for so long, Olivia."

"I guess I'm Miranda now. Or about to be."

"Miranda, then. By whatever name, you will always be dear to me."

And then I lost it. My vision blurred, and the tears spilled over and down my cheeks. "I could stay," I said, my voice coming out all squeaky and quivery. "I'd like to stay, if you want me to." I swiveled back toward him.

"'If I want you to.'" Stephen laughed, a short, bitten-off sound.

"Well. Do you?" I gazed up at him, willing him to say it. Even if I couldn't stay, even despite all the obstacles, I wanted him to want me to.

"Miranda, you have become my other self. When I am not with you, I am thinking of you. But I must let you go, even though it is the last thing I want."

"Come back with me, then. We could make it work." I rushed my words, afraid he'd stop me. "You lived in the present before, and this time I'd be able to help you fit in. It would be easier than when you were all alone."

Stephen grasped my arms. "Do you imagine I haven't thought of that? That I haven't worked out every possibility in my mind?" Abruptly he let me go and leaped to his feet. He walked a few steps away, and then spun back toward me. "I am a man of this era, made for this time. This is what I know." He gestured expansively. "This is my world. You are a young woman of your time, one I am not accustomed to."

"Why can't I stay here, then?"

"Ask yourself if that is what you truly want. Never to see your family again. To give up your dream of acting. To be deprived of all opportunities offered to young ladies of your century." He walked back over, pulled me up, and wiped my tears away with the handkerchief that had held the pendant.

"Aye, you could stay. We could marry, have a family, and you could do all the work a dutiful wife must do, while I supervised the farm and tenants. But I know that would not make you happy."

"Yes, it would!"

"We are . . . you are too young. If I allowed you to stay, my heart would break to see the unhappiness in your eyes. I . . . cannot go through that again."

I dabbed at my wet cheeks with his handkerchief. As much as it hurt to admit it, I knew he was right. I would love him with all my heart, but in the end, it wouldn't be enough. I'd long for everything I couldn't have, and that would kill the love between us. Not right away, but someday.

His arms slid around me, holding me close. "I love you, Miranda. God knows, after Mary died, I never thought to say those words again. But I do *love* you. And that is why I must send you back." He stepped away, and his expression looked agonized. "You do not know it, but I was lost from the first time I caught sight of you. 'Twas one of the reasons I chose you. You bewitched me."

"I did? So you loved me all along? All this time, and you never said anything."

"How could I?"

"You violated your own 'no personal gain' rule."

"So I did. I could not help myself."

"You told me when I first arrived that time stood still in the present while I was in the past. There must be a limit on that. If I stayed, time would go on, wouldn't it, eventually? I'd be declared missing or something?"

"Aye. And we are pushing against the limit. I have to get you back within a few days of the new moon, or your time will move on without you."

"Something else you neglected to mention."

"You had enough to worry about. I knew I could deal with that particular problem."

I wondered what else he hadn't told me. What more there was about this journey I'd never begin to fathom. I wiped my nose with the handkerchief. "When you disappeared for those days, I started to think about going back. Seeing the people and places I missed. And acting."

"It was one of the reasons I left. I needed to give you the time to separate from me and begin to think about going home. I hope you will mend things with your mother."

"Thank you for helping me sort through . . . my issues . . . with her. I think maybe the two of us can make a new start."

He stroked my hair, pressed sweet kisses on my head, then held me away from him. "I believe you no longer have such self-doubt as you once did. Regarding both your mother and acting."

I smiled, my spirits lifting a little. "It's true. I've had a lot of time to think about both."

He went on. "When I brought you back, even though I was so taken with you, you were a means to an end. I had to prevent something from happening, and I had no clear idea of how to do it. I apologize to you, Miranda, for using you cruelly."

"You mean wanting me to seduce Shakespeare?"

He winced. "I am ashamed of what I asked of you. It was not the act of a gentleman."

"You've already apologized. Remember? And I'm sorry for being so . . . difficult. I *have* mellowed a little, haven't I?"

"Indeed, you are all goodness now."

I smacked his chest playfully, and he caught hold of my wrist. "Now, sweet, 'tis time."

"Stephen, no." I could feel love pulsing up through me, making my eyes shine with it.

He pulled me close and we clung to each other for a moment, shutting out the world, both our worlds. Brushing my lips gently, he clasped my hand and led me toward the tower. "You must climb to the top," Stephen said.

Clutching my backpack, I jolted to a stop. "Wait! Do you have the astrolabe? Are you sure you know what you're doing? I'm not going to end up in a harem in Constantinople, or on the *Mayflower* or something, am I?"

"Be assured, I have everything I need. I know what I am about."

I swallowed hard as he backed away from me. "What should I do when I get to the top?"

"Nothing. I will take care of . . . the rest. Look out over this English countryside so that you'll remember it always. And one thing more. I had the pendant inscribed for you. Read it."

I fumbled for it, but Stephen stopped me, shaking his head. "Not now. Do not read it until you are at the top."

"All right," I agreed, despite my overwhelming curiosity. I reached out for him once more, our fingers barely connecting as he moved farther away. Clutching my backpack, I dragged in a ragged breath and began climbing the narrow stone stairs, a shiver of fear shooting through me. Once at the top, I did as Stephen said. I whirled around, marking the countryside in my memory. The slant of the sunlight on undulating fields and flowering bushes. The gentle swell of the land, reaching up to meet a serene sky.

Dizziness rose up, and I grabbed hold of the iron railing surrounding me. I sensed an imperceptible shift, and my hands and feet began to tingle. Desperately, I raised the pendant and read the inscription.

Farewell! Thou art too dear for my possessing. . . .

At the last moment I screamed. "Stephen!"
And was gone.

Chapter Thirty-Three

Boston, Present Day

STRUGGLING UP FROM THE DEPTHS OF SLEEP, I opened my eyes and squinted at the sunlight streaming into my room. I lost the struggle, rolled over, and sank back into oblivion.

Later, my cell phone woke me. Not moving from my prone position, I twisted my neck until I spotted my backpack near the bed. I stretched out an arm and grabbed it. By the time I'd unzipped the right compartment, the ringing had stopped. I hadn't really wanted to answer it anyway.

I flopped back down, only then noticing I'd slept in my clothes. The full realization of parting from Stephen was beginning to catch up with me. I was home, in Boston, feeling profoundly depressed. I vaguely remembered standing in the street near the Dennis School sometime during morning rush hour, seemingly only minutes after leaving Stephen. Everything had seemed out of sync. I hailed a cab, the sound and speed of the cars scaring me. The concrete sidewalk and asphalt streets felt unwelcoming beneath my feet. Intense exhaustion had overtaken me, along with a stupefying awareness of the time shift. After barely making it through the front door of our home, I'd gone to my room, thrown myself on the bed, and fallen asleep.

Why had I let myself be talked into leaving him? *You agreed to this, Miranda. Remember? You weren't talked into anything.* A sound, something like a moan of agony, burst out of me.

I resisted the urge to sink back into sleep, and instead sat up and tugged my boots off. Then I padded over to my desk and started up my laptop. I wanted to see what date and day it was. When the desktop came up, the bar across the top told me it was Saturday, March 22, 1:11 p.m. So Stephen had been right; I'd only lost a few hours. I had a performance tonight. I raked my hair with both hands, trying not to freak out. Was I really home? It seemed impossible.

I found my cell phone and checked to see who the missed call was from. I listened to the message. "Miranda, it's your grandfather." As if that voice could belong to anyone else. "I know you must have had a late night, but check in with us when you're feeling human again." *If he only knew the truth . . .*

Until I'd had a shower, I wouldn't feel human again. Flipping on the bathroom light, I recoiled from its glare. I'd have to readjust to the brightness of artificial light. Candlelight was soft, and so forgiving. Looking at myself in the harsh glow of modern lighting, I sensed that I looked different in some way. More grown-up. I turned the shower on and stripped, and it wasn't until then that I remembered the necklace. My body heat had warmed it. The thin red ribbon curved around my neck, the oval resting just above my breasts. I unknotted the ribbon, flipped the pendant over, and read the inscription once again, even though I had committed it to memory: *Farewell! Thou art too dear for my possessing.* Did Stephen really believe that?

The sting of the hot water spiking from the showerhead seemed almost like an invasion of my body. And in a way, a betrayal. I was washing off all traces of my time with Stephen. I tilted my head back and let the water pour over my hair and face. Hot tears joined with the streaming water, and I allowed myself a bout of uncontrolled weeping.

I dressed—fresh, soft clothes felt wonderful against my skin, no denying it—and headed for the kitchen to make coffee. As I waited for it to brew, I fingered the pendant and thought about the inscription. If I had to guess, I'd say it was the first line of one of Shakespeare's sonnets. I'd have the rest of my life to work it out. Right now, I simply wanted to treasure it.

After pouring a cup of coffee, I carried it to the kitchen table, where I had an expansive view of the backyard. Daffodils and tulips bloomed profusely all around the boundaries of the yard. The grass was greening, and the crab apple trees showed off their gorgeous pink blossoms. I slid open the patio door and stepped outside. It was a mild day, perfect for a run. I'd call my grandfather afterward.

I went for that run, took a second shower, and made the call. Tears flooded my eyes when I heard my grandfather's voice. "Hi, Gramps!" It seemed like so long since I'd talked to him.

"Miranda, my dear. Glad to hear you're among the living." I loved that he had such old-fashioned manners and called me pet names like "my dear."

"How are you feeling?" he asked. Not too obvious, but definitely worried about whether I was obsessing over last night's performance.

"I've thought things over today, and I think I have a better grasp of Katherine."

"Good. She was 'young and beauteous / Brought up as best becomes a gentlewoman.' Don't forget that. Katherine was a gentlewoman before she became known as a shrew."

"There are great subtleties in her character. I understand that now." *Now that I've had a month or so to think it over.*

"Believe in yourself, child. You have the inner strength to get it right."

"Thanks, Gramps. You're the best."

He chuckled. "One more thing. I didn't know whether I should tell you or not, because they wanted to surprise you, but your mother and father will be in the audience tonight. I thought it would be too great a shock if you happened to spy them in the middle of a big speech."

"What? But they're in Rome . . . aren't they?"

"They're flying home to see you play Katherine."

I bit down hard on my lip, feeling as if I'd been sucker punched.

"I'm sorry. Perhaps I shouldn't have said anything."

I pulled in a long breath. "No, you're absolutely right, Gramps. I would have frozen if I'd seen them, probably forgotten my lines. I'm glad you told me. I'll do my best to act surprised."

"Break a leg tonight, my dear."

"Are you okay?" Macy asked as I stepped into the dressing room and threw down my backpack. She was already wearing her Bianca dress.

I smiled. "I'm fine. Thanks for worrying about me." I gave her a hug, and when I stepped back, I could see the surprise in her eyes. I was normally not given to hugging. "How was the party?"

"Great, except everybody missed you and kept asking me where you were. John was bummed. Finley was afraid you were sick and Bridget would have to play Katherine."

"She'd do okay." I laughed when Macy winced. "I'm feeling better about everything, Mace."

Her face lit up. "Good! I'm so relieved." She glanced up at the wall clock. "You better get dressed. It's only an hour till curtain."

"I will. One more thing, though. I wanted to tell you how great you were last night. I'm sorry I didn't say anything afterward. You were enchanting as Bianca, just the way she's supposed to be."

She couldn't hold back a huge grin. "Don't worry about it. You were . . . upset."

I carried my things to the bench in front of the row of cupboards and grabbed my first gown off the rack. Someone, bless their organized heart, had carefully rearranged all the costumes in the correct order.

Before driving over here, I'd rummaged through my mother's jewelry box and found a silver chain that matched the pendant perfectly. My dress was cut low, and I debated whether or not to leave the pendant on. But in my heart, I knew there was no way I was walking out on that stage without it. Macy came over and fastened me up the back. When I turned around, she gasped.

"What is that? It's gorgeous!" She moved her hand as if to touch the pendant, and I spun around, pretending I needed something from my pack.

"Just a piece of costume jewelry. I thought it might be fun to wear it for the performances."

"Well, it doesn't look like costume jewelry. It looks authentic. Are you sure that's not a real sapphire? And those pearls—they're not the weird color of fake ones."

"I'm sure, but thank you. Good to know it looks all right."

"Oh, before I forget, Steve Langford hasn't shown up. He didn't even call—can you believe that? Jake Ryan is playing Lucentio."

I plunked down on the bench, the breath rushing out of me. Of course Stephen wouldn't be here for the performance! If Macy hadn't reminded me, I might have totally lost it when I first saw Jake.

Katherine isn't in Act I, so after the curtain went up, I had some time alone to compose myself. I thought about my mom and dad changing their plans and flying home just to see me. A miracle. I was sure they'd have to fly right back. It was a major sacrifice, one I would never have expected them to make. Long flights were definitely tough on actors. However it had come about, I was happy they were here.

I closed my eyes, breathed deeply, and summoned the spirit of Will Shakespeare. Then I gathered up the tangled strands of Katherine's character and weaved them together. All that I'd learned, both in the present and in the past, began to meld. Gramps was right about her—she *was* raised as a gentlewoman. In some respects she was similar to Jennet, forced to do her father's bidding. And then, ironically, Petruchio's. In the end, Katherine's newfound passion, purpose, and serenity began to surface, allowing her to be at peace.

A sense of calm washed over me. I felt much more prepared and much less nervous than I had on opening night.

"Miranda?" It was Derek, Mr. Finley's assistant. "Time to get in position. The first act is almost over."

"Thanks, Derek. I'm coming."

I joined Bianca onstage to begin the second act. With every line, I felt a new confidence. I allowed the language, rhythm, and meter to control my speech and my interpretation of Katherine. I wanted her love for Petruchio to shine from within. In the end, with her "advice to the wives" speech, I let the audience decide if she was being irreverent and ironic, or subdued and obedient. Perhaps something in between.

When we took our bows, the applause overwhelmed me. Cries of "Brava" shook the house. It seemed unreal. I'd never experienced anything like it. When I looked out at the audience, I glimpsed my mom and dad, on their feet with everybody else.

The curtain came down and the cast surrounded me, patting me on the back, hugging me, telling me how wonderful I'd been. When I tried to congratulate them, my voice was drowned out. Mr. Finley actually grabbed me by the shoulders and said, "Brilliant!" I laughed, feeling almost giddy. And then I spotted my mother and father making their way toward me. "Excuse me," I said quickly, and ran to meet them.

My dad caught me up in a big hug. "Oh, Miranda, you were magnificent. Never has there been a truer Katherine."

"I can't believe you came all the way from Rome, but I'm so happy you did."

He let me go, and there stood my mother, eyeing me with an odd expression on her face. Her beautiful dark hair looked ruffled from her travels, but her eyes were bright. With tears, I realized. When she spoke, her voice was soft. "I am so proud of you, darling. You made Katherine come alive. You own the role, now and forever."

Wow. I'd never heard such high praise for anyone from my mother.

Then she pulled me against her and hugged me tightly.

"Now, dear, I do have a few suggestions for you. . . ." I looked at Dad, and he rolled his eyes. I choked back a laugh.

"I'm sure you do, Mom. Come back to the dressing room with me. The cast will want to say hello."

It seemed like hours before everyone left. I'd convinced my family to allow me a little time alone, but I was due at home for a celebration within an hour. Stretching it out for as long as possible, I removed my makeup, changed, and cleaned up. When I finished and there was nothing left to do, I stood utterly still and listened. Maybe I'd hear Stephen's voice, or his footsteps. For a brief moment, I wondered if I'd dreamed him.

After a while, I sank down on the bench and reached for my pendant. I rubbed my thumb over the surface, tracing the facets of the sapphire and the roundness of the pearls. Then my fingers brushed over the inscription. *Farewell! Thou art too dear for my possessing.* I knew he wasn't coming. I rose, reached for my backpack, and flipped out the lights.

"I will see you again someday, Stephen." *I will see you again. . . .*

Author's Note

FROM WILLIAM SHAKESPEARE'S BIRTH in 1564 to his arrival in London around 1590, no diaries or letters related to his personal life exist. Shakespeare scholars often refer to this period as "the lost years." Other than the records of his baptism, marriage, and the births of his children, there are only a few inconclusive hints upon which to build a picture of his life.

One of the more intriguing theories about Shakespeare's youth places him in northern England, serving as a schoolmaster. John Aubrey, in a seventeenth-century work called *Brief Lives*, was the first to make this assertion, which has been mentioned as an acceptable theory in many of the major biographies of Shakespeare since. There is some circumstantial evidence that Shakespeare's father, once prosperous, was struggling financially at that time, and a university degree for his oldest son would have been out of the question. It makes sense that Will would have sought employment, especially if he lacked enthusiasm for his father's trade as a glove maker. The family of John Cottom, one of Shakespeare's schoolmasters in Stratford, lived near the Hoghtons in Lancashire. If asked, Cottom might have recommended Will for the post of private schoolmaster at Hoghton Tower.

A potential clue has been found in the will of Alexander Hoghton, the man who may have employed Shakespeare in 1581. Hoghton asked his neighbor and relative, Sir Thomas Hesketh, to be friendly to "William Shakeshafte nowe dwellynge with me." Although it is not universally accepted that William Shakeshafte is Shakespeare, some scholars believe they are the same person.

A number of experts think Shakespeare had a means of continuing his studies. If he didn't attend university, he almost certainly had access to a great library. The collection at Hoghton Tower would have fueled his intellect and imagination and helped fill in some of the gaps in his education.

About Edmund Campion, a renowned Jesuit priest of the time, we know more. By all accounts, he was a man of keen intellect, sharp wit, and great personal charm. He was educated at Oxford University and, after joining the Society of Jesus in Rome, returned to England in 1580 disguised as a merchant. At the time *Kissing Shakespeare* takes place, he was working on a document called "Ten Reasons," in which he denounced Protestantism, proclaiming Catholicism the one true religion, and addressed Queen Elizabeth personally, exhorting her to renounce the new Church of England. Printed in secret, the small volume was brazenly placed on the benches at Oxford University's Church of St. Mary before Commencement in 1581.

Ultimately tracked down by Francis Walsingham's spy network, Edmund Campion was arrested in July of 1581 and sent to the Tower of London. He was tried, convicted, and sentenced to death as a traitor. Executed on December 1 of the same year, at the age of forty-one, he is considered to be a martyr by the Catholic Church. Campion was canonized in 1970 by Pope Paul VI.

Alexander Hoghton died in August of 1581, around the time of Campion's arrest. His heirs continue to reside at Hoghton Tower, an Elizabethan manor house open to the public. It is near the city of Preston.

And the young Will Shakespeare? By the age of eighteen, he was living in Stratford, his birthplace, and married to Anne Hathaway, with whom he had three children. Eventually he made his way to London, where he was an actor in the theater companies for which he wrote his plays. In 1613, he retired to Stratford and died there in 1616, at the age of fifty-two.

Shakespeare remains the most celebrated writer in the English language.

Acknowledgments

I AM INDEBTED TO the many people who helped shepherd *Kissing Shakespeare* to publication. First, to my agent, Steven Chudney, whose encouragement and guidance were essential, and to my editor at Delacorte Press, Françoise Bui, whose insightful analysis of the story enabled me to find its heart. Thanks also to copy editors Nancy Elgin and Colleen Fellingham for their meticulous reading of the book, and to Stephanie Moss for the striking cover design. I would also like to thank Irene Gorak for reviewing and commenting on the author's note.

Sir Bernard de Hoghton, whose family home, Hoghton Tower, provided the setting for *Kissing Shakespeare*, kindly answered numerous questions, not only about the house and grounds, but also about the intriguing story of the Shakespeare connection. Others on his staff generously shared their knowledge as well.

Stephen Greenblatt's book *Will in the World* started me on this journey. For further explication of Shakespeare's possible connection to the Jesuits, I depended on an essay by Richard Wilson called "Ghostly Fathers: Shakeshafte and the Jesuits," which appeared in his book *Secret Shakespeare*. For an understanding of Edmund Campion, I relied on Evelyn Waugh's well-known biography.

Without the help of my critique group, the Wild Folk, this would have been a different book. Their influence is evident on every page. I can never thank them enough. Along the way, my family, including my sisters, Janis Stubbs and Susan Dettling, provided encouragement and rallied me during the difficult times. Many friends cheered me on, and their interest and support has never flagged.

My daughter, Katie Mingle, read and critiqued the manuscript and served as my contemporary language authority. The pride that she and my stepdaughter, Dana Zedak, have in me brings me great joy.

And most of all, I want to thank my husband, Jim Mingle, my first reader, most thoughtful critic, biggest supporter, always-willing listener. Your love has guided me every step of the way.

About the Author

Pamela Mingle, a former teacher and librarian, lives in Lakewood, Colorado. She and her husband enjoy traveling to Great Britain, where they love taking long walks. It was on one of those walks that she discovered Hoghton Tower, the setting for her first novel, *Kissing Shakespeare*. Visit her at PamMingle.com.